GRIMM END

S T Cameron

BAKALOO MEDIA

S T Cameron / Bakaloo Media
524 4th Street S
Moorhead, MN 56560
www.bakaloo.com

Publisher's Note: This is a work of fiction. Names, characters, places, and incidents are a product of the author's imagination. Locales and public names are sometimes used for atmospheric purposes. Any resemblance to actual people, living or dead, or to businesses, companies, events, institutions, or locales is completely coincidental.

Ordering Information:
Quantity sales. Special discounts are available on quantity purchases by corporations, associations, and others. For details, contact the "Special Sales Department" at the address above.

Grimm End / S T Cameron. – 2nd ed.
ISBN 13: 979-8-88623-314-8

To Kay for her love, support, and encouragement

Chapter 1

The sun had already set when Molly Blair slipped down the servant stairs to the kitchen. It had been several hours since the evening meal and she found the kitchen clean and deserted. She checked again to make sure that she had the neatly folded old papers in her pocket. This is the last time, she thought to herself. After tonight, her debt is paid.

She glanced out through the dining room as she passed the swinging door that had been propped open for the night. The chandelier's crystals refracted the last light of the evening, sending little dots of colored light here and there throughout the room. She hurried to the door leading outside. That door served as the servant's entrance to the house as well as the door where delivery men would drop off sides of beef, cases of wine and packages of all shapes and sizes supplying the household with everything it needed. At that time of night, it was as forgotten as the kitchen. A moment later, she was out in the cool evening air and running across the yard to the trees.

Once she was concealed in the woods that surrounded the yard, she stopped to catch her breath. She looked back at the house. While most of the people who lived there referred to it as "The House", it was actually a large mansion that was built on a bluff overlooking the town and lake below it. The turrets towering high above the grounds and the grotesque gargoyles lining the roofs made it seem almost menacing in the growing darkness.

To the townspeople, the mansion was known as Grimm End. It was the name they had for the rocky bluff that jutted out over the lake where Alphonse Grimm, the founder of Shadow Bluffs, met his fate.

The mansion, build on that same outcropping of land, inherited the name.

She could see that lights were on in several of the windows of the mansion. It didn't seem as if anyone had taken notice of her leaving.

If she had been going to town on mansion business or if she had the night off, she could have gotten a ride into town. The business she had in town that night, however, was not something that she could let anyone in the mansion know about. She took one last look at the house and started on her long hike into town.

She didn't like walking through the woods anytime, let alone at night. She always had that odd feeling that someone was watching her. She didn't want to follow the cobblestone driveway down to the iron gates, though. If someone discovered that she was walking to town, there would be questions asked that she wouldn't want to answer.

Her employer was C. J. Kask, an elderly man who had made his money early in life traveling the world in search of strange artifacts. He put them on display in one the many museums that he owned around the world. In recent years though, he rarely left his room, let alone the country. However, he still had secrets. Secrets that other people were willing to pay for. Or blackmail for.

She heard something rustling through the leaves close by. She instantly stopped and looked around. Whatever it was stopped at the same time. She held her breath willing herself to be as silent as possible. Then she heard it again, a rustling movement coming closer. She almost screamed when a small dark shape rushed out of a bush nearby. It stopped when it saw her and then turned and ran. She recognized the faint white stripes down the creatures back as it fled. It was only a skunk. She let out her breath and almost laughed out loud.

She made it to the gates without seeing anyone or anything more and was soon off the mansion grounds and on the road into town.

A chilly breeze blew along the road, and Molly pulled her jacket tight around her. It was early May and, in Minnesota, that meant the days were warm, and the evenings were still cool.

It had been almost a year since she had come to work for Mr. Kask. She was an upstairs maid which meant that she cleaned a lot of bedrooms and bathrooms. It also meant that she had access to Mr. Kask's private study just off his bedroom and she was in that study earlier that evening.

C. J. Kask had been a man of habits. And despite the illness that had confined him to his bed since before she started at the mansion, his meals remained punctual, and his visitors arrived on time for appointments and never stayed beyond their allotted time. One of the habits that Molly had come to count on was that he would meet with his son, Matthew, privately for one hour in the afternoon. After that meeting, at exactly 6 pm, his usual dinner would be served in his bedroom. Each night of the week had its standard menu that never changed. That night, it had been pork chops, mashed potatoes and gravy with apple cinnamon cake for desert. After his dinner, his son would leave, and he would rest again until morning.

At a little past seven, Molly would then be free to search around the study under the pretense of cleaning. Several times, she had found information that she thought would be worth smuggling out. Most of the time, there was nothing valuable. That night was different.

That night she found his will. And while many people would be interested in the long list of possessions that were being divvied up in the document, she knew that the information that would settle her debt was the list of names and addresses of the people who stood to inherit from the old man. She folded the document up, put it away in her pocket and waited for her opportunity to deliver it to town.

She saw lights approaching on the road. She would have ducked into the woods, if the driver hadn't already have seen her. That would call more attention to her than being caught out on the road at night. As the car neared, it started slowing, and it stopped next to her. It was a Raven County Sheriff's Department patrol car. Sheriff Richard Marco smiled at her from the open window.

"Getting some air?" Marco asked. He was a large man; muscular, not overweight. He filled the driver's seat of the car. His teeth were yellow from years of chain smoking and coffee drinking.

However, it was his eye that disturbed her. The pupil of his left eye was almost entirely colorless. It didn't affect his sight. It just made other people uncomfortable, and the Sheriff seemed to enjoy that.

"Uh, yeah. Just out for a little walk." She tried to smile back at him.

"Lonely piece of road," he said nodding down the road behind her.

"I guess."

"Don't want anything to happen to you. You never know who may be out looking for trouble."

"There isn't much crime around here."

"I don't necessarily mean that kind of folk."

She knew what kind he meant. Shadow Bluffs was very different from the outside world. There was something in the air, or in the water, probably in everything, she thought. Whatever it was, in Shadow Bluffs, magic was real, some people could turn into animals and the dead did not rest.

"You mean the shape shifters?" Molly asked in a quieter voice.

"Shifters, yes," the Sheriff said. "But not just them. The Dead don't look too kindly on the living either."

"If we were anywhere else, I'd say those are just old wives' tales."

"Well, I ain't an old wife. I know that they are real. It's best not to push your luck when they're concerned."

"I can handle myself. I took a self-defense class."

"Uh huh. Heard anything from that brother of yours?"

"Jack? Not since he left town." She kicked at a rock with her foot. Her brother was the last thing she wanted to talk to the Sheriff about.

"That's a long time. Been a year, hasn't it?" he asked.

"Just about. We never were very close," she said. They hadn't been close. She knew that he wouldn't come back to town even though she had managed to clean up the mess he had been in. Still, it wasn't like her brother not to call once in a while even if it were just to ask for money.

"You know, I never had much against him. Rounded him up a couple of times when he was a boy trespassing on Mr. Kask's land. But nothing like that last trouble."

She remembered him sneaking off to play in a little cave by the stream running through the mansion's property. He said it was a fort, and he was guarding it.

"He was always a good brother," she told him.

"I know. Well, you be careful out here." He flashed his yellow teeth at her again.

"I will," she said and started walking toward town. She heard the car drive away down the road behind her. She didn't look back.

It was almost a half hour later when she arrived at the western edge of Shadow Bluffs. There, the road took a long loop around the old Elmwood Cemetery. Elmwood was the oldest and largest cemetery in the area. It was rarely used anymore and had become overgrown and decayed. The newer Rosemont Cemetery in the south part of town was the place where people were buried now.

Normally, during the day, she would take a shortcut through the cemetery rather than follow the road as it twisted around it. At night, it was a different story. As she followed the road around the cemetery, she could see the shadows of figures moving slowly through the tangled underbrush between the headstones. She pulled her jacket close around her and hurried along until she left the cemetery behind and arrived at the square in the center of town.

Shadow Bluffs was just a small town of only several hundred people. When the sun went down, everything closed up. Everything, that is, except for the little cafe on the square.

The sign across the building proclaimed it to be Carson's Diner, home of Della's World-Famous Meatloaf. Della Carson had been the owner of the diner until she died about twenty years ago. Her son, Willie, was the owner now.

There were a good number of people in the diner, as usual, maybe having a late dinner of their world-famous meatloaf or just having a little coffee and a slice of their fresh baked blueberry or apple pies.

All the businesses on the main square were well kept and clean. Places where customers would be comfortable and even proud to shop. At night, the light from the diner and the street lights around the square gave it a warm, comforting glow.

As she was passing the fountain in the middle of the square, something came running at her from one of the side streets. She only noticed it at the last moment, when it jumped up at her and caused her to stumble backward. She ended up sitting on the edge of the fountain with a large brown and white dog practically sitting in her lap.

The front half of the large dog was perched up on her lap as its tail wagged and tongue hung out of the corner of its mouth. Molly relaxed and rubbed its ears.

"You gave me quite a scare," Molly told it.

Although it appeared to be a normal dog, she wondered if it actually were. She looked for a collar or tags. It had neither.

"Where did you come from?" she wondered aloud.

"Here, boy," a voice called. Molly saw a young boy crossing the street to the fountain.

"Is this your dog?" Molly asked the boy. He had jet black hair that hung down so she couldn't see his eyes. His face and clothes were dirty, and he wore no shoes.

"Nah," he said. "We just play together."

"Well, you better take him and go on home now. It's pretty late."

"I know," he said. He pulled the dog off her lap and ran off with him.

Molly brushed herself off and turned to go. She was interrupted by his tiny voice again.

"Miss," he called from the corner of the Great Northern Bank building. "Be careful where you go tonight."

She was going to ask him what he meant by that, but he was gone around the corner before she could say anything. She might have gone after him if it weren't for her appointment. She hurried off in a different direction.

The darker streets that ran just behind those on the square may have been only a block away, but the shops there seemed like they were a world away. Many were run down, and most were disreputable. The shopkeepers there would be just as willing to steal your wallet as sell you something. Molly's destination was on one of those streets.

Chapter 2

She glanced down both directions on the street before she tapped on the old wooden door of the Golden Lamp Pawn Shop. The windows were dark, and the sign was off. She knew her arrival was expected. It was not expected quite as much as required. Despite the cool night breeze blowing through the town, she was starting to sweat.

The street was almost deserted, except for a pair of dark figures that were ambling along toward her. They were bundled in dark coats with their hoods pulled over their faces. They were murmuring to each other, but Molly couldn't catch what they were saying.

As they passed the door, Molly pressed her back against it and watched them. The hoods turned toward her for a moment, the blackness inside undisturbed by the little bit of light from the street lamp nearby. Then, they were past her and moving further down the street. Molly caught a hint of mint in the air after they had gone. The mint, she knew, was used to cover the smell of decay that often accompanied the presence of the Dead.

She tapped again a little louder. She stepped back and looked up at the second floor windows. It wasn't surprising that no light shone out onto the empty street. She'd only been up to that room a handful of times, but day or night, the windows had always been covered with heavy draperies with no sign that they were ever opened.

The loud thunk of the door's deadbolt sliding open startled her. She closed her eyes and tried to will her racing heart to slow down. She took a deep breath, let it out and opened her eyes again. The door was partly open, and a dim light spilled out onto the sidewalk in front of the small shop.

She gently pushed the door open a little more and slipped into the building's entrance. It was an old building with white plaster walls, high ceilings and a colorful mosaic tile floor faded into dullness over the years. A door to the side had the name of the pawn shop stenciled on beveled glass. Hanging from a suction cup on the inside of the glass was a sign stating that the shop was closed. Ahead of her was a steep stairway leading to the second floor of the building. Standing on the third step, staring blankly at her, was a dark-haired Asian girl who was eight or nine years old.

"Good Evening, Asami," Molly said softly as she closed the door.

The girl made no reply. She simply turned and headed up the stairs. She had no difficulty climbing the steps rapidly despite the long brown dress that she wore. All three of the women who lived there wore dresses made of the same plain brown fabric. It made Molly think of the robes worn by ancient druids who worshiped nature. Except these druids lived in an apartment above a pawn shop.

She followed the girl up the stairs and paused for a moment at the top landing. Asami held the door to the apartment open for her. The acrid smell of incense billowed out from inside and the light transitioned from a dull white light in the stairwell to a red-tinted one inside the apartment.

The little girl tilted her head toward the open doorway and waited. Although Asami seemed innocent enough, Molly was afraid of her. She was afraid of all the Moira sisters. She took a quick breath and went inside.

Piri was seated at a small round table covered with a dark red table cloth. There were only two lights on in the room. One focused down on the table where Piri was seated crocheting and the other next to the hallway where Molly entered illuminating a comfortable, burgundy, winged-back chair. Piri motioned for her to sit.

Molly sat and waited. An unkempt black and gray cat jumped up into her lap and stared at her with its bright yellow eyes. She brought her hand up to pet it. It bared its teeth and hissed at her until she moved her hand away.

Piri appeared to be working on a pink, baby bootie. Suddenly, Piri threw the partially finished bootie onto the table next to two other finished ones and stood up. She snatched a cane that leaned against a chair beside her and made her way over to Molly. She was a tall and slender woman with white-gray hair that contrasted with her dark skin. The hand that she held out to Molly was as wrinkled as the old woman's face.

Molly carefully pulled the folded sheets of paper from her coat pocket, trying not to disturb the cat, and handed it to the woman who promptly turned and settled herself back at the table. She unfolded the papers, smoothed them out on the table and squinted down at them.

The room looked the same as the first time she'd come to them. Her brother had been in trouble. An elderly man had been attacked and ended up in the hospital. His wallet and a small amount of cash were stolen. The old man later identified her brother as the attacker. He recognized the blue jacket and Twins baseball cap that her brother always wore.

The Sheriff investigated her brother and found the wallet in her brother's apartment. He denied having anything to do with the attack and had no explanation of how the wallet had gotten there. He was facing a long time in jail.

Molly came to the sisters because they had a reputation for being able to make problems go away. And they did. The charges were dropped, and her brother was advised to leave town.

Shortly afterward, she was asked to come see the sisters again. That was when they asked for their payment. She was to get a job at Grimm End and try to find anything she could on the whereabouts of Kask's family. They never told her why, and she never asked.

Now that she was able to get them a list of his family members' names and addresses, she felt she had more than paid for their services with those papers and a year of her life.

Molly looked at the three women. She always wondered why they were known as sisters when the three women couldn't be more different. Asami was Asian and just a child. Piri was an ancient black woman and would have been more of a grandmother or even a great-grandmother than a sister to Asami. And then there was Dior.

"Is it anything useful, Piri?" The voice came from a shadowy corner near the front draped windows. From her voice, Molly had always pictured Dior as a young woman, but she had never seen her in the light.

"It's what you wanted, names and addresses," Molly said. "That should be enough to—" Molly stopped when a small hand touched her shoulder. She looked up at Asami who merely shook her head. Piri had stopped reading and was glaring at her, as well.

She sat back in the chair as Asami pulled another chair up to the small table and sat by the old woman. The cat leapt off of Molly and jumped up in Asami's lap where it curled up and purred as Asami stroked it's back. She and Piri looked over the papers before Piri finally spoke.

"Yes," Piri said scowling up at Molly. "It tells us what we wanted to know."

Dior rose quickly and stood behind the old woman. Molly saw the woman's hand as she picked up the papers. There was a ring with a dark ruby stone on her ring finger, but the little finger was missing. Molly gasped.

The three women stiffened. Piri and Asami looked at Molly and then up at Dior. Dior slowly set the papers on the table and backed out of the light. Molly could feel the air in the room change. She began to sweat again.

"So?" Dior asked from the shadows. Molly could hear the edge in her voice. "You feel you have fulfilled your end of the bargain?"

"Yes, you wanted me to find out where they were, and I did. That should make us even," Molly said, looking down at her hands in her lap. Her voice sounded more confident than she felt. She braced herself for an angry outburst.

"We are more than even," Dior said quietly. Molly looked up at her shadowy form in surprise. Even Asami and Piri abruptly turned toward her.

"More than even?" Piri asked.

"Yes, this information is worth far more than the trivial favor we did for Molly's poor brother," Dior said and sat back down on her chair in the corner. "Thank you for your help, Molly. You are free to go."

Molly stared at Dior. Only when Asami and Piri turned back to look at her did she move.

"Thank you, Dior," Molly said and quickly turned to leave.

"No," Dior said. "Thank you, Molly." Just as Molly was about to open the apartment door, her heart skipped a beat.

"Oh, and Molly," Dior called. Molly stopped with her hand on the doorknob. She slowly looked back toward the place she thought the woman was sitting. "You have nothing to worry about. You've done well. We will take care of you."

Molly smiled faintly and then hurried out into the hallway. She rushed down the stairs and out into the street. Only then did she allow herself to relax.

The three women were silent after Molly left. After they had heard the door to the street close again, Piri stood up to face Dior.

"What was all that about?" Piri asked. "She found this little bit of information, and suddenly we're all best friends?"

"She did get us what we wanted. We needed leverage on Kask, and she provided it. What was the name of that family? Cross?"

"Yes, Mary Cross," Piri read. "And her children, Thomas, Sara and Daniel."

"They will provide us the leverage we need."

"The leverage you need," Asami corrected her. "I'm still not sure this is the best path for us."

"I'm sure," Dior told her.

"Either way," Piri said. "We have to do something about Molly."

"I know. I know," Dior said. "Before she even came here tonight, I knew that we were done with her. Those papers she brought were just a lucky break."

"You knew?" Asami asked. Her eyes narrowed.

"We can't be," Piri said angrily. "She knows too much about us."

"Ah, but we are done with her, Piri. I told her that we'd take care of her and, true to my word, I have already arranged for her to be taken care of."

Piri sat back down at the table and frowned at the papers still lying there. Asami looked up from rubbing the cat's neck and smiled.

Chapter 3

The road back to the mansion wound up through the hills above the little town for a couple miles. Molly never liked sneaking out to see the Moira women. It always meant a long walk to town and back.

When she was almost back to the gate leading up to the mansion, she saw that there was a car parked at the side of the road. It wasn't running, and its lights were off. She crossed to the opposite side of the road to pass it.

When she was alongside it, she realized that it was the Sheriff's patrol car and the driver's door was open. The Sheriff was nowhere to be seen. She hurried ahead to get away from the road and back to the mansion as fast as she could.

She saw something move slowly out from the trees ahead of her. She stood still in the middle of the road. The gate to the mansion's driveway was still several hundred yards ahead, and the creature was between it and her. It was too far back to town. She didn't know where to run.

It raised its head, and Molly realized it was just a deer. It looked towards Molly and froze. She let out a sigh of relief.

"It's OK," she said aloud, more to herself than to the deer. It started to lower its head again and then snapped back up as Molly began to take a step. It suddenly bounded up the road, and within seconds, it was past the gate and disappearing into the darkness.

"You don't have to be afraid of me," she called to it.

She had just taken another step when a low growl rumbled from the road behind her. She turned around, and took a sharp breath as she saw a massive mountain lion that stood just paces from her. The moonlight gleamed off its eyes making it appear even more hellish to her.

With terror welling up inside her, she turned and ran as fast as she could up the road toward the gate. She had just reached it when the creature slammed her against the metal bars with its powerful body. Pain shot through her head and chest, and she fell backward onto the ground. She tried to catch her breath. The force of the impact and the pain shooting through her chest every time she took a breath made it difficult.

The big cat circled around her. She knew that if she didn't do something quick, she would die right there by the gate. Then, she saw that the impact had caused the gate to open a little. She only hoped it would be enough. She felt around in the gravel next to her until she found a good sized rock.

As the animal circled back around toward her head again, she flipped toward it and brought the rock down on its head as hard as she could. The creature was knocked to the ground, and in that moment, she pushed herself up and stumbled toward the gate, fighting the pain that wracked her body. She slipped through the opening and slammed it behind her. As she slid the bolt to latch it, the giant cat leapt at the gate. The gate held, but one of the cat's claws caught her arm, ripping a long gash into it. She cried out in pain and stumbled back. She gripped her arm in agony.

The cat was on the outside of the fence pacing and looking for a way past it. It tried to leap over. She was amazed and horrified at the height that the cat could jump. Fortunately, it only succeeded in injuring itself on the pointed posts that lined the top of the fence.

The cat stopped its pacing and jumping. It just stood there, growling and staring at Molly. It was then that she saw it. The cat's left eye was almost totally white. Her mouth opened in horror. No sound came out. It couldn't be, she thought.

She turned and ran up the road toward the mansion. She was feeling weak from the pain and loss of blood. She pushed herself as hard as she could.

She had only gotten a couple hundred yards up the driveway when she heard something running fast through the forest to her right. It passed her rapidly, and a few seconds later, the cat sprang out of the trees and landed on the pavement ahead of her. It stood and glared at her. She barely could bring herself to look at its colorless eye.

She plunged into the trees to her left and ran wildly through the underbrush. Twigs and branches caught at her, and she stumbled over dead branches on the ground. She pushed on. Now and then, she could hear the cat behind her, sometimes off to her left and sometimes off to her right. It seemed as if it were herding her through the forest. Then she heard the sound of the little stream ahead of her.

She remembered her brother's cave. If she could get to it without the cat seeing her, she could hide there until it went away. She ignored the pain searing through her limbs and ran harder toward the sound of the water.

She came to the stream only a short distance from location of the cave. She ran along the stream until she was above it and then leapt down in front of the hole. She rolled backward into the cave and laid still. She tried to muffle her breathing by pulling her jacket over her mouth.

Quickly, she realized it wasn't her jacket. It was a darker color, and she gagged at the terrible smell. She eased her key ring out from her pocket and shined her key light on the material. It was a rotten sleeve of a dirty blue jacket. Worst of all, there was a bony hand still in the sleeve.

She quickly sat up and shined the light on the place she had been laying. The body of a man was sprawled where she had come to rest. The head, which had been separated from the rest of his body, still wore a Twins baseball cap. Even in the dim light, she knew that it had been her brother. He had never left town.

A growl from the entrance brought her back from the horror of discovering her brother. The cat stood at the entrance.

"You wanted me to find him, didn't you," She yelled at the beast. "Didn't you. You killed him." She got on her knees and started throwing any rocks that she could find at the cat. It tried to avoid them, but after a couple of good hits, it screamed with anger. The small cave echoed with the terrible sound.

The cat leapt at the girl. The girl, her own anger masking the pain, pushed herself up. She met the creature's body in mid-leap and knocked it aside against the wall of the cave. She then lunged for the cave opening.

She only got her upper body through the opening before another horrific pain shot through her as the animal bit into her left shin. She tried to kick, but the pain from her injuries was finally overwhelming her. The animal's jaw locked onto her leg and pulled her back down into the cave.

The animal released her leg, and she rolled over to face the creature. It stood over her snarling, the one eye holding her attention and flooding her with terror. She tried to scoot backwards using her elbows. She missed the opening and ended up with her back to the cave wall. The creature stepped forward toward her.

"Please," she pleaded. "Please don't."

The cat leapt at her again. She tried to roll to one side. She only ended up face down in the mud with her back to the beast. It scratched at her back tearing through her clothes and ripping at her skin.

The pain and the terror overwhelmed her as the beast's powerful jaw clamped down on her neck from behind. The pain became the only thing that she was aware of.

It was also the last thing she was aware of as the creature crushed the bones and ripped through the arteries in her neck. She lost consciousness just after the beast began to feed.

Chapter 4

M r. Joshua P. Dunlap was ready for his shave. On a normal day, he would have used his electric razor to clear all the stubble from his face and neck and then he would use a trimmer to edge around the neat mustache and goatee for which he was well known. He was the owner of Dunlap Ford, one of the largest car dealers in a three county area. And he had been the face seen in Dunlap Ford's television commercials for over 30 years.

But it wasn't a normal day. Mr. Dunlap was dead. According to the coroner, it was a heart attack. Rather than lying comfortably in his own bed, he was lying on a cold table under bright florescent lights covered only with a sheet. The cold didn't matter to him, though.

The cold didn't matter to Thomas Cross either. It was his job to prepare Mr. Dunlap for his viewing the next morning. He had already washed the man's silver hair and cut his nails. It was time to give him his last shave. He lathered up the shaving cream in a cup and applied it liberally to Mr. Dunlap's face and neck. He then used a straight razor to give him a close and clean shave. Most preparers would use a safety razor. Thomas felt the old-fashioned straight razor was somehow more dignified and gave a cleaner shave.

Even though he was just an employee of Gibson Brothers Funeral Home, Thomas always thought of the people he prepared as his clients. And, he always tried to make his clients look good for their funerals. It was the last time that anyone would ever see them again, so he felt that they should look their best.

The Gibson Brothers felt that the services that Thomas provided were just an expense that they were obligated to include, and they complained about having to pay Thomas each and every payday. Thomas didn't let it bother him. He knew that his services were important for the family and, in some way he couldn't quite articulate, he thought it was important to the dearly departed too.

His phone chimed. It was 6 pm. He wouldn't normally be at the funeral home that late in the evening. However, Mrs. Dunlap had moved his funeral up a couple of days because she had a hard time living in such a big old mansion without the husband she loved so much. She wanted to go away for a while and go through the grieving process at their vacation home in the Bahamas. It was short notice, and Thomas knew Mr. Dunlap needed to be ready.

He quickly finished shaving the man and was working on detailing his black mustache and salt and pepper goatee when he heard a slight creaking noise. He paused for a moment with the trimmer poised over Mr. Dunlap's ample nose. He listened for any more noises. There weren't any.

Thomas' station was located in the far corner of the basement below the funeral home. There was a swinging door at the bottom of the stairway that led to the upper floor and normally, it would open and swing shut with nothing except a slight whooshing sound. Thomas was used to it creaking like that every once in a while.

He finished Mr. Dunlap's facial hair. Then, he cleaned up the shaving equipment and grabbed the suit that Mrs. Dunlap had provided for Mr. Dunlap to wear into eternity. Thomas laid out the clothes and started dressing the man when he heard another creaking sound. This time, it wasn't the door. He covered Mr. Dunlap again with the sheet and turned his attention toward the stairway.

The basement was filled with caskets. The Gibson Brothers used the basement as their showroom. The most expensive caskets were closest to the stairway, and they got less expensive the farther away from the stairs they were located. The caskets closest to Thomas' work area were the discounted and bargain basement ones.

All the caskets were as they had been, except for the Crown Royal next to the stairway. It was the most expensive casket that the Gibson Brothers had ever carried. It was made of the finest elegant mahogany highlighted with a hand rubbed high gloss finish. Every inch of metal hardware was plated with pure 24 carat gold. And the interior was top of the line champagne velvet. It was the elder Gibson's goal either to sell it or to be buried in it.

The lid of the Crown Royal was open. It hadn't been open a few minutes earlier. The younger Gibson wanted them to remain closed to prevent dust from settling on the linings. Now, it was open. As Thomas watched, the lid slowly began to close again.

He made his way through the line of caskets and placed his hand on the handle of the Crown Royal. After preparing himself, he quickly opened the lid and grabbed the body lying inside by the shirt and hauled him out.

"I told you not to play around in the caskets," Thomas told his brother.

Daniel Cross laughed as he was hauled out and unceremoniously dumped on the floor. He may have been fifteen, but the sandy haired boy often acted far younger.

"What are you doing here?" Thomas asked.

"The carnival, remember," Daniel said as he got back up on his feet.

"Is that tonight?"

"Yeah. We talked about it yesterday. Mom wants us to go home for dinner before we head over there. Are you ready?" Daniel opened the lid of a casket that had a white interior and silver handles.

"I can't yet," Thomas said as he pulled his brother's hand off the casket lid and closed it again. He looked back at Mr. Dunlap lying under the sheet. He had to be ready in the morning. "You go ahead. I'll meet you at the carnival later."

"Mom's not going to like that," Daniel told him.

"I have to finish this," Thomas said and headed back to work.

Daniel watched his brother go. The dark-haired boy was Daniel's opposite in many ways. The worst one, to Daniel, was that he never wanted to have fun. He seemed like an old man rather than a nineteen year old.

Daniel left his brother to finish Mr. Dunlap's preparations. He wished that he had an excuse for skipping the family dinner.

Chapter 5

S ara Cross pulled the lid off the pot that was boiling on the stove. The spicy aroma of chili billowed out along with the steam that had been trapped inside. She breathed in the delicious smell and stirred the chili again.

"Almost ready," she called to her mother.

She put the lid back on the pot and gathered up the shredded cheddar cheese, nacho cheese tortilla chips and sour cream. She joined her mother in the dining room and set the food around the table. The table was set for four people. However, her brothers hadn't arrived yet.

Mary Cross was staring off into space while she slowly swished the wine around in her glass. Sara wasn't sure how many glasses she'd had that night. Three, she thought.

She was concerned with the amount of drinking her mother was doing. She never drank at all when their father was there. Since he left, the single glass of wine once in a while became one every evening and now several per night. She sometimes wondered if it were limited to the evening.

The wine bottle on the table was empty, and she hoped that her mother wouldn't go open another one.

"If you want to talk about it, you can," Sara told her.

"Hmm? Talk about what, dear?" Mary asked, her thoughts coming back from wherever they had drifted.

"About Dad," Sara said.

Joe Cross walked out of the house seven years earlier to go to work and never came back. After an initial frenzied search by the Wakina Police Department, the investigation eventually wound down and even though it remained open, it hadn't been active for a long time.

She put her glass down and patted Sara's hand.

"That's ancient history."

"It's OK to talk about it, Mom," Sara said.

"I'm fine," Mary said sharply. "Your father is gone, and I don't want to talk about him."

"Yes, Dad is gone," Sara said quietly. She wanted to say, but, we're still here.

"And we're just fine," Mary said.

"We don't spend any time together as a family, except for dinner. Thomas and Daniel are rarely home at all."

"Well, the boys are growing up. They don't need their mother so much anymore. And you, you're seventeen, almost a woman."

"Daniel and Thomas do need you. They might not admit it, but they do. It hurts them. It hurts all of us to see you like this."

The sound of the front door opening interrupted the moment. Daniel came into the living room and dropped his jacket on a chair.

"I'm here," he said. "Let's eat."

He sat down at his place and looked at the two women.

"Did I interrupt something?" he asked.

"No, dear. Sara was just going to get the chili," Mary told him and looked at Sara. When she didn't move right away, Mary tilted her head toward the kitchen. Sara rolled her eyes at her mother and got up from the table with an exasperated sigh.

"Where's Thomas?" Mary asked.

"He had some work to do," Daniel said. "He's going to meet us at the carnival."

Sara stopped at the kitchen door.

"What," Sara said. "He knows he's supposed to come home for dinner."

Daniel shrugged. "He's got work."

"But," Sara started to say. She was interrupted by her mother.

"It's OK, Sara," Mary said softly. "If he has work, that's more important."

"No it's not," Sara said, flushing with anger. "Nothing is more important."

"Than dinner?" Daniel asked.

"No," Sara said. "Than family." She stormed out into the kitchen

Mary got up from the table and followed Sara. She found her sitting on one of the kitchen chairs, her head in her hands.

She pulled a chair closer to her daughter. She sat down and put her arm around Sara.

"Everything will be OK, Sara," she told her, holding her tightly and stroking her arm.

Her mother always could make her feel better by holding her like that. Ever since she could remember, whenever she'd get upset or hurt, her mother would hold her tight and whatever that was wrong would seem far away. Her tears dried, and she relaxed and leaned against her.

After a few minutes, Mary kissed her forehead and suggested that they eat. Sara nodded and got up. She always felt a pang of uneasiness when her mother let her go. She was never sure why. After a moment, the feeling passed.

She brought the chili to the table, and they each began to fill their bowls and add whatever other toppings they liked.

Daniel finished first and pushed his bowl away from him.

"I'm stuffed. Ready to go?" he asked Sara. He could see that her bowl still more than half full.

"Not yet," Sara told him between spoonfuls.

Daniel leaned back. He knew it would be a little while still. He thought that she was actually eating extra slow just to annoy him. And it was working. He didn't want her to know, so he just tried to relax and ignore her.

He stared at the flowers in the middle of the table. They used to be daisies, he thought. It was hard to tell. His mother's green thumb must have turned black.

While growing up, he couldn't remember a time when their house wasn't full of plants. They had plants hanging in every corner. Gardens surrounded the house from May until September. They even had potted trees in the living room.

That seemed to change after their dad left. She didn't seem to care anymore. Eventually, the greenery turned brown, and after the leaves were vacuumed up, the pots were taken out to the garage.

Every once in a while, she would buy a plant, like the daisies and put it on the table. Soon, they would go the way of the other plants and end up dead in the garage.

"Help take stuff out to the kitchen and then we'll go," Sara said, interrupting his thoughts.

They cleaned the table and put away the food. Mary told them that she would do the dishes so they could go out and have fun at the carnival. Sara gave her mother a hug and thanked her.

When she turned around, Daniel was already out the door, heading to her car. She shook her head and followed him out.

Chapter 6

For most of the year, the fairgrounds in Wakina, Minnesota stood empty and forgotten, except for sleigh rides in December and three days in May. For those three days, the Salenski Carnival transformed the fairgrounds into a playground of blinking lights and calliope sounds with the smell of popcorn and funnel cakes wafting through the air.

And for those three days, the fairgrounds would be packed with teenagers, families and carnies.

Thomas found Daniel eating cheese curds by the First Lutheran Church food booth. Sara was talking on her phone nearby. She was wearing her Wakina Lions baseball hat and jacket. She had been the first girl to earn a place as pitcher on the boys' baseball team for their high school team.

"Who's she talking to?" Thomas asked.

"Mom. She probably doesn't want us to stay out too late," Daniel said.

Sara snapped her phone shut. She turned to go sit down at the picnic table with her brothers and ran into a tall man wearing gray overalls.

"I'm sorry. I guess I wasn't looking," she said. She looked up at his face. She was startled because his face seemed odd. His skin had a grayish coloring and was lined. She couldn't tell whether it was wrinkled or scarred. His eyes were dull and sunken with dark circles under them.

"Be careful," he told her and walked away into the crowd. Before she could say anything more, he was gone. Sara sniffed. He must like mints, she thought.

"Weird," she said to herself. She noticed Thomas was there. "Now that you're finally here, we can have some fun."

The next hour or so was a blur of rides. They took their chances on the High Roller, a steel coaster with a 40 foot drop and a single loop. The ride was just under a minute, and they would have gotten on it again right away, but the line was just too long.

Then they decided to try out the Alien Horror, an ancient haunted house decorated with various bulbous aliens chasing and zapping unsuspecting humans across the front of the ride.

In its day, it could have been a fun ride. The lack of maintenance over the years made it a joke. Many aliens were replaced with bright flashing lights and loud horns designed to startle. Most of the ones that remained, although realistically detailed, either flopped around like a fish out of water or just didn't work at all.

"That was disappointing," Daniel said when they got out of the ride. "Those horns gave me a headache."

Sara admitted she had one also.

They had more fun on the Zipper. Daniel and Sara were in one car, and Thomas ended up by himself in another. As the cars made their way around, Daniel did his best to flip their car over and over to the discomfort of Sara. Thomas just let his car do what it wanted to.

Sara dragged her brothers on the bumper cars next. Daniel and Thomas weren't enthusiastic about the ride especially when Sara did her best to slam into their cars.

It was when they were swinging back and forth on the Pirate Ship that Sara noticed him again. The man in gray overalls was standing by an electrical shack watching the ride. She pointed him out to her brothers.

"There's the guy I ran into over there," she said. "It's as if he's watching us."

The boys looked to where she was pointing. They saw him standing there facing their direction.

"He probably works for the carnival. Maybe he's just checking the ride," Thomas told her.

A large group of kids walked by in front of him. It was a birthday party judging by the number of balloons the kids were carrying. She lost sight of him behind the balloons and kids for a moment, and when they moved on, he was gone.

"Where'd he go?" Sara asked her brothers. They just shrugged.

When they got off the ride, she looked for him again. He was nowhere to be seen.

"Let's go play some games," Daniel said and headed for the midway.

"Hey, kid. Show your girlfriend what a wimp you are," a voice on a loudspeaker said. The three of them glanced around. Across the walkway was a dunking booth. A sad clown wearing an old fashioned checkered swimsuit sat on a board over a tank of water.

"Yeah you. Show her what a wimp you are," he called to Thomas. "I bet you can't dunk me." He motioned at the target next to the tank. The sign above it read "Drown the Clown." A Carny in front of the booth held out three baseballs to him.

"She's my sister," Thomas called back to him.

"I didn't know that was legal here," the clown said and let out a loud, obnoxious laugh.

"Two dollars for three tries," the Carny told them.

"Quick, make a decision. Don't let your mind wander. It's too little to be left out alone." The clown's laugh blasted out again.

Thomas paid the man and took the three baseballs. Daniel grabbed his arm.

"Let Sara do it," he told Thomas quietly. "She's the all-star." They all smiled as Thomas handed Sara the first ball.

"She must be the man of the house," the clown said as Sara stepped up to pitch.

She went into her pitching routine, wound up and threw a hard, fast ball. It caught the edge of the target. The target didn't move. The ball hit the backdrop of the booth with a resounding thwack.

"You couldn't hit the ground without gravity," the clown joked.

Sara was frustrated that she had missed. She tried to shake it off and motioned for Thomas to give her another ball. Thomas handed Sara the second ball. Again, Sara started her routine.

Sara wound up and threw the ball at the target. There was a metallic whine as the ball again caught the edge of the target, causing it to vibrate. Still the target didn't move, and the clown stayed where he was.

"Do you want me to throw that for you?" The clown laughed uproariously.

Sara kicked the front of the booth. Thomas could see that she was angry. He handed the third ball to her. She tried to snatch it from him, but she accidentally dropped it. It bounced against the front of the booth and rolled up against Thomas' feet.

"A girl throws better than you." The clown's laughter echoed across the midway.

Thomas picked up the ball. He tossed it in the air. He looked at Sara, and she nodded, motioning for him to give her the ball. He tossed it in the air again and looked at the clown. He was still laughing. Finally, he tossed the ball to Sara.

In one smooth motion, Sara grabbed the ball out of the air and threw it as hard as she could at the target.

"A Swing and a," the clown started to say. A loud clang rang out in the night air. The clown dropped into the tank and disappeared into the water.

"You got dunked by a girl," Sara called to the clown who was trying to climb out of the tank. He looked like a wet dog.

The Carny was staring at the target. The target arm was bent back from the impact, and the ball was embedded in the target's face plate. It was obviously broken, and there was going to be a lot of work to put the dunking booth back into working order.

"Excuse me? Can I try again?" Sara asked.

"Go away, kid," the Carny said and turned away from her.

"Hey, I've got money," she said, digging some out of her pocket. "I want to try again."

The Carny turned back. "You'll be lucky we don't call the cops and have you pay for the damage you did." He went to examine the target.

"Hey," Sara called to him.

Thomas and Daniel took her by the arms and led her away. She called back to the Carny several times before giving in to her brothers.

"How about we go on the Ferris Wheel," Thomas suggested. Daniel agreed.

The brothers guided her into the line for the ride. In a few minutes, they were seated on one of the sixteen yellow and red gondolas. Sara was seated between her brothers.

"Now this is relaxing. Cool night air. We can see all the lights," Daniel said, glancing at Sara.

Sara sat with her arms folded. She knew her brothers wanted her to calm down. She didn't want to. She sat glaring straight ahead, ignoring them.

The gondola went up, and they could see the lights of the town beyond the fairgrounds. Then the gondola went back down again, and Sara could see both the Carny and the clown wrestling with the target arm. She smiled to herself.

She stared out onto the midway as the gondola returned to the top and started back down. Out of the corner of her eye, she saw him again. The man in gray overalls was standing next to a ticket booth watching the Ferris wheel.

"There he is again," Sara said, "by the ticket booth." She pointed him out for her brothers. As the gondola dropped closer to the ground, the ticket booth where he was standing disappeared behind the Octopus.

"I don't see him," Thomas said.

"I don't either. Are you sure it was the same guy?" Daniel asked.

"Just wait. When we go back up, you'll see him right over there."

The gondola started rising again, and the ticket booth came back into view. The man was gone.

"He was there just a minute ago," she said.

The brothers looked at each other and shrugged. The gondola went around several more times and then slowed to a stop. They had to wait for three other gondolas to be unloaded before they were let out of theirs.

"Hey, this is boring," Thomas said. "Let's do some faster rides." Daniel liked the suggestion.

A while later, Daniel stumbled into the fence around the Tilt-A-Whirl. It was the third spinning ride in a row, and he was starting to get a little queasy. Thomas roughly guided him through the gate and back out onto the midway.

"Just don't barf on me," he told Daniel.

"I shouldn't have eaten those cheese curds," Daniel said with a hand on his stomach. "I've had enough of the rides for a while, let's do something else." He suddenly pointed at the colorful trailer ahead of them. "Hey, how about getting our fortunes told?"

Chapter 7

The trailer had a banner across the top that announced Madame Zella, Psychic and Cosmic Soothe Sayer. A number of symbols were scattered across the face of the trailer including a deck of cards, a hand and a crystal ball. A sign on a post near the door said that Madame Zella would look into your future for only $10.00 per 15 minute session.

"There's no line. Want to go in?" Thomas asked.

"That's all just bull," Sara said and started walking toward the Himalaya.

"I'd like to see my future," Daniel said.

"If you want to waste your money, go ahead," Sara said and sat down on a bench nearby.

"Come on, Tabby. Let's all go in together," Thomas said. Daniel nodded in agreement.

Sara hated when Thomas would call her by that name. Her middle name was Tabatha and anyone who knew it would tease her about being named after a TV witch. She didn't mind the name that much. She just didn't like the nickname Thomas used.

"As long as I don't have to pay for it," Sara said and followed them into the trailer. "And the name is Sara," she reminded Thomas.

Inside, they were greeted by Paula, Madame Zella's assistant. She took the money from Thomas and led them through a curtained doorway into what appeared to be an old Victorian parlor. A large round table was in the center of the room with an ornate stain glass light shining down on it.

There were several high-backed wooden chairs with plush cushions around the table and a larger chair that would be more at home in a throne room than a parlor. The larger chair was swiveled to face away from the table and the room's entrance. Paula motioned for them to sit in the wooden chairs and then left the room.

On the table in front of them were a deck of cards fanned out, a bell and something the size of a bowling ball under a cloth near the larger chair. The rest of the room was dark.

They waited for several minutes for the psychic to come in. Sara looked at her watch. Thomas and Daniel looked at each other. Daniel shrugged.

"Madame Zella has the power to see into the future and know what your fortune will be," a woman's voice said. "What is it that you want Madame Zella to find out for you?" The voice had an exaggerated accent like one from some Eastern European country. The larger chair swiveled around, and Madame Zella was revealed.

She wore a dark purple dress with a black spider web lace covering. On her head, she had a golden turban with an emerald clasp in the front. Each finger of her hands had a ring and each wrist was adorned with a number of gold bracelets. She wore large dangling earrings, and it was hard to tell where her earrings ended, and the myriad of necklaces around her neck began.

"We want to know our sister's future," Daniel said pointing at Sara.

"What?" Sara looked at her brothers.

"Yes. Tell us what the future has in store for her," Thomas said, laughing.

"Very well. And how do you want me to divine the future? Should I read your palm? The Tarot cards? Or, should I consult my crystal ball?"

The three teenagers were amazed that she was able to say all that with a straight face.

Even though Sara didn't believe in any of it, she picked the crystal ball simply because she wanted to see what it looked like.

"Very well," Madame Zella said. She pulled the covered ball toward herself and centered it in front of her. Then, she slipped the cover off and draped it over the arm of her chair. It looked like a clear glass ball about 10" in diameter except for the dim glow that could be seen in the center.

"Spirits of the Netherworld," Madame Zella commanded as she started to wave her hands around the ball. "I call on you to communicate to me the future of this young girl."

Daniel began to giggle. Thomas kicked him under the table.

"A window into the future is opening," Madame Zella said. She peered closely at the crystal ball. The glow in the center began to get brighter. The three siblings leaned closer to try to see something, anything, inside the ball.

"There is an important competition in your future, Miss Cross. It is Miss Cross, isn't it?" she asked. Sara nodded and rolled her eyes at her brothers. She pointed to her name on her jacket.

"I see a field. A baseball…" Madame Zella suddenly stopped. Her eyes grew wide as she looked into the glowing ball which started to glow even brighter. The three teenagers couldn't see anything in the ball. It had become too bright for them.

"No. That's not a field. It's a, a cemetery." The woman, speaking without a trace of an accent, seemed entranced with the vision. "There are many people around a small building. A mausoleum, I think. You're inside. You aren't dead though, no, you are very much alive."

"You say something to the crowd and then go back inside. They come toward the door and…" She suddenly stopped and looked at the ball in horror. "Oh, my god," she screamed and shielded her face with her arms.

She turned her face from the crystal ball and quickly grabbed at the cloth hanging from the arm of the chair. She tossed it over the ball. She covered her face with her hands. "No, No, No," she repeated as she rocked in her chair.

Just as the three of them stood up to see if they could be of any help to her, Paula came into the room and rushed over to Madame Zella.

"What's wrong Zella?" she asked. Zella waved her off and continued to rock. Paula turned on the teenagers. "What did you do to her?"

"We didn't do anything," Daniel said.

"No more today, Paula," Zella said between sobs. "No more."

"What did you see," Sara demanded.

"Out. All of you," Paula yelled at them. "We're closed."

Zella tried to say something.

"What is it, Zella," Paula leaned closer.

"Give them their money back," Zella said and then laid her head back down on the table.

Paula pulled a wad of cash from her pocket and searched for a ten dollar bill. She passed up several tens before producing one near the bottom. Apparently, Sara thought, she was looking for the one they paid with.

"Here's your money," she said. "Now out with you."

"What did you see?" Sara asked Zella again.

"She saw nothing. Just go." Paula herded them out the doorway and then down the front steps of the trailer. She slammed the door shut. A sign hung on the outside that said, "Madame Zella is consulting the spirit world. Please come back later."

"Why wouldn't she tell us what she saw?" Sara asked her brothers.

"I don't know," Thomas said.

"It was probably just a scam," Daniel said.

Thomas looked at his watch. "It's almost midnight," he said. "Let's just go home."

Chapter 8

Sara was quiet all the way to the parking lot. Daniel did stop on the way out and buy a caramel apple dipped in peanuts. Thomas and Sara said they weren't hungry. When they got to their cars, Thomas broke the silence.

"Daniel will ride with you, Sara."

"I'm fine," Sara told him. She got into her Mustang and started it.

Daniel was going to ride home with his brother in his Charger. When he saw Thomas nod to Sara's car, he reluctantly went over to it.

"Wait up, Sara. I'm going with you," he said.

Sara weaved her way through the parking lot and then turned toward town. Thomas pulled out of the parking lot behind her and followed them home.

"I'm sorry you had a bad night," Daniel said after several minutes of silence.

"I'm OK," Sara said and sighed. She looked over at the partially eaten apple. "Can I have a little?"

"Have all you want," Daniel said handing her what was left. He had eaten most of the bottom half with the peanuts. There was still a good portion of the top left, though.

"Thanks," she said and took a bite. Nothing more was said until they got home.

The house was dark when the three of them got there. Sara pulled slowly into the driveway and stopped.

"That's odd," Sara said. Although it was late and their mother was probably in bed sleeping, she usually left the front light on for them.

That night, it was off.

Thomas parked across the street from the house and met them at the door. He unlocked the door and switched on the front hall light. It flashed and immediately went off again. He flicked the switch several more times. The hallway remained dark.

"It must have tripped the breaker," Thomas said. He went through the living room, the dining room and finally into the kitchen. He tried lights as he went. They all remained off.

"Maybe the power is off," Daniel suggested.

"I'll check the breakers," Thomas said and headed for the basement stairs.

"I need something to drink," Daniel said. He opened the refrigerator and rummaged through the darkness inside. "Everything is still cold."

"I'm going to bed," Sara said and headed upstairs to her room. The light in the stairway didn't work, and the upstairs hallway light wouldn't turn on either.

When she got to the top of the stairs, she noticed that there was a soft glow coming from her mother's bedroom. She wondered why she had light in her room when the power seemed to be out everywhere else in the house. She went to see if she were still up.

"Mom," She called softly as she neared the doorway. She sniffed. Is that mint, she thought.

Just as she passed her bedroom, a gloved hand clamped over her mouth. Before she could react, both of her arms were pinned behind her back. She tried to struggle.

"Do you want to live," the man's voice whispered harshly into her ear. She nodded. "Then be quiet."

She thought about how she could get away. But she needed to warn her mother and brothers. She looked in her mother's room. It was then that she noticed that the glow wasn't an electric light. It was moving. Maybe a candle, she thought?

As the light came into her view, she took in a breath to scream. The man felt her stiffen.

"Don't make a sound," he whispered. She barely heard the words.

The thing was roughly the size of a small man, maybe five feet tall. Although it was shaped like a person, it seemed to be made up entirely of flames. Sara had the impression that it was looking for something despite the fact that it had no facial features that she could see.

Sara's mind tried to comprehend what she was seeing. Then she remembered her mother. She was in the room with it. She began to struggle and call out to her. The man pulled her tighter.

"Quiet," he hissed in her ear. "Or it will find you."

Sara stopped struggling as that realization sunk into her. Find her? Was that horrible thing, whatever it was, looking for her?

It slowly made its way to the hallway. It didn't walk like a human, it moved along the floor like a flame would dance along a log in a fireplace. As it got closer, panic started to well up inside her. She began to struggle again.

"Stop," the man commanded quietly.

The lights came on in the hallway. When it saw Sara, the flames suddenly grew in size until it filled the doorway and lapped against the ceiling.

The man shoved Sara down the hallway toward the stairs. She stumbled and fell against the wall and landed on the floor. She immediately was up on her knees and looked back toward her mother's door.

It was the man in gray overalls from the carnival. He stood facing the flame creature. He had a bag in his hand, and he poured what appeared to be a white powder into his other palm. As the flames billowed out toward him, he blew the powder into the air between them.

As the powder came into contact with the flames, she heard a shrill cry and the flames died down and backed away. She felt a blast of cold air blow down the hallway.

Though the flame creature had retreated, the flames on the ceiling continued to burn, and they were spreading to the walls.

"Go. Now," the man called back to her.

"My mom," she yelled back. "She's in there."

"I'll get her out," the man told her. "You must go."

The man disappeared into her mother's room. She heard the shrill cry again and another cold wind blew down the hall. Sara got up and ran to the doorway, shielding herself from the growing flames around it.

"What the hell," Thomas said from the top of the stairs. He stood staring in disbelief at his sister standing under a canopy of fire at their mother's bedroom door. Daniel stood below him trying to see around him.

"I'm getting mom," she told them. "Call 911."

She looked back into the room to see the man had the fire creature trapped against the bedroom window. Most of the room was in flames. Her mom was unconscious on the bed, the edges of her blanket were already burning. She ran to the bed and pulled the blanket off her.

The man blew another handful of powder at the creature. The creature seemed ready this time and leapt out of the way. It rushed at Sara. Sara raised her arms to ward off the flames. The heat enveloped her just briefly before she felt a freezing blast of cold and heard the scream again all around her. She fell to the floor, holding her hands over her ears.

Thomas and Daniel pulled her up off the floor. She looked around wildly. The fire creature was gone, but the house was still on fire. The man in gray overalls had picked up her mother and was carrying her to the doorway.

"Out of the house," he shouted at them.

Thomas and Daniel pulled Sara with them down the stairs and to the front door. Thomas threw open the door and herded Daniel and Sara out. The man followed them with their mother in his arms.

They hurried across the street and turned back to the house. The fire was spreading rapidly through the second floor.

"Did you call 911?" Sara asked.

"They're on their way," Thomas said trying to reassure her.

The man placed their mom down on the boulevard and checked her for injuries.

"They must have done something that made her sleep. She doesn't seem hurt," the man told them.

Sara was pacing around on the grass. She was breathing fast and wringing her hands.

"What was that thing?" Sara asked. The man could hear the rising panic in her voice.

"Everything is OK, Sara," the man told her in a quiet voice. "It's gone now. Why don't you sit down and try to calm yourself."

"How can I calm down? Something tried to kill us. Our house is burning down, and you, I don't even know who you are. You tell me to calm myself?"

"My name is Franklin," he said. "I'm a friend."

"And what was that?" Thomas asked, pointing at the house.

"It was a Fire Djinn," he said.

"A Djinn? Like a genie?" Daniel asked.

"Something like that. This was an evil creature. It was sent to kill you."

"Sent to kill us?" Thomas asked. "By who?"

"I don't know. I was told you were in danger, and I was sent to watch over you."

"Who told you that we were in danger?" Sara asked.

"My grandfather sent him," their mother said. She was sitting up looking at them.

"You never told us that we had any relatives that were still alive," Thomas said.

"He and my mother decided that it was safer that way. We pretended he didn't exist, and he pretended that we didn't exist. That way no one would know about you."

"Why?" Daniel asked.

"Because he has enemies and he feared that they might try what they did tonight."

They all looked at the house. The flames had spread to the main floor. A distant siren could be heard getting closer.

"Why didn't you just tell us?" Sara asked, turning back to Franklin. He was gone.

"Where did he go?"

"It's best that he doesn't get involved," Mary said.

"But, what if he's hurt? He should've waited for the ambulance," Sara said. The fire truck with its siren blaring and lights flashing came around the corner and pulled up in front of the house. The firemen jumped off and immediately went to work getting the hoses hooked up to the fire hydrant.

"He could have been killed," Sara said, absently, watching the house being ravaged by the fire.

"No," Mary said. "You can't kill someone who's already dead."

Chapter 9

The Cross family spent the night sitting across the street from their house watching it burn to the ground. Mary's car was in the garage, and that was engulfed in flames. Sara wasn't sure how her car would fare in the driveway. Thomas parked his car on the street so at least they had transportation. Everything else except what they were carrying was gone.

Their neighbors across the street, Orville and Olive Gilmore, woke up to the sirens and hurried out to check on the family who were camped out on their lawn. The elderly couple stood on their lawn dressed in their pajamas and slippers with their white hair sticking out in all directions, watching in horror as the house across the street was consumed by the fire.

The couple offered to have them come inside away from the fire and rest. Mary politely declined. The only comfort that they accepted was a couple of blankets and a pair of Olive's pink slippers. Mary, who was dressed only in a nightgown put on the warm, fuzzy slippers and wrapped a heavy blanket around herself as protection against the cold night breeze.

Sara sat most of the night with the blanket in her lap and her knees pulled up against her chest absentmindedly rubbing the blanket's smooth, satin edge against her cheek and rocking gently. Several times during the night she went to her mother and cried in her arms like she did years earlier when she was told her father would not be coming home again.

Daniel spent the night sitting by himself. He tried to be composed. However, there were several times the tears couldn't be held back.

Mary tried to comfort him once. He pulled away and went for a walk to be by himself. He didn't walk very far though because he wasn't sure that fire creature was truly gone.

Thomas was the only one that didn't allow himself to mourn the loss of their home or possessions. He never knew creatures like that existed except in horror stories. Now, he knew that some monsters were real, and they needed to keep an eye out for them so they wouldn't be caught unprepared again.

By the time the first light of morning began to dawn, their tears had been temporarily cried out, and everyone except Thomas had dozed off for a short period of time.

"You are lucky to have gotten out of there alive," Wallace Compton told them. Compton was the Fire Chief for the Wakina Fire Department. He looked over his shoulder at what was left of their house. "Unfortunately, we weren't able to save it. It's the damnedest thing. That fire just didn't want to be put out."

The sun was just starting to come up, and the firefighters were packing up their equipment. In the early morning light, they could see that the house was a total loss.

"Thank you for trying, Wallace," Mary said.

"Any idea what might have started it?" He asked her.

"No. I was sleeping, and the kids just came home from the carnival. They called 911 as soon as they saw the fire."

"Did you leave any candles burning?"

"No candles," Thomas said. "The lights didn't work though."

"The lights?"

"When we came home, the front hall light flashed once and then all the power seemed to be off after that."

"Might have been an electrical short then," He told them. "My men will take a look and see what they can find out."

"Thank you, Wallace," Mary said. She could see a young police officer standing by his squad car watching them from across the street.

"Have you made arrangements for a place to stay for a while?" The Fire Chief asked.

"Hmm?" Mary asked, rejoining the conversation.

"A place to stay? Do you have one?" He asked again.

"Oh, no, not yet."

"You should try to do that first. And call your insurance agent," he said. "Then check with your church or the Red Cross. They should have something to help you get back on your feet."

"I'll do that, thank you," she told him.

"I'm sorry for the loss of your house, ma'am," he said and left to supervise the equipment cleanup.

"What are we going to do, Mom?" Sara asked.

"Are you waiting to talk to us, Jason," Mary called to the young police officer.

"Yes, ma'am," he said and hurried over to them. "I'm Officer Wells with the Wakina Police Department."

"Yes, I know," Mary said.

Although Mary had never met Jason Wells in person, she had heard all about him from Sara. He had graduated from High School with Thomas a year earlier, and he and Sara had played on the same High School baseball team for two years before that.

"I just have some routine questions about the fire," he told them.

"That's fine."

"Who was home when the fire started?" he asked.

"I was upstairs sleeping," Mary said. "Sara and the boys were at the Carnival until late. Did you go to the Carnival, Jason?"

"No, ma'am. I was on the late shift last night. Were the doors and windows locked and shut?"

"Yes. I locked up everything and turned on the porch light for them when they came home."

"Did you see anyone in or around the house just before the fire started?"

"Well, I was asleep. Did any of you see anyone?" Mary asked her kids. They all shook their heads no.

"OK. Some of your neighbors reported that a man carried you across the street. Who was that?"

"Oh, I never saw him before," Mary said.

"He was just jogging by when we helped Mom out of the house," Thomas said.

"Yeah, he came over and helped carry her across the street," Daniel added.

"Before we could thank him, he left. We don't know who he was," Sara said.

Jason paused to write down what they had told him. When he was done, he looked back up at the three kids.

"He was jogging by? He was said to be wearing overalls," Jason said.

"Not that I saw," Thomas told him. Sara and Daniel shook their heads too.

"OK. Did you see him around before you went into the house?"

Thomas and Daniel looked at Sara. "No," Thomas said. "We didn't see him until after. Do you think someone set the fire?"

"I don't know. I'm just trying to cover all the bases," Jason said. "How long after you discovered the fire did you call 911?"

"I was the one that found it," Sara said. "I yelled to Thomas to call, and I went in to get my mom out."

"I had just seen it when Sara told me to call," Thomas said. "And I called right away."

"And you went into a burning room to get your mom?" Jason asked.

"Yes," Sara told him.

"That was a dangerous thing to do. You both might have been trapped in the fire."

"I couldn't leave her there."

"I know. I probably would do the same thing," He told her. "Officially, I can't condone what you did. But personally, I think you were extremely brave." He smiled at her. Sara smiled back.

"Do you have any more questions?" Thomas asked after a long pause.

"Oh. Just one more, I think," he looked down at his notebook to find his place. "Oh, yeah. Are your insurance payments up to date?"

"Yes, they are," Mary told him.

"Thank you, ma'am," he said. "I'll get in touch with you if there is anything more we need."

"Thank you, Jason," Mary said.

"Bye," Sara said as Jason walked back to his squad car.

"Bye, Jason," Daniel said, mocking Sara.

"Shut up," Sara said and shoved him.

"I need some breakfast," Thomas said, and the rest agreed.

After a quick stop at a department store for some clothes for Mary, they soon were seated in a booth at Joey's, one of their favorite places for breakfast.

Mary just ordered a coffee and a blueberry muffin. Sara had a bacon and cheese omelet while Thomas had a vegetarian one. Daniel didn't care for breakfast, so he ordered a burger and fries.

"What are we going to do, Mom?" Sara asked.

"I don't know," Mary told her. "We've lost everything, our house, our stuff." She dropped her knife on the plate startling everyone around them. She cradled her forehead in her hands. Sara could tell that she was trying to hold back her tears. She was having a hard time.

"I know that losing our home and our things is upsetting. I'm sad about it too," Sara told them. "I'm very happy that we are all still alive though. And I'm worried about staying that way."

"You think they will come after us again?" Daniel asked.

"I don't know. We need to salvage what we can from here and leave."

"Where will we go?" Thomas asked her.

"To talk to great-grandfather."

"Have you ever met him?" Thomas asked.

"When I was young. The last time I saw him, I was a teenager. My mother and I went to visit him. I stayed in the car, and she talked with him briefly on the porch. We never went back. I wasn't even sure he was still alive until last night."

"If he's got enemies, why would they be after us? We didn't do anything to them," Daniel said.

"I don't really know much about him," Mary said. "He was an explorer back in the 1930s and was famous for going to all sorts of strange places. He'd come back with fantastic stories about black magic and monsters. And he'd bring back the strange things that he'd found. He put those on display in his museums. People called them Museums of Terror, I think. I suppose somebody thinks there's some truth to his stories."

"He was around in the 1930s?" Daniel asked. "What is he? 100 years old?"

"He'd have to be close to 100," Mary said. "I don't know exactly how old he is."

The waitress checked to see if they needed anything more. When they told her that they were done, she waved to the manager who was just finishing up with another customer. He quickly strode over to their table.

"I saw the report about your house on the news this morning, and I am very sorry for your loss," He told them. "Please, don't worry about the bill. Your breakfast is on me this morning. I hope the rest of your day is much better."

"That's very nice of you. Thank you," Mary said. The three kids added their thanks. The man smiled and returned to the cash register to help another customer.

"Well, we'd better get going," Mary said. "I have to stop at the bank to get some cash. We also need to have our mail held until we get settled in Shadow Bluffs. Then, we'd better get on the road."

"Shadow Bluffs?" Daniel asked. "What's that?"

"That's where your great grandfather lives," she told them.

"There's something I want to do before we leave," Sara said.

"What's that?"

"I want to see that psychic again."

"That's a waste of time," Thomas told her.

"Maybe, but if it's for real, I have to know."

"Know what?" Mary asked her.

Sara told her about what happened with the fortune teller the night before.

"It's about a three hour drive to Shadow Bluffs," Mary said. "I want us to be there before dark."

"You three go ahead. I'll just stop out there and see her for a few minutes. I'll be right behind you."

"Could you ride with Sara?" Mary asked Daniel. "I'd rather not have anyone be alone."

"But…" Daniel started to say. His mom didn't let him finish.

"Daniel, I need you to do this," she said.

"OK."

"I'll call you when we get there," Mary told them. "Before dark, OK?"

"Before dark," Sara assured her.

Chapter 10

Sara and Daniel found the midway quieter than it was the night before. Although the crowds were still large, it had a more laid back atmosphere than at night when the lights come on, and the music is turned up.

They made their way down the midway to where the fortune teller trailer was. They were almost there when Daniel called Sara's attention to something across the midway.

"I'm going over there," he said.

He pointed to the huge banners along the west side of the midway that formed the front wall of the Nature's Oddities attraction. Each of the four banners highlighted one of the four creatures hidden within the tents; the Fiji Mermaid, the Two-Headed Bull, the Fire-breathing Dragon and the Reclusive Sasquatch. In case there were any doubts about the authenticity of any of the attractions, a large red circle with the word "Real" was emblazoned on each of the banners.

"OK," Sara said. "Meet me at the fortune teller's before too long." She continued on her way.

Daniel just nodded. He didn't want to hang around with his sister, he thought.

There was a man with a megaphone standing in front of the entrance to the attraction. He looked like he had just stepped out of an old movie with his straw hat, red striped blazer, bow tie and cane. He called out to the crowd pointing to several with the tip of the cane.

"Come on over folks. Gather around." The man waved his cane at the area in front of the attraction. "The show is starting right now. You've read about it. Everyone has been talking about it. And here it is, right now."

Daniel walked over to the front of the Sideshow along with several other people from the midway.

The man pulled a covered cage from behind the podium and set it on the table next to him. He pulled up the cover on the side facing him and checked on the contents. He then looked back at the crowd nodding as if everything were ready for the show.

"Inside you'll see the beautiful and frightening Fiji Mermaid. She is a creature of the depths and rarely seen on dry land except right here. And we have Sasha, the two-headed bull. Go ahead and touch him. He won't bite with either head."

"That's not all. We also have a real fire-breathing dragon. You won't be able to touch that one. No, it'll be behind a fire-proof wall with glass 2 inches thick. Don't worry. You'll be safe." He flashed the crowd a smile that Daniel thought would be worn by a snake oil salesman.

A large crowd had gathered by that time. People were glancing around to make sure that they weren't the only ones who wanted to see the freak show.

"We've saved the best for last. People have been looking for him for decades, and we have him. The mysterious and reclusive Sasquatch. You won't find him anywhere else except here, right now."

Daniel didn't take his eyes off the covered cage still sitting on the table.

"I want you to see all of the creatures that we have right inside, so I'll tell you what. Forget about the $8.00 that it says on the sign. For the next 5 minutes, I'm going to let you all in. Everyone who is standing right here. Everyone goes in for just $5.00. That's right, you can see all the creatures inside for just $5.00, but you have to go now."

Daniel pushed forward with a number of other people from the crowd and paid his money. The crowd slowly moved through the entrance into the Sideshow.

"That's right folks. The tickets are going fast so come on in right now. There are only four more minutes to get in for only $5.00."

He entered the darkness of the first tent just inside the entrance. It was then that he realized that the man never revealed what was in the cage.

When Sara got to the trailer, she found that it was still closed. She knocked several times, but neither Paula nor Madame Zella answered.

There were several game booths nearby, so she went over to the nearest one.

A large man with a handlebar mustache was running the ring toss. A grid of bottles filled the center of the booth and a multitude of stuffed animals hung from every available space around it.

"Ten rings for $3.00," he said holding out five rings in each hand.

"Sorry. I just had a question. Will Madame Zella be back soon?" she asked him.

"Madame who?"

"Madame Zella, the woman who does the fortune telling over there," she said pointing to the trailer.

"How should I know? Do you want ten rings or not?"

"No, thank you," she said and went on to the next booth.

"No guts, huh," the man called after her. "Your loss." He sold the ten rings to a group of nine year olds. They came close but failed to ring even one bottle.

The next booth was a balloon dart game. The back wall of the booth was lined with balloons. It was two dollars for three darts. If you were able to pop a balloon, you got a prize. The more balloons popped the bigger the prize.

The man running the game was tall and had a short mustache and beard. A cigarette hung from his lips. A younger man was standing in a narrow opening between the back wall and the side. He probably ran the game on the other side, she thought.

"Could you tell me if the fortune telling booth over there will be open again today? It seems to be closed right now."

"Do I look like some kind of psychic? I run this game and that's it. Go ask someone else unless you want to try your luck?" He showed her three darts.

"No, thank you," she was about to turn away when she saw the young man waving her to come around to the other side.

She walked around to find that the other side of the booth was also a balloon game. In this one, the players would spray water into the mouth of a clown which would inflate the balloon on his head. The first person to pop their balloon got a prize. There wasn't anyone waiting to play.

"You're looking for Zella?" the man asked.

"Yes. Will she be back soon?"

"I don't think it will be open at all today. I heard that she was sick.

Got sick last night."

"Sick?" Sara asked.

"Yeah. So rumor is that it won't be open at all today."

"I have to see her. She found out something about my future. She wouldn't tell me what it was. I have to know what she saw."

"Hey, I'm sorry to have to tell you this. It's just an act. She doesn't see anything. She just makes it up."

"No. That's what I thought too. But right in the middle of it, she saw something. It scared her, and she asked us to leave. I need to know what it was."

The young man looked at her for a moment. Then after glancing around, he pulled out a sign saying that he'd be right back and quietly told Sara to follow him.

They sneaked between a couple of rides and left the midway. Behind the rides, the trailers that served as homes to the carnies while on the road stood in tight rows. He took her down one row, cut between two trailers and then down the next. He stopped in front of one and knocked on the door.

After a moment, a voice inside asked, "Who is it?"

"It's Cal, Zella," the young man said. "I have a visitor for you."

A moment later, Zella's face appeared in the window of the door. Her face clouded when she saw that it was Sara was standing with Cal. She opened the door.

"What do you want?" she asked Sara.

"Now, Zella. This girl says that you actually saw her future," Cal tried to soothe her. "She just wants to know what it was. I think that if you did see something, you should tell her. It might help you feel better too."

Zella looked at Cal and then back at Sara. She closed her eyes for a moment and then seemed to relax a little.

"OK, Cal," she said. She backed up into the trailer and motioned to Sara. "Come on in then."

"I hope she has the answer you want," Cal said.

"So do I. Thank you," Sara told him and went into the trailer.

Chapter 11

For Daniel, the first three tents were disappointing.

The Fiji Mermaid in the first tent appeared to be a strange experiment in taxidermy floating in a large fish tank. The tank had become so green that you hardly could see the thing floating in it. Three kids wearing name brand hoodies stood right in front of it. The eleven or twelve year-olds pounded on the front of the tank while the rest of the people looked on uncomfortably and then drifted off toward the next tent.

"Wake up," the kid with the red hoodie yelled. He waved a short walking stick over his head.

"It's fake," another kid said. He pulled the hood of his gray hoodie over his head. He pounded the glass one more time and then walked off.

"You think it's fake?" the third kid in a blue hoodie asked. After a quick glance at the thing floating in the water, he followed the other two to the next tent.

In the next tent, Sasha, the two-headed bull did have two real heads. However, one was useless to Sasha except for a few automatic muscle reactions. Daniel felt sorry for the poor animal.

While most people were fascinated by the strange animal, many didn't go near it. The three hoodie kids quickly surrounded it. A Carny sat on a chair nearby. He was more interested in his phone than watching out for Sasha. All three started to grab at it.

"This isn't fake, is it?" Blue Hoodie asked.

"Nah, it's real," Gray Hoodie told him. He pulled on the ears of the useless head. "But this head's dead."

Red Hoodie pulled the mouth open. "This head couldn't bite you even if the cow wanted to."

"Leave it alone," Daniel told them.

"What's it to you," Gray Hoodie said. "You work here or something."

"No, I wish I did," Daniel said and glanced over at the Carny. Whatever he was doing on his phone had his full attention. "I'd kick you out of here."

"I'd like to see you try," Red Hoodie said.

"I don't think so," Daniel said and moved within inches of the boy. Daniel was eight or nine inches taller than the boy which forced him to look up at Daniel. The boy was silent for a long moment. Daniel kept an eye on the walking stick in case the boy tried using it.

"The cow ain't fun anyway. Let's just go," he said and turned to leave the tent. The other two boys frowned at Daniel and followed the other boy into the next tent.

The fire-breathing dragon, in the third tent, was actually a Komodo dragon in a pen behind a wall with a small square of glass. Each visitor would look through the glass and, right on cue, a ball of flames would billow up behind it. The flames came from below though, not from the animal. After a quick look through the glass, everyone went on to the next tent.

Daniel wasn't sure he wanted to see the next one. He wasn't happy how the carnival treated the two animals so far, and the three kids probably weren't the only ones mistreating them. Daniel loved animals and volunteered at the Wakina Park Zoo every summer. The animals there might not be free, but they were treated well and cared for.

There was a scream from the next tent just as Daniel pushed through the tent flap.

Most of the people were running toward the exit. Daniel could see Red Hoodie with his back to the bars of a cage. A hairy arm was holding him against the bars two or three feet in the air. The other two kids were pulling on his legs trying to free him.

Daniel rushed over to the cage. The Sasquatch was nothing more than a large orangutan. It was angry. However, it only held the boy immobile. Its other hand held the walking stick the boy had been carrying. It was roughly poking it at his back.

The boy was crying. Except for being poked in the back, Daniel could see that he wasn't hurt.

"It's OK," Daniel said to the orangutan in as soothing a voice as he could. "You can put him down. He won't hurt you anymore."

The orangutan looked at Daniel and waved the stick around. It made some guttural noises and then poked the boy with the stick again.

"I know," Daniel said. "He won't hurt you anymore. Will you?" Daniel looked up at the boy.

"No. No, I won't hurt you. Please let me down," the boy whimpered.

"See. You can put him down," Daniel said. The orangutan looked at the boy and slowly lowered him to the ground. He released him. The orangutan took the stick in both hands and broke it in half.

A Carny came rushing in with a rifle just as the orangutan threw the pieces at the boys. Daniel moved to stop the Carny while the three boys ran from the tent.

"Don't shoot him. He won't hurt anyone," Daniel told him.

"That's for someone else to decide," the man said and shot a dart into the ape. It screamed and pulled at the dart. Within seconds, it was on the ground. It held a hand out toward Daniel.

"I'm sorry," Daniel said softly and touched its hand.

Sara had to squeeze by Madame Zella to get into the fortune teller's trailer. Once she did, she found herself standing in a narrow aisle between a worn brown couch on one side and a small kitchenette on the other.

Two more steps would take her to the other end of the trailer where a dinette was located. That was where the woman motioned for her to sit. Zella sat across from her.

The table was piled with a number books and notebooks. From what Sara could see, they were about astrology and the occult. A Tarot deck was also spread out on the table. Zella started to gather the cards together.

"I have a confession," Zella said. She tapped the deck on the table and straightened the cards.

"What's that?" Sara noticed that Zella looked far different than the Madame Zella she met the night before. She was wearing a simple t-shirt and jeans. And she was also not draped in jewelry.

"I'm not a real fortune teller." She didn't look at Sara. She kept her eyes on the deck in her hands.

"I didn't really think you were."

"It's just a job," she said. "And the job is just to entertain you. I go through the motions. I don't see the future. I tell you a few things you want to hear and then you go on your way, ten dollars poorer, and hopefully little happier."

"That's not what happened last night," Sara said.

"No. Last night was different."

"What do you mean?"

Zella didn't say anything right away. She placed the deck of Tarot cards in front of Sara.

"Shuffle the cards," she said.

Sara wasn't sure she wanted to. She looked at the cards and then picked them up. If she needed to shuffle cards to get her to talk, she thought, that's what she'd do. She shuffled the cards several times and then handed them back to Zella.

"Tell me what you saw," Sara said.

"I've never seen anything in the crystal ball before," she said. She turned up a card. It showed a beautiful woman in white with purple robes and a golden headdress. "This is the High Priestess," she told her. "This symbolizes your present. It signifies intuition, wisdom and secret knowledge." She placed the card in the middle of the table.

"There is a light inside the crystal ball that can be operated from my chair. I can dim it or make it brighter." She turned up another card. It depicted a demon on a field of fire. "This is the Devil. This symbolizes the obstacles you face. It can signify any number of evils like temptation, greed, lust or just plain danger." She placed that card across the High Priestess.

"I could see your baseball jacket and I assumed it was your last name on it. So, I went with that." She turned up another card. It depicted three swords on a field of battle. "This symbolizes your past influences. It signifies a painful disruption and loss of balance." She placed the card below the middle two.

"I started to tell you about your baseball game, and I was going to tell you that you'd win your next one." She turned up a fourth card. It depicted a castle tower on a hill being hit by lightning. "This is the Tower. It symbolizes past events. It signifies an unexpected event or catastrophe and irreversible change." She placed it to the left of the middle cards.

"I stopped because something happened that has never happened before." She turned up the next card. It depicted seven cups floating over a blue lake. "This is the Seven of Cups. It symbolizes your future influences. It signifies illusions and deceptions." She placed it above the rest of the cards.

"I actually saw something in the ball. A vision of a cemetery." She turned up a sixth card. It depicted five wooden sticks on a green field. "This is the Five of Wands. It signifies discord and conflict." She placed it on the right side of the other cards.

"I saw a crowd of people gathered around a mausoleum. They seemed angry." She turned up another card. It was the Three of Cups. "This symbolizes how you affect the world. It signifies bonding, friendship, community." She placed the card to the side in front of herself.

"You were in the vision. You were standing at the door of the mausoleum." She turned up an eighth card. It depicted a woman pouring water from a pitcher in each hand with a bright star overhead. "This is the Star. It symbolizes how the world affects you. Because the card is upside down, it is considered reversed. It signifies disappointment, bad luck and imbalance." She placed it to the side above the Three of Cups.

"You said something to the crowd, and then you shut the door to the mausoleum." She turned up a ninth card. It was the Five of Cups. "This symbolizes your hopes and fears. It signifies loss and regret." She placed it above the Star.

"The angry crowd started to close in on you and then I saw the most terrifying thing I've ever seen." Zella drew a final card and held it in front of her with the back toward Sara. She closed her eyes, and when she spoke, her voice was unsteady. "This card symbolizes the outcome. This is the fifth time today that I have dealt the cards to see your future, and it always comes out the same."

"What did you see? Please. I have to know," Sara insisted.

Zella shut her eyes tight as if she had just seen the vision again. Her voice was low and strained. "I saw the building disintegrate in a fiery explosion," she said and placed the last card on the table.

Sara sat stunned by what Zella had said. She looked down at the table and her breath caught in her throat.

The last card was the Death card.

Chapter 12

Jefferson Potts checked his watch. He knew it was seven even before he looked. He'd heard the chimes from the town's clock tower down the street just a moment before. Like most people, though, he relied on his watch rather than his senses to tell the time.

He began the process of moving his produce carts back into his shop for the night. Mr. Potts had, what he liked to consider, the best grocery in town. He knew that no one in Shadow Bluffs would disagree because he also had the only grocery in town.

During the day, the carts of brightly colored fruit and lush green vegetables attracted more than one person to stop and purchase a delicious snack and maybe a few more things on their way from one place to another. At night, he brought them back into the shop.

After maneuvering a cart full of tomatoes and onions through the door and down a side aisle, Potts returned to the sidewalk to find a young boy with longish, unkempt hair looking at the cart of apples and oranges. The jet black hair hung down and almost obscured his eyes.

Mr. Potts had seen the boy many times before. He always wore the same worn, brown clothing, his face was always dirty, and he never wore shoes. The oddest thing about the boy was that his feet seemed always to be clean despite wandering around the city barefooted.

He didn't know where the boy lived or who his parents were. No one that Mr. Potts had talked to knew that. Someone, Polly Weathers he thought, asked the police to look into it. Nothing ever came of it. At least, nothing that he had heard about. All that he knew was the boy's name was Luca and that he was around 10 years old. Or at least, he thought so.

"Good Evening, Luca," Mr. Potts said to him. "In the market for some oranges?"

Luca looked at his feet and fidgeted. "No, sir. I don't have any money."

Potts looked at the boy and sighed, "I'll tell you what. If you help me take the rest of these carts into the store, I'll let you have an orange for free. OK?"

Luca's face brightened. "Really?"

"Yes. But be careful with them. Just push them inside and down the aisle over there," he said motioning toward the right side of the store. He turned around to grab the cart of corn and cucumbers. Luca was already pushing it into the store. He turned back to where Luca had just been standing and scratched his head. Shrugging, he started to push the cart with apples and oranges into the store.

As he came back out onto the sidewalk, he was saying, "Only three more carts to…" He stopped and stared at the empty sidewalk.

"All done, Mr. Potts," Luca called from inside the store.

Mr. Potts found all of the carts just where they were supposed to be for the night. He scratched his head and wondered how the boy had done it. He looked at the small boy and then at the four large carts standing neatly in a row along the counter. He looked at the boy again and then shrugged.

"You did a good job, Luca. Which one would you like?" Mr. Potts asked, waving the boy over to the oranges.

"This one," Luca said and grabbed one from the bottom of the pyramid of oranges.

Mr. Potts realized what was about to happen and tried to stop him. It was too late. The pile of oranges came apart and rolled one-by-one onto the floor, bouncing under the cart, out onto the sidewalk and all around the clean feet of the little boy. One even rolled almost all the way to the back of the store and stopped by a barrel of potatoes.

"I'm sorry," Luca said and looked at the floor. Mr. Potts looked down at the boy and started to laugh.

"It's OK, Luca," Mr. Potts patted him on the back. "Help me clean them up, and we'll call it even."

Luca wiped his tears and smiled up at Mr. Potts. He then started grabbing every orange he could find. It didn't take long for the oranges to fill up the cart again even if it weren't a neat pyramid anymore.

"Thank you, Luca. You hurry on home now, OK?" Mr. Potts

showed Luca to the front door of the store. "Did you get that orange you wanted?"

Luca held up the orange to Mr. Potts to show him that he had. He turned down the street and skipped away.

Mr. Potts smiled after him, closed the door and locked it. He'd have a funny story to tell Polly Weathers in the morning. He laughed to himself as he flipped the sign in the front window from Open over to Closed and finished turning off the lights in the shop. She'll get a laugh out of it.

Polly Weathers would have gotten a laugh out of it, except, in the morning, Mr. Potts wouldn't remember his encounter with the boy. Mr. Potts had an excellent memory, but he never remembered the boy helping him roll the carts into the shop even though it happened almost every night.

Luca skipped down the street and stopped at the fountain in the town square. He sat on the side, spun around and planted his feet in the water. The cool water always felt good on a warm day.

Luca pulled out the orange that Mr. Potts had given him and then three more from under his shirt. He got out a bag and put three of the oranges in it for later. The fourth, he started peeling right away.

There was a little bit of a breeze blowing across the fountain toward him. It carried with it a slight spray of water. He ignored it though because he was hungry. The orange was gone in minutes.

"Still no service," Sara said as she checked her phone again. She had been trying to get through to her mom or brother since they left Wakina. At first, her calls simply weren't answered. For the past hour, though, she had not been able to make a call at all.

Their mom had promised to call when she got to Shadow Bluffs, but Sara and Daniel had not heard from her since they left. Daniel could see that Sara was worried.

"I'm sure they got to the town just fine. They just don't have any service either," he assured her.

"I know," she said. "I'm just anxious to get there."

"Me too. There are only a few miles left."

They arrived in Shadow Bluffs just as the sun was setting. The streets were mostly deserted, and the few people they did see just stared at them as they drove by. The highway into town ended at the town square and although many shops around it were already closed, a few still had their doors open including a small cafe. They parked the car and headed over to it.

A boy was sitting with his feet in the fountain. When he saw them looking toward him, he waved to them and smiled. Sara gave him a half-hearted wave back.

"There's his car," Daniel said pointing to Thomas' orange Charger parked off the square on a side street. "They must be around here somewhere."

"Probably in the diner," Sara said.

"She is," a cheerful voice said from behind them. "I don't know where he went."

The two of them turned to find the black-haired boy from the fountain standing on the sidewalk behind them.

Quiet little rascal, Sara thought.

"What's that?" Daniel asked.

"The lady from the car over there. She's in the diner. The boy was in there too. He left a while ago."

"Thank you," Sara said. She started toward the diner. Daniel followed her.

"You're new here," the boy said.

"Yes," Sara said over her shoulder. "We just got here. We're going to meet up with my mom and brother."

"My name is Luca," he said, trying to keep up with them.

"We're glad to meet you," Daniel said. They crossed a street and turned toward the diner.

"And you are," Luca prompted them.

"Sorry, I'm Sara."

"And I'm Daniel."

"It was nice meeting you, Luca," Sara said. "We have to go find our mom, now."

"Can I go with you?" Luca asked.

Sara stopped and looked back at the boy. "Shouldn't you be getting back home?" She asked. "It's getting pretty late."

"Heck, no. I stay out late all the time."

"Don't your mom and dad get worried if you're out too late?"

"No," he said. He suddenly got a faraway look. "They're not home much."

Sara looked over the boy. By the look of his clothes, face and hair, he was probably telling the truth about his parents, she thought. They probably left him to fend for himself most of the day. She could see that the boy was very thin. "Did he even get regular meals?" she wondered.

She looked at Daniel. He just shrugged.

"OK," she said and turned back toward the diner. "We'll introduce you to our mom."

As they neared the diner, a patrol car pulled up to the curb in front and a large, uniformed man got out. He headed toward the door and reached it just before they did. He held it open for them. Sara hung back and let Daniel and Luca go in first.

Except, Luca wasn't there. She glanced up and down the sidewalk. There was no sign of him.

"Something wrong?" the man asked.

"Nothing, it's just that we were talking to this boy, and now he's gone," Sara said.

"This boy?" The man asked.

Sara looked up at him. She was going to describe the boy, but then she saw that the man's right eye had no color. Her mouth opened, and no sound came out. After a moment, she realized that she was staring at it.

"A little boy," she said, finally. She looked away. "I guess he went home."

The Sheriff looked closely at her. "Must have," he said.

Sara quickly turned away and went into the diner. The Sheriff glanced around the street. He did not see any boy. You won't be able to hide much longer, he thought as he went in and let the diner door close behind him.

Chapter 13

It was almost as if Sara and Daniel had stepped back in time more than fifty years. The red and white booths along three walls of the diner and the matching red and white metal stools that lined the lunch counter were straight out of the 1950s. The floor was a black and white checkered pattern. An open kitchen dominated one side and was surrounded by the counter. A row of tables ran down the middle of the diner from the door to the back. A jukebox by the front door was playing "Riders on the Storm."

They saw their mother sitting in a booth at the back of the diner. They passed the Sheriff who had taken a seat on a stool at the counter. An elderly man on a stool at the far end eyed them suspiciously. They slid in opposite their mother. She had a glass of pop in front of her. There was a second glass that still had a little ice in the bottom.

"Where's Thomas?" Sara asked her.

Before Mary could answer, a teenage girl stopped at their table with a couple of menus and an order pad.

"Can I get you something to drink?" she asked.

"I'll have a root beer," Sara said.

"What about you?" she asked Daniel.

Daniel looked up at her. The girl had bright red hair with thin black streaks. Her eyes were a gray blue and at the moment, caused him to forget what he was going to say. She gave him a crooked little smile. Sara jab him with her elbow.

"Oh. I'll have a, uh," he stammered and looked down at the menu, "a Dr. Pepper."

"I'll get that right away," she said and giggled as she walked away.

Daniel suddenly just wanted to leave, preferably before the girl got back with their drinks.

"Where did Thomas go?" Sara asked again once the girl was back behind the counter.

"Our cell phones don't work here," Mary said. "He went to look for a pay phone."

"Our phones don't work either. They must not have towers here," Daniel told her.

"Who's he calling?" Sara asked.

"The last time I was here, I was just a little girl. I don't know where my grandfather lives. He's calling information," Mary said.

"Maybe you can ask someone here." Sara said.

"We have to be careful. We don't know who to trust."

"No one to trust," the old man at the counter said loudly to himself and took a bite of a toasted cheese sandwich.

"Here are your drinks," the red-haired girl said, suddenly appearing at their table. She dropped off the two drinks.

Daniel glanced up to try to see if she had a name tag. There wasn't one pinned to her shirt. He heard her giggle and looked up to see her smiling at him again.

"It's Gwen," she told him. She turned to Mary. "Are you folks just passing through?"

"We're just visiting some family," Mary told her.

"Well, you picked a perfect time to visit. Tomorrow's the Spring Social."

"The Spring Social?" Sara asked.

"Yeah. It's to celebrate the end of winter. Nothing fancy. Just a little party with food and music."

"We don't know what our plans are yet," Mary said.

"Well, most everyone goes for at least part of it," she said. "Come on over if you have time. I hope to see you there." This last part was directly more at Daniel than the other two.

"We'll try to make it," Daniel said, reddening.

"Well, welcome to Shadow Bluffs," a young man's voice said from behind Mary. They looked to see two boys sitting at the table behind them. One was wearing a green and gold letterman jacket. The other boy had on a Minnesota Vikings jersey. The remains of burgers and fries littered the table.

"Thank you," Mary said and turned back to her kids. Sara and

Daniel just nodded to them.

Both boys slid out of the booth. The boy in the letterman jacket seemed like the star quarterback type to Sara. The boy with the Vikings jersey was more than a foot taller and probably 100 pounds heavier than the quarterback, so he was probably one of the defensive linemen. They grabbed chairs from a table nearby and straddled them, leaning on the backs to talk with the three newcomers.

"I heard that you have family here. Maybe we know them," the quarterback said.

The lineman glared at Daniel and said nothing.

"Maybe," Mary said. "But we don't know you."

"We don't know you," the old man at the counter said and pushed his plate away.

"Oh, I guess you're right," the quarterback laughed. "I'm Vincent, Vincent Sterling. Gwen there? She's my sister." He slapped the lineman on the back. "And this here's my best friend, Mason."

"Gwen's my girl," Mason said quietly leaning closer to Daniel, his glare unwavering.

"No, I'm not, you slug," Gwen said as she whacked him over the head with her order pad.

"Gwen, stop it," he whined shielding his head with his arms in case she tried to hit him again.

"Leave him alone," Vincent said and grabbed her arm.

"Leave her alone," Daniel told him. Vincent looked at him curiously and then let her arm go.

"I don't know anything about you," Vincent told Daniel. "You could be a nice guy. Then again, you might not be. Until I know for sure, just stay away from my sister."

"Yeah," Mason said, "We don't need your kind hanging around."

Daniel was about to ask Mason what he meant, when Gwen whacked Vincent over the head.

"And you. You don't decide who I can talk to and who I can't. Why don't you two just finish your burgers and get out of here," she said.

As Gwen returned to the kitchen, the Sheriff got up from his stool and made his way over to their table.

"Is there a problem here, boys?" he asked, putting one of his large hands on a shoulder of each boy.

"There's a problem here," the old man repeated and slammed his fist on the counter.

"No, Sheriff Marco. Just welcoming these fine people to town," Vincent told him.

"Really? Sounded like you were hassling them. Were you hassling them, Mason?" He looked down at the bigger boy.

"No, Dad. It was like Vincent said."

"Well, why don't you two boys go on home now? I think they've been welcomed enough."

Mason frowned at Daniel as the two boys got up. They pushed the chairs back to the table where they belonged and quickly left the diner.

"Sorry about them boys. They don't mean any harm, really. My name is Sheriff Richard Marco." He tipped his hat to them.

"I'm Mary Cross. These are my children, Sara and Daniel." The Sheriff nodded to each one in turn as they were introduced.

"Welcome to Shadow Bluffs. I understand you have family here?"

"Yes, my grandfather," Mary said.

"Can I ask his name?"

Mary looked at her two kids. She really didn't want to say, especially in such a public place as a diner. But, the Sheriff might be suspicious if she refused to tell him.

"C.J. Kask," she said trying not to be too loud.

"C.J. Kask is dead," the old man at the counter announced and then bowed his head.

"Hush up, Claude," the Sheriff told the old man. "He is not dead."

"That's right, Sheriff Marco," an elderly woman in a flowery dress said from her seat several booths away. An even older woman sat across from her absorbed in a book.

"What's that, Miss Emily?" The Sheriff asked.

"C.J. Kask. He's not dead."

"That's right, Miss Emily," the Sheriff agreed.

"He can't be dead," she told him.

"Why do you say that?"

"We haven't heard the Banshee. He can't be dead," she said.

"The Banshee's coming," Claude threw back his head and yelled to the ceiling.

"Now, Miss Emily, you know there's no such thing as a Banshee," the Sheriff said.

"Of course there is. Why I remember when I was a little girl, back in, uh, what year was it, Agnes?" she asked the older woman sitting with her. "Agnes?"

"Eh?" Agnes asked, looking up from her book.

"Miss Sadie. What year was she taken?" Miss Emily asked her.

"1958," Agnes said and went back to reading.

"Yes. That was it. 1958," Miss Emily continued. "It was in the fall. Agnes and I were sitting on our porch enjoying some tea my mama had made. I had just poured each of us a fresh cup when we heard it."

"The Banshee?" Daniel asked. He turned sideways on the bench with his feet out in the walkway to listen to the old woman's story.

"No, not the Banshee, dear boy, the siren. Apparently, Miss Sadie had fallen ill and C.J. had called the ambulance. You know, Miss Sadie had never been the same after their son was taken."

"By the Banshee?" Daniel asked.

"Oh goodness, no. The Banshee doesn't take anyone, child. The Banshee just announces their imminent, uh, departure so to speak," Miss Emily told him.

"And what does Miss Sadie and the ambulance have to do with a Banshee?" the Sheriff asked.

"Oh, it really doesn't have anything to do with the ambulance. No, the ambulance was on its way up to the house when we heard the Banshee's wail. It was terrifying. Wasn't it terrifying, Agnes?"

"Eh?" Agnes asked. This time she didn't look up.

"Wasn't the Banshee's wail terrifying?"

"Terrifying, yes," Agnes said, continuing to read.

"It was terrifying," Miss Emily repeated. "When the ambulance returned to town with Miss Sadie, it didn't use its siren. Miss Sadie was gone. We were sad to see her go. Weren't we Agnes?"

"Yes, Emily. We were sad," Agnes said and turned a page.

"That's why I know C.J. can't be dead. The Banshee has been heard every time someone in his family died, and we haven't heard the Banshee in many years now."

"She didn't come when Matthew was taken," Agnes said.

"That's because Matthew didn't die," Miss Emily told her.

"Who's Matthew?" Daniel asked.

"Oh, Matthew was their son. When he disappeared, it broke Miss Sadie's heart, and she was never the same again, pour soul," Miss Emily said sadly.

"Thank you for that history lesson, Miss Emily," the Sheriff said. He turned back to Mary. "Have you been up to see Mr. Kask since you got into town?"

"Not yet," Mary told him. "I haven't seen him in years, not since I was a little girl. I'm sorry to say that I don't even know where he lives."

"It's easy to find, ma'am," the Sheriff said chuckling. "Just go outside and look up. It's the mansion on the hill. You can't miss it."

"Oh, thank you. When we tried to call information, we found that our cell phones don't work," Mary said.

"Yeah, we had service several years ago. Lightning struck the tower, and they never sent anyone out to fix it."

"Great," Daniel said.

"Nice meeting you, ma'am, all of you," the Sheriff tipped his hat again and returned to his stool at the counter.

"We'll head up there as soon as Thomas gets back," Mary said to them.

"He's been gone a long time. Where did he go?" Sara asked her.

"I don't know. He was just going to find a phone to use."

"Should I go look—" Daniel began. The rest of the sentence was cut off by a woman's scream, a long ear-splitting screech coming from outside the diner. When it finally died off, everyone sat stunned.

"Did you hear that? Someone is in trouble," Sara said, getting up and rushing to the front door. She looked back at everyone still sitting where they were. "Don't just sit there. We need to help her."

"Yes, dear. Someone is in trouble, and I'm afraid that someone could be C.J.," Miss Emily said sadly.

"No, out on the street. The scream. Someone is getting hurt," Sara pushed open the door and went out into the night. Daniel followed her. Mary grabbed their things and went to the cash register to pay for their drinks.

"No, dear," Miss Emily said quietly. "That's the Banshee."

Chapter 14

The square outside the diner was quiet. No one was on the street, and there was no sign of the woman whose scream they heard so clearly in the diner.

Daniel and Mary joined her on the sidewalk, and all three listened carefully for any sound of commotion. None of them heard anything.

"It was so close," Sara said. "Where could it have come from?"

"I don't know. I wish Thomas would get back here," Mary said. "We shouldn't be out so late like this."

"I'm getting a bad feeling too," Daniel said.

"I think we should try to find him as quickly as we can," Mary said. "I'll leave a message for him in case he returns to the diner." She went back in.

"Wait here," Sara told Daniel. "I'll get the car."

Sara was almost to the car when she heard someone call her name. She turned to see Thomas crossing the square toward her. He waved and called her name again.

"Thomas," Sara called to him. "Did you hear that scream?"

"No," he said. "I didn't hear anything."

"Head over to the diner," she told him. He had just crossed the street to the fountain in the center. "I'll pull my car over there."

She unlocked the car and started to get in when she saw the boy she had met earlier step out from in front of the car.

"Look," he said, pointing to the street where Thomas had been.

A dark figure of a woman was standing there. She raised one of her arms and moved her hand in a circle as if she were stirring something in the air.

"Oh, no," Luca said. Then he yelled to Thomas. "Run!"

Sara looked at her brother. As he was passing by the fountain in the center of the square, she saw something that made her hair stand on end. A column of water rose up out of the fountain. As it grew, appendages emerged from the sides forming a human-like shape with thick arms the size of tree trunks. The arms reached out toward Thomas.

"Thomas, look out," Sara yelled. It was too late.

It wrapped its arms around Thomas and pulled him backward toward the fountain. Terror gripped at Sara's mind. She wanted to run away, but she felt as if she were frozen standing there by the car. Then she was running. Running toward the fountain, not away.

The creature pulled Thomas into the fountain and pushed him down under the water. When Sara reached the fountain, it lifted one of its arms and swung it at her. She didn't have time to duck before it caught her in the midriff and knocked her backward onto the ground.

She winced from the pain. She couldn't believe that it had been just water. She got up quickly and tried to catch her breath. Thomas was struggling near the surface. It turned back toward him and pushed him down again. The last thing she saw was his arm sliding down into the water. Just as his hand was disappearing, she dove into the churning water and grabbed it.

The water was like a whirlpool. Sara was buffeted around as she tried to hang on to her brother's hand. Thomas was dragged farther down, and Sara was being pulled down with him. She found his other hand and tried to pull him away from the creature. It was too strong. She began to run out of air, and she could see Thomas was too.

Suddenly, something like a tentacle wrapped around her chest and squeezed her. She tried to hold on to Thomas with one hand as she clawed at the tentacle with the other. While the tentacle held her fast, it didn't seem to be solid. It was a column of swirling water like the tail of a miniature water spout wrapped around her body. She could see Thomas beginning to panic. He expelled the air out of his lungs in a violent jet of bubbles and then the water rushed into him. His eyes went wide, and his mouth opened and shut as his body tried to get air. The tentacle tightened around her again, and her last air was squeezed out of her mouth. As the bubbles swirl around her head, she descended into darkness.

In the darkness, Sara was suddenly aware of a distant voice. It was a woman's voice. She didn't know who it was or where it was coming from. She opened her eyes or at least she thought she did. In the darkness, she wasn't quite sure. She tried to move her body. She wasn't able to.

"I will give you one chance," The voice was saying. "I gave your brother the same chance, and he refused."

"Where is my brother," Sara tried to ask. However, she was also unable to speak.

"You will see your brother again soon," the voice said. It seemed to drift around her and fade in and out as it spoke.

"You came here to see your great-grandfather?"

"How did she know that?" Sara wondered.

"There is a great deal that I know," the voice replied.

She can hear my thoughts, Sara realized. Am I alive or is this heaven? Or Hell? Her thoughts trailed off.

There was a light laughter in the darkness.

"There is a box in your great-grandfather's house. It belongs to me. He refuses to give it to me. So now, you must get that box and bring it to me," the voice told her.

"Who are you?" Sara wondered.

"You will know that when it is time for you to know," the voice said.

For a moment, Sara could see a box in her mind. It was a wooden box with metal straps. It seemed to be made of one solid piece of wood with no latch or hinges. In the center of the top, there was a circular design with a slot in the shape of a cross.

"Bring me this box," the voice said.

And if I refuse, Sara thought defiantly.

"You will end up like your brother," the voice said.

"My brother? Where is he?" Sara wondered.

There was another laugh and then it faded away.

Suddenly, Sara felt as if she were rising up. She was being pushed up faster and faster. She was aware of water rushing past her body and then she was up and out of the water. She landed on the street near the fountain and rolled several times. She heard something land nearby.

Sara lay there coughing up water and trying to catch her breath. She could hear voices all around her. She rolled over and opened her eyes. Her mother was kneeling beside Thomas, clutching his limp body to hers and murmuring softly to him.

"Sara. Sara, are you all right?" Daniel asked her.

"Thomas," Sara tried to say and coughed again. "Thomas?"

The Sheriff pushed his way through the crowd that had gathered around the fountain and tried to take charge of Thomas. Mary would not let him.

"I can make him better," she said rocking him in her arms. "I can make him better."

Finally, with the help of Daniel, the Sheriff was able to pull Thomas away from her and lower him onto his back. He knelt over Thomas and, after checking for a pulse, began CPR on him. Thomas' right arm was stretched out on the ground almost as if he were reaching for Sara. She took his hand and held it.

Daniel was crouched by Thomas. Tears were streaming down his face. Sara could see the girl from the diner standing behind him. She placed one hand on his shoulder. She held her other hand over her mouth as her eyes filled with tears.

A man pushed his way through the crowd to where they were lying. He looked at Sara and then at Thomas.

"I'll take over, Sheriff," the man said.

"OK. Doc," the Sheriff moved back, and the doctor examined the boy.

"Thomas," Sara softly called to him. He didn't respond. He just laid there in a puddle of water, his dark hair matted to his head and his clothes soaking wet.

"He needs a blanket. He's cold," Sara said weakly.

"It was the strangest thing," someone was telling the Sheriff. "They weren't anywhere to be seen and then suddenly, POW. They came out of the water as if they were shot out of a cannon."

Sara looked back at the fountain. It was just as it had been earlier. The spray was gently falling on the calm surface. Nothing different at all.

She looked across the fountain to find the woman she had seen earlier, but a crowd had gathered, and she would have been just another face among many. She saw the boy, Luca. He was looking at her, and he looked as if he were about to cry. As she watched him, he backed into the crowd and disappeared.

After what seemed like hours to Sara, the doctor stopped doing CPR. She turned to him. He was checking Thomas' neck for a pulse. He pulled a stethoscope out from his coat pocket. After he pulled open the boy's shirt, the doctor listened to his heart. After a few moments, he sat back on his heels and pulled the stethoscope from his ears.

"Doctor?" Mary asked. Sara could hear the desperation in her voice.

"I'm sorry," the doctor said. "He's dead."

Chapter 15

Sara sat in the ambulance and paid no attention to the paramedic who was checking her blood pressure. Her attention was focused on the black bag strapped to a gurney next to the fountain. The doctor and sheriff loaded it into the back of a station wagon. Although she couldn't read the words on the side of the car through her tears, she knew that it belonged to the coroner.

The body in the bag was jostled and bumped as they roughly situated it in the back of the car. She wanted to yell at them. Show some respect, she thought, that's my brother. Or was my brother. Thomas had been there a short time ago. Now he was gone. She buried her face in her hands.

When she looked out again, she saw the fountain behind the station wagon. Two people in uniforms were searching around in the fountain with their pant legs pulled up to their knees. The water appeared to be no more than a foot deep.

She could see her mother and brother. Daniel paced back and forth with his hands jammed into his pockets watching them search the fountain. Her mother stood frozen staring at the black bag that contained Thomas.

"Come on out, guys," the Sheriff called to the men. "There isn't anything more you can do in there."

They got out and put their shoes and socks on again.

"Thanks for your help," he told them. "I can take it from here."

"How are you feeling?" the paramedic asked.

"I'm OK," she said. "Can I go now?"

"I don't think there will be any lasting effects. You just took in a little water. You probably should go home and rest."

He helped her out of the ambulance, and she hurried over to her mother.

"I can't believe he's gone," Sara said as the coroner's station wagon pulled away.

"I can't either," Daniel said.

Their mother just pulled her jacket tighter around her without saying anything.

After they had some time and the tears had slowed, the Sheriff approached the three of them.

"My office is just down the way there," he told them pointing at an official looking building just off the square. "Why don't we go there and I'll get your statements about the drowning. Then we can get you up to Mr. Kask's so you can rest."

Sara and Daniel began to follow the Sheriff. Mary just stood there looking at the fountain.

Sara took her mother's arm. "Let's go, Mom," she told her.

Mary looked at her with a confused expression, but allowed herself to be led away from the square. Daniel waited until they passed and then following behind.

"What about the thing that killed Thomas?" Sara asked the Sheriff.

He slowed for just a moment and then continued on. "The thing?" he asked over his shoulder.

"Yes, the thing in the fountain that grabbed my brother and drowned him."

The Sheriff stopped. He turned around to face Sara. "There's nothing in the fountain except a foot of water and some change," he said. "He must have fallen in and hit his head on the bottom."

"He didn't fall in," Sara insisted. "I saw something come out of the fountain and grab him. It pulled him down and drowned him."

"We took a look at that fountain," the Sheriff told her. "I even had the highway patrol walking around in it. There's no way something could have been hiding in that shallow of water. Besides, what here would want to attack your brother?" He turned back toward the office.

"If it were anything like what burned our house down, I'd say it was a Water Djinn." Sara said.

The Sheriff quickly turned back to her in surprise.

"A water," he started to say and then the surprise was gone. "I have no idea what you're talking about. Besides, the coroner has already ruled it an accidental drowning." He resumed walking toward the Sheriff's Office, picking up the pace.

She dropped her mother's arm. Mary stopped as Sara hurried ahead to grab the Sheriff's arm. "It was not an accidental drowning. Thomas was murdered," Sara yelled at him.

She wasn't able to catch his arm because at that moment, the Sheriff fell forward on the street as if he had been pushed violently from behind. After he fell on the ground, he rolled several times before coming to a stop flat on his back.

Daniel looked in amazement at the Sheriff. Mary just stared curiously at Sara.

The Sheriff stood up and dusted off his uniform. He gave Sara a stern look.

"Why don't you come back in the morning to give your statements?" the Sheriff asked. He continued to scowl at Sara. "Then you can sleep on what you want to say."

"I think that would be for the best," Daniel agreed and took Mary's arm. Sara saw that the Sheriff wasn't going to listen and reluctantly agreed.

The Sheriff gave Thomas' keys to Daniel. He told them that he would return the rest of his possessions after they gave their statements in the morning.

Sara stared out at the tree-lined road as she followed Daniel up the hill toward the mansion. She looked over at her mom. She was looking out the side window at the trees flashing by. Sara was worried about her unusual silence.

"How are you doing?" she asked.

Mary didn't say anything and continued to stare out the window.

"How do you think he'll react when he sees us?" she asked.

Even without a response from her mother, she continued to talk just to break the awful silence in the car.

"He knew we were in danger and sent Franklin to help us. I think he'll be expecting us. Especially when Franklin told him about what happened," she said.

"You probably met Franklin when you visited your grandfather."

"How old do you think he is?" Sara asked.

Mary didn't answer.

"I suppose he was dead long before you knew him," Sara said, slowing the car.

Daniel pulled up in front of the black, iron gate leading to the mansion grounds, and Sara pulled up behind him. He jumped out to open it for the two cars.

As he slid the bolt to unlatch the gate, he noticed something red on it. He stepped aside to let the headlights from the car fully illuminate it. There was clearly something red splashed on the bolt. Paint maybe, he thought.

He pushed open the gate and pulled Thomas' car through. After Sara passed and continued up the drive, he closed the gate again and latched it. He noticed a red and black striped bobcat sitting on the road looking at him. He slowly moved around the back of the car to the driver's door. The bobcat continued to watch him. He quickly got back in the car and continued up the cobblestone driveway after Sara. He looked in his rear view mirror and saw the wild cat stand up and walk along the road until it was out of his view.

As she drove on, Sara reached over and squeezed her mother's arm. She neither moved nor spoke. After a short time, Sara continued her one-sided conversation.

"Doesn't that freak you out? I mean, dead people walking around?" Sara asked her mom.

"I'm freaked out by him," Sara said when she got no answer.

"I'll probably get used to him," she said quietly, "someday."

The driveway broke free of the trees and both sat in silence looking at the massive building in front of them. The mansion was mostly dark though there were a few lights on in rooms on the main floor.

"Wow," Sara said looking up at the enormous building. Mary looked, but didn't say anything.

The driveway widened as it circled the front lawn. They stopped in front of the house, and Daniel pulled up behind them.

Chapter 16

They gathered at the bottom of the steps and hesitated a moment before Sara led them up to the front door. They didn't know what to expect from a man that they had never met nor even knew was alive until the night before. Now, they were on his porch and were looking for a place to stay. And looking for protection from his, and now their, enemies.

An outdoor light was on, illuminating the porch and the pair of massive, carved-oak front doors with tarnished brass handles and lion head door knockers. Daniel carefully pulled on one of the lion heads almost expecting it to take a bite out of his hand and let it drop against the door. It gave a loud bang against the brass plate.

The sound of the knocker hadn't died out yet when the dead bolt was unlatched and the door swung open. They waited for the loud creaking sound that all old doors had in the movies. This one opened quietly.

A stocky, bald man with bushy, black eyebrows stood in the doorway. He was impeccably dressed in the classic uniform of an English butler. His eyebrows rose as he saw them and he stepped back to allow them to enter.

"Please, come in. Mr. Kask is expecting you," he said.

They stepped into a large room, and the man closed the door behind them. The room was two stories tall with a wide stairway in the middle climbing to a balcony that circled the upper part. There were several doors leading off from the room on both levels.

The walls were filled with paintings, carvings and strange objects from all over the world. There were African masks, Egyptian figurines, Renaissance paintings and Chinese embroidery among others.

The man noticed that they were staring at the room. "This is the Grand Foyer," he told them.

"Do you want us to remove our shoes?" Daniel asked the man as he took in the polished wood floor in the room and the plush carpeting on the stairs.

"No, that is not necessary," he said. "My name is Bramwell. I am the head of the household staff. We are very happy that you are finally able to join us here. If there is anything you need during your stay, please let me know."

They weren't sure how genuinely happy he was because no emotion marred the stoic look on his face. They followed him to a set of double doors on the main floor.

"Mr. Kask has asked that you wait for him in the front parlor," he said and opened the doors for them.

The front parlor was a large room with several sofas and chairs gathered around a massive fireplace. There wasn't a fire prepared, which, considering their adventures the night before, was a relief for them. Above the fireplace was a painting of a beautiful woman wearing a yellow dress. Her hands were folded in her lap, and her eyes stared out at them with what seemed like a hint of sadness.

Sara helped her mother to a chair. Mary gazed up at the painting.

"Who is she?" Sara asked. Her mother didn't say anything and Daniel just shook his head.

"That was your great-grandmother, Sadie," a voice behind them said. They turned to find an older man standing at the door. He was bald, like the butler, but he had a large white mustache that ended with a loop at each end. His blue eyes flashed from one person to another.

Sara introduced the three of them. The man greeted Sara and Daniel with a vigorous handshake. When he greeted Mary, she just looked at him. Sara told him about Thomas and that her mother was not doing well. He said that he understood. He took her hand in his and welcomed her. She gazed at him and didn't say anything. Sara sat on a chair near her mother and Daniel sat in a wing-backed chair across from the one the old man chose for himself.

"My name is Matthew Kask. C.J. is my father," the man told them.

"Grandfather?" Mary asked in a quiet voice.

"Yes. C.J is your grandfather," he told Mary. "Your mother, Sarah, was his daughter and my sister."

"My grandmother's name was Sara too?" Sara asked.

"Sarah with an 'h', yes. Didn't you know that you were named after her?" Matthew asked her. He looked at Mary in surprise.

"No. They thought it best that we didn't know anything about our grandparents," Sara told him. "To protect us," she added.

"I understand. Unfortunately, our attempts to keep you all safe didn't work. I am terribly sorry to hear about Thomas and your mother."

Sara leaned toward her mother and patted her arm. Daniel sat back in the chair and distracted himself with several coasters that were piled on the table beside him.

"Thank you," Sara said. "We had nowhere to go after our house burned down, so we came here. We were hoping C.J. could help us decide what we should do."

"That was just what you needed to do. Of course, you will be staying with us until we can get this resolved. I'm sure that after what you've been through over the last day, you will need to rest. Bramwell will show you to your rooms."

"We won't be seeing C.J. tonight?" Sara asked him.

"Unfortunately, C.J. is not doing well," he said. "He has been confined to bed for several months now, and I'm afraid that we can't be disturbing him at this late hour. Perhaps he will feel up to visiting with you tomorrow. Would that be OK?"

"I really wanted to talk to him," Sara said.

"Grandfather?" Mary asked again, looking at Matthew with a pleading look.

"We can wait until tomorrow," Daniel said. Then he helped Mary to her feet. "We will see him tomorrow." He told her.

Sara realized that questions about the box were best left until she could see her great-grandfather alone.

"I just wanted to meet him, that's all," she said quietly.

"You will," Matthew said. "Very soon."

They heard the front door open and then close. There was the sound of boots clomping across the floor and a moment later a tall and extremely thin man in dirty work clothes appeared at the doorway. His dark hair was matted down with sweat and dirt.

"I'm sorry. I didn't know we had company," he said trying to fix his clothes and hair. "I just wanted to let you know that I'm done for the night."

"That's fine," Matthew told him. "Please, I would like you to meet my niece, Mary, and her two kids, Sara and Daniel. This is Peter Jacobs. He's C.J.'s archivist. He keeps track of all the things that C.J. kept after he closed the museums."

"Which was just about everything. Nice to meet you all," Peter said. "I apologize for my appearance. I've been doing a little bit of amateur archeology on a high mound I found on the property."

Daniel and Sara greeted him politely.

"They will be staying with us indefinitely," Matthew told him.

"It will be nice to have more people in the house. It's a pretty large house for such a small family."

"Yes," Matthew said looking at the painting of Sadie.

"Is it some kind of burial mound?" Daniel asked.

"Oh no. I wouldn't disturb a burial mound. That could open up a bunch of problems that we just don't need. No, the mound that I'm excavating is older than a typical burial mound. There's a cedar tree growing on it that was there during the Roman Empire in Europe."

"There are no trees that old around here." Sara said.

"Yes, there are. Not many, I grant you, but there are some."

"What's so special about the mound?" Daniel asked.

"I was out doing a little survey of the land around the mansion when I discovered it. As I approached, my compass started to go wild. It just spun around and around. When I walked away from the hill, the compass would go back to normal. There is something magnetic in that mound of dirt, and I'm trying to find out what."

"Cool. Have you found anything yet?" Daniel asked.

"Not yet."

"Can I help?" Daniel asked.

"Sorry, I've got the dig pretty well shored up. However, there still is a danger of a cave-in. I don't want to be responsible for anyone getting hurt."

"It's been a long day," Matthew broke in. "I'm sure everyone could use some rest."

"You're right. I'm sorry I'm keeping everyone up. Goodnight and welcome to Grimm End."

"Peter," Matthew said abruptly.

"Sorry, bad habit. Welcome to 'This Old House'," he joked. "I hope you enjoy your stay here." Peter returned to the grand foyer and soon his boots could be heard clomping up the stairs.

The old man stood up and motioned to Bramwell to show them to their rooms. Sara was helping Mary follow the butler back out into the grand foyer when she suddenly stopped and turned back to Matthew.

"I'm very glad to meet you finally. Growing up without a family can be a lonely thing," she told him.

"We are happy to have you with us at last," Matthew told her.

"And I'm glad that you're back," Daniel told him.

"Back?" Matthew asked.

"Yeah. A lady at the diner said that you disappeared when you were younger."

"Disappeared? I don't know anything about disappearing," Matthew thought for a moment. "Oh. I wonder if she meant when my father sent me out east to a boarding school for a couple of years. I bet that's what it was. He thought that a little discipline was good for a boy, so he sent me to a boarding school run by a retired general."

"And Great Grandmother didn't want you to go?" Sara asked.

"Yes. She was against it. After she passed away, he decided that it had been a mistake and brought me back home."

"Well, some people think you're dead," Daniel said.

"Daniel," Sara said.

"Well, they do."

"Goodnight. My father's physician will be visiting shortly," Matthew said, looking at his watch. "I'll have him stop in and visit with your mother." He followed them out into the grand foyer.

"Thank you," Sara said.

In the grand foyer, Sara noticed a figure in gray overalls standing in the shadows of a doorway beside the stairs. She had Daniel take their mother's arm and take her upstairs while she went over to the man.

Bramwell led the others up the stairs to show them to their rooms.

"Franklin," she said looking up into the man's scarred face. "You weren't hurt in the fire, were you?"

"No," he said, shaking his head. "I wasn't injured."

"I appreciate what you did for my family," Sara told him. "Thank you."

His expressionless face changed, and he appeared to have a hint of a smile toward Sara. "You're welcome," he said.

Then, Sara lowered her voice to a whisper. "Can I talk to you tomorrow sometime?" she asked.

"About what?" he asked, the little smile faded and his eyes narrowed.

"You knew my mother when she was a girl. I thought that maybe you could tell me a little about that time," she said.

"I see," he said. "Very well."

"Thank you," she said and hurried off to catch up with the others.

The room that Bramwell showed Sara was, like the rest of the house, filled with fine, old furniture, ornate carpets and decorative wallpaper. The dark four-poster bed that looked tiny in such a large room would have practically filled her entire bedroom at their house in Wakina. She pulled open the heavy drapes to find a door that opened out onto a balcony.

She stepped out onto the balcony and felt the cool breeze coming off the lake. The balcony overlooked the grounds at the back of the mansion. There were wide, well-kept lawns with gardens planted here and there. And at the back of the yard near the trees was a large hedge maze. She thought that would be interesting to check out in the morning. She leaned over the balcony to see a patio area below them.

"Hey look. There's a cemetery," Daniel called to her from a balcony outside his room. He pointed out toward the lake.

To the east of the mansion on the edge of the bluff overlooking the lake was a cemetery. There were quite a number of headstones lined up throughout the cemetery. However, it was the large mausoleum in the center that caused a chill to run up her spine. "Was that the mausoleum she was to die in?" she wondered.

She was going to say something about what the psychic saw, but Daniel had already gone back into his room. Sara took another look at the cemetery and returned to her room.

"You'll be just fine," Dr. Cameron was telling Mary when Sara and Daniel joined them in her room. Their mother's room was similar to theirs except it faced the front of the house and had a view of the town below.

Mary was cradling a pillow in her arms and didn't seem to be paying any attention to the doctor. Sara went to her mother and sat down on the edge of the bed. She took her mother's hand and held it.

The doctor packed his instruments in his case. "Your brother's death was a tremendous shock to your mother," he told them. "And to protect herself, she has withdrawn, a little, from that reality. What she needs most right now is rest."

"How long until she comes out of it?" Sara asked him.

"She may be fine in the morning. Or it may take a little while. I don't know," he said, looking at Mary sadly. "I'll stop by tomorrow and see how she's doing."

Sara thanked him and then the doctor excused himself and left.

"You'll find some toiletries in your bathrooms," Bramwell told them, "and there are some clothes in the wardrobe."

"Thank you," Sara said. "We don't have much more than the clothes on our backs."

Bramwell nodded. "Mr. Kask has arranged for you to go into town tomorrow to purchase clothes and whatever else you'll need."

"Thank you."

"Not at all," Bramwell said and bowed slightly. At the door, he turned back to them. "If you need anything in the night, just pick up the phone and press the 'Staff' button."

"No bell ropes," Daniel joked.

"No, sir. The house may be over two hundred years old. That doesn't mean we are," Bramwell said. Except for a slight crinkling around the edges of his eyes, his face didn't betray his humor. He turned away and closed the door behind him.

Sara went to her mother and gave her a hug.

"Are you going to be alright?" Sara asked her.

Her mother looked at her for a moment and then looked away again.

"I can't believe he's gone," Sara said, almost to herself.

"I know. It all seems like a bad dream that we can't wake up from," Daniel said. They were all silent for several minutes. Sara was on the verge of tears while Daniel stood looking out the window at the town. He barely could make out the fountain in the square.

"Are we safe here?" Daniel asked.

No one had an answer for him.

Chapter 17

There were no lights on in the grand foyer when Sara descended the steps. She had spent more than an hour trying to sleep and then gave up and decided to take a walk around the old house.

The east wing where they had their rooms seemed to be mostly bedrooms. Except for the three that they occupied, they were all empty. The west wing was probably where Matthew and C.J. had their rooms. Since she didn't want to disturb them, she decided to head to the main floor instead.

The two-story grand foyer was well lit with the moonlight shining through the windows on the second floor. She found that there were six doors that opened into the hall besides the front door. She made her way from one to the next.

The first room was the front parlor where they met their Great Uncle Matthew. The next was a large dining room. The last one on that side of the steps was to a hallway that led to the back of the house by the kitchen. That one likely went to the servant's quarters, so she decided not to go there.

She had just peeked in a room that appeared to be some sort of study when there was suddenly a rumbling sound and a moment later, the floor shook violently for a moment. An earthquake, she thought. No, she decided, there weren't earthquakes that strong in Minnesota.

She moved on to the next room. Just as she touched the doorknob, there was another rumbling sound and again the floor shook. This time it shook so violently that she almost lost her footing. It lasted a little longer and just as quickly, the rumbling and shaking stopped.

Suddenly, a light turned on in the room behind the door. Her feet were lit up from the light that shone through the crack at the floor. She jumped back off the patch of light in surprise. Cautiously, she put her hand on the knob again and opened the door.

A young man was standing at a fireplace with his back to Sara looking at some pictures that stood on the mantle. His brown hair was slicked back, and he was dressed in old-fashioned clothes as if he were at a costume party.

"Hello," Sara said.

The man jumped, knocking a picture over. The picture slid off the mantle, but the man was fast enough to catch it before it fell to the floor. He placed the frame back on the mantle and turned to face Sara.

"Oh, it's you," he said apparently relieved.

"Who are you?" Sara asked him.

"Me?" he asked. He seemed somewhat confused by the question. Then he smiled. "Oh, yes. I see. My name is Matthew Kask."

"Matthew Kask?" Sara asked. "Are you related to my Great Uncle Matthew?"

"Great Uncle Matthew? Yes, I am. He's been like a father to me," Matthew told her. "Please, Sara, sit down." The man sat in one of the chairs near the fireplace and motioned to Sara to take one of the other seats. She sat in a blue one near the door.

"Were you at some sort of party?" Sara asked.

The man appeared puzzled again. Sara motioned at her clothes indicating the way he was dressed.

"Oh, my clothes, yes," he said smiling. "Yes, I was at a party. Best way to spend a Friday night, don't you think?"

"Last night was Saturday."

"Really? The 7th?"

"No, the 19th."

"Of June?"

"May. Don't you know what day it is?"

"Of course I do, Sara," he said. He glanced at the clock on the mantle. "What are you doing up so late?"

"I couldn't sleep," she said. "Hey, you know my name."

"I do?"

"Yeah, how do you know my name?"

"You told me."

"No I didn't," she protested.

"Well, no matter. I know your name, and that's the end of it."

The sound of rumbling returned. Sara grabbed onto the arms of the chair.

The young man looked around wildly. "Already," he said. Then the floor started to shake again. As soon as it stopped, he was on his feet hurrying to a small desk at the side of the room.

"I know that this may sound a little confusing. Please promise me something," he said.

"Promise you something?" Sara asked.

"Yes," he said, slamming a drawer shut and turning toward her with a silver bladed letter opener.

Sara jumped up and stood with her chair between them.

He advanced toward her, flipped the handle toward her and placed the letter opener on the table by her chair.

"Keep this with you at all times," he said.

"A letter opener?"

"Yes, it's not the best choice, but we have to make due," he told her. "Keep this with you and the next time you see me, give it to me."

"Give it to you? Why don't you just take it now?"

"It wouldn't do any good," he said. The rumbling started again. "Please, just promise you'll do it."

Sara wasn't sure what to think of this Matthew, but the thought of the room shaking again scared her more. She turned for the door.

"OK. I promise," she called to him. She opened the door and stood in the doorway. She watched the chandelier in the grand foyer rock gently as the floor shook. She held onto the door frame until the shaking stopped.

"Are you OK?" she asked as she turned back to the room. There was no one there. She checked behind the couch and the drapes. The man was gone. There was only one door, and she had been blocking it. Where could he have gone?

She stopped at the chair where she had sat and looked down on the table. The letter opener was there just as he had left it. She carefully picked it up and looked at it.

It had a pearl handle and a silver blade. She took one last look around the room and turned off the light. She was uneasy in the dark room not knowing where he'd disappeared to, so she quickly went back out to the grand foyer.

She had just decided to go back to her room and try to sleep again, when she heard someone coming down the hallway from the west wing. With everything that had happened in the last day, she decided to duck back into the small parlor where she had met the younger Matthew to avoid being seen.

From the darkness of the room, she saw a bald man leave the west wing and descend the stairs. As the man turned and passed the doorway, she recognized him as her great uncle. She was curious about where he was going to at that hour, so she decided to follow him.

She peeked out into the hall and saw him go through a doorway to the back of the house on the east side behind the stairway.

She crossed to that doorway and checked around the corner. She could see him ahead walking along a long dark hallway. His familiarity with the house allowed him to find his way in the darkness.

Sara caught glimpses of him in the moonlight cast into the hall from side rooms as he passed. He seemed unaware that she was following him. She tried to move slightly faster to close the gap between them.

Then, Kask stopped and pulled something away from the wall and disappeared behind it. It wasn't a door. At least it wasn't any kind of door that Sara knew of.

A light was switched on and gleamed from behind whatever it was he went through. She hurried down the hallway, keeping her eyes on the spot he disappeared and stopped in front of it. In the dim light, she could see that the wall was covered with a tapestry. It had some kind of design on it, but she couldn't tell what it was.

She took one edge of it and slowly moved it until she could see the opening behind it. It was another hallway similar to the outer one except it was only about twenty feet long. It was empty except for five large tapestries, one at the far end and two on either side of the hall. She saw no sign of her great uncle.

She went to the first tapestry on her left and pulled it back. She jumped back in alarm as she came face to face with someone staring right back at her. It took her a moment to realize that it was her reflection in a mirror behind the tapestry. She quickly glanced behind each of the other four tapestries and found that each of them covered a full-length mirror.

Her great uncle had disappeared.

Chapter 18

The Sheriff was at his desk when Sara and Daniel arrived at his office the next morning. He was filling out some paperwork and didn't notice them come in.

An elderly man was sweeping around one of two other desks in the office, neither of which appeared to be used by anyone. He looked up at them and narrowed his eyes.

"Visitors," he said. The Sheriff looked up.

"Oh, yes. Please come in," the Sheriff told them. "I have a little paperwork to finish up. Jackson here will take you to our conference rooms."

"Of course," Jackson said. And then he added under his breath. "What else do I have to do around here but take visitors to the conference rooms?"

"Just do it, please," the Sheriff told him without looking up.

Jackson took them down a hall and stopped in front of a door with a small window in it. He pulled a large wad of keys from his belt. Almost without looking, he chose a key and inserted it into the lock. The lock clicked, and he opened the door.

"One of you can wait in here," he told them after flipping on the lights.

"One of us?" Sara asked him.

"Yeah."

"Why just one of us?"

"That's what the Sheriff wants. 'Jackson.' The Sheriff said to me. 'I want to talk to each one by him or herself.' That's what the Sheriff wanted, so that is what we're going to do."

He stood there with the door open and waited. Daniel decided to go in.

"The Sheriff will be with you shortly to take your statement," he told him. He then closed the door and locked it again.

"Why did you do that?" Sara asked him.

"Standard procedure, Miss," he said. "These doors are to be kept locked at all times. Follow me." He continued down the hallway.

He stopped in front of an identical door with an identical small window. He pulled out his keys, and again he selected a seemingly random key and unlocked the door. He flipped on the lights and waited. Sara stared at him for a moment and then went in.

"The Sheriff will be with you shortly to take your statement," he said and closed the door.

Sara heard the door lock behind her.

The room contained only a table and two chairs. The walls were bare except for one. The upper half of that wall was made up almost entirely of a mirror. She figured that someone used that to watch suspects as they were being interrogated. Except that she wasn't sure who that someone would be since the Sheriff would be the one doing the interrogating.

She sat in the chair on the opposite side of the table so that she could face the door. She sat with her hands folded on the table and waited.

Close to twenty minutes later, she heard the door unlock and the Sheriff came in with a manila folder. He smiled at Sara and sat down across from her with the folder in front of him. Sara heard the door lock again behind him.

He flipped the folder open and inside were two printed sheets of paper. He slid the top one over to her and asked her to read it and sign it.

Sara read the statement.

It said that Thomas had been running past the fountain when he tripped and fell in. Sara witnessed him falling into the fountain and ran to help him. After reaching the fountain, she tried to help Thomas. She lost her footing and also fell into the water where she hit her head on the bottom. She was able to get both Thomas and herself out of the fountain where she collapsed on the ground afterward. Her head injury contributed to her inability to recall any events between falling in the fountain and lying on the ground after leaving it. Despite all efforts, emergency personnel were unable to resuscitate Thomas and he was pronounced dead at the scene.

"It didn't happen that way," Sara told him after reading it. She pushed it back across the table.

"Really?" The Sheriff raised his eyebrows. His white eye was locked on her. "I have numerous witness accounts that corroborate this statement." He pushed it back to her.

"That's not what happened, and I'm not signing it," she told him.

"Well," he said taking the other sheet of paper from the folder and sliding it to her. "You have the option to sign this statement instead. I also have witnesses that will corroborate this statement, if necessary."

Sara took the second paper and read it.

That statement told a completely different story. In it, Sara confessed that she was arguing with Thomas by the fountain. Thomas had discovered that she had set the fire at their house in Wakina, and he was going to turn her in. In a fit of rage, she hit him, and he fell into the fountain. She then jumped in after him and held him under water until he stopped moving. Afterward, she pulled him from the fountain and collapsed next to him on the ground feigning her own injuries. Despite all efforts, emergency personnel were unable to resuscitate Thomas and he was pronounced dead at the scene.

Sara dropped the paper on the table. She couldn't believe what she'd just read. She looked up at the Sheriff, and her mouth opened to say something, but she stopped..

"I understand," the Sheriff said with a slight smile. "You need some time to think. I'll just go talk with your brother and give you a few minutes to decide." He stood up and knocked on the door.

"When I come back, I expect one of those papers to be signed," he told her. Jackson unlocked the door, and the Sheriff left the room. Sara looked back down at the two papers as the door was locked again.

She felt terribly alone in the room. All she wanted to do now was get Daniel and get out of there. She looked at the second page again. How could he accuse her of killing her own brother?

She looked up at the mirror. "Was there someone watching her?" she wondered. "Watching to see how she reacted?"

Then, the lights went out. The room was totally dark except for the little bit of light coming from the small window in the door. "Now what?" she wondered.

"Are you trying to scare me?" she said aloud. There was no answer.

She looked back at the mirror and was startled to see a shadowy shape of someone looking out at her. After recovering from the scare, she almost laughed. With the lights off, there must have been enough light in the room behind the one-way mirror so that Sara could see the person watching her.

However, with the little bit of light coming through the small window in the door, she could see the figure's legs all the way down to the floor. It wasn't behind the mirror. It was in the room with her.

She stumbled up out of her chair and moved around the table away from the figure. It slowly walked toward her. She backed around to the door and pounded on it.

"Jackson! Open the door," she yelled. "Jackson! Let me out of here!"

It was about to step into the light from the door when it stopped. Sara backed up to the mirror.

"The box," a hushed woman's voice said. "Find the box or someone else will die."

"Leave my family alone," Sara yelled at it.

"Or maybe I'll just kill you," she continued. "And have your brother get me the box."

Sara turned and pounded on the mirror, calling for help again. The figure's laugh was interrupted by the sound of a key in the door. As the door started to open, the shadowy figure stepped behind it.

The Sheriff pushed past the old man and shoved the door open. He flipped the lights back on. Sara shielded her eyes for a moment.

"There's someone behind the door," she yelled to the Sheriff. The Sheriff drew his gun and slammed the door shut again.

There was nothing behind it. He put his gun away and glowered at her. He waved her back to the table. Sara slowly went to where her chair lay on its side, looking about the room all the while. She righted the chair and sat down again. He pushed the page with the accident report over to her.

"I've had enough of these shenanigans. Just sign the damn paper," he told her.

Sara signed the paper and looked up at the Sheriff again. He grabbed the paper and waved for her to leave. She cautiously got up and made her way around to the door making sure not to turn her back to the Sheriff. She stopped with her hand on the door knob.

"Go," the Sheriff bellowed.

She pulled open the door and slammed it shut behind her. Daniel was standing in the hall waiting for her. He asked her what was wrong. She decided not to tell him about what had happened.

"Let's just get out of here," Sara said.

Chapter 19

They met Bramwell in front of the Sheriff's office, and they spent the next several hours in one shop or another around the square purchasing things that they would need for the next several weeks during their stay at the house.

They each also picked out an outfit appropriate for Thomas' funeral. And to their surprise, the funeral had already been scheduled for later that day.

"That's awful quick," Sara said after Bramwell announced the plans.

"I understand," Bramwell said. "With the Reverend's busy schedule and the severe weather that we'll have later in the week, Mr. Kask simply felt the sooner, the better."

"Where is he going to be buried?" Daniel asked.

"Mr. Kask thought that your mother would want him interred in the family crypt overlooking the lake here at the house," Bramwell told her.

"We've never really thought about those kinds of things before," Sara said.

"Mr. Kask said to purchase whatever you need for the service."

"Thank you," Sara told him.

They were just finishing up their errands when Sara had a question for Bramwell.

"Is there a bookshop in town?"

The Reverend Ronald Kincaid led Matthew and Mary across the lawn to the small cemetery behind the house. Mary clutched the small book that Sara had purchased. Daniel and Sara followed behind them.

A crowd was waiting on the lawn for the funeral. Although none of them knew Thomas, they were there to pay their respects to the Kask family. As the procession approached, they parted to allow them into the cemetery.

A narrow walking path wound among the headstones and ended at the foot of the steps into the marble mausoleum. The two metal doors of the mausoleum stood open beneath the pillared archway that protected them from the elements. The words "Vita Aeterna" were engraved in the marble above the doors.

Sara stopped at the outside door. She wasn't sure that she wanted to enter the small building. It was a mausoleum. And there was a crowd standing outside. They weren't actually surrounding the building. "Still, was this when it would explode?" she wondered.

Daniel noticed that she had fallen behind and pulled her onward.

The group moved through a four foot long hallway to the main gallery inside. A pair of barred gates was folded against the sides of the hallway.

Inside the mausoleum, there were three marble tables. Thomas' casket was set on the center table. The lid was open. Thomas, dressed in a stylish dark blue suit, lay with his hands together on his chest and a white Calla Lily in his lapel.

Matthew supported Mary who seemed about to faint. Sara wanted to be strong and hold back her tears. Only one tear escaped. Daniel also tried to be strong. But, as soon as he saw Thomas, he could no longer hold back, and he wept.

Matthew took Mary to Thomas, and she gazed down at him. She gently touched his hair and then his cheek. She bowed her head for a moment and used a tissue to wipe her eyes. She then took the small book that Sara had given her and slipped it under Thomas' hands. Then, she kissed her hand, touched it to his cheek and turned away from her son.

Sara was the next one to visit Thomas. She looked at his face and thought about how peaceful he looked. The last time she had seen him, he was frantically looking to her for help. She had failed him. She dabbed her eyes and quietly said, "I'm sorry, Thomas." She looked at the book that her mother had placed in the casket. It was the Adventures of Tom Sawyer, his favorite book from when he was a little boy. Her eyes filled with tears again as she turned to join her mother.

Daniel approached his brother in the casket. Thomas appeared to be simply sleeping. He knew this time, it was different. Thomas would not be waking up again. He had been close with his brother, and now there would always be a something missing from his life. He reached in and straightened his brother's tie. "Goodbye, Thomas." He said and went to his mother's side.

Reverend Kincaid began the service. Sara didn't listen to what he was saying. She looked about the room and at the small plaques that were mounted on walls. Each plaque stated the name, birth date and date of passing for the person who was sealed up in the wall behind it. Some of the plaques even had a short, pithy saying that was meant to sum up the life of that person.

She wondered how anyone's life could be summed up by one short phrase. Thomas was only nineteen and still, his life couldn't be boiled down to just a few words. He cared about people, even dead people who were beyond care. He was good at art and music and sports even though he never actively pursued any of those activities. He was a good son. And he was a good brother to her. Her tears began again.

Daniel's attention was on the opening in the back wall of the mausoleum. It was just large enough to slide a casket into. He could see that there were spaces for twenty caskets in the wall. Eleven had markers placed on them. Thomas would be number 12. Soon, his brother would be sealed into the wall, and they would never see him again. He bowed his head and closed his watering eyes.

The Reverend Kincaid finished the service with a prayer and then went to each family member with words of hope for Thomas' eternal life. They all thanked him for his kind words, and he took his leave.

The four of them continued to stand there as the casket was closed and sealed. Four men lifted the casket to the vault opening and slowly slid it in. One of the men then placed a metal plate in the opening and fastened it with screws.

They were in the process of lifting a marble outer cover to close the vault when Sara decided she couldn't watch it any longer. She ran from the small room back out into the bright sun of the afternoon. Daniel looked at his mother. She clutched Matthew's arm and wept. He turned and hurried after Sara.

Sara stood on the steps of the mausoleum trying to catch her breath. Her heart was beating madly, and it felt like she couldn't breathe.

Daniel went to her and put his arm around her. She looked at him and gave him a weak smile of appreciation.

She looked out at all the people gathered on the lawn just outside the little cemetery. Almost all of them were silently staring at the two of them.

"Why are all these people here?" she whispered to her brother.

"To pay their respects," he said.

"They never knew Thomas. Why do they just stand there gawking? Why don't they just go away?"

Daniel just shook his head and shrugged. There were two faces in the crowd he recognized. The Sheriff was one that he was not thrilled to see, but Gwen was one that he was.

"Is that him?" Sara asked.

"Him?" Daniel asked.

"Great Grandfather," she said, "Up, on that balcony."

Daniel looked at the balconies along the back of the house. On a balcony in the west wing, a figure was bundled in a blanket sitting in a wheelchair watching the cemetery. He wore a wide brimmed hat which obscured his face. Bramwell was standing beside him.

"I guess so," Daniel said.

"Maybe we can talk to him today."

"Why is it so important to you that we see him?"

Sara wanted to tell him about what happened in the fountain and that she needed to talk to their great grandfather about the chest. Daniel was looking at her expectantly. She couldn't shake the feeling that he would think that she had just dreamed it. Or worse yet, she was losing her mind.

"He's our great grandfather," she said, looking away from Daniel and back toward the balcony. "We didn't even know he was alive until yesterday. I figure we should try to get to know him. Before anything happens."

"Before what happens?" Daniel asked.

"Well, he is over a hundred years old, you know," Sara said.

Their mother and Matthew came out of the mausoleum and followed the path back out of the cemetery and into the crowd which began to form a line to give them their individual condolences.

"I don't want to go through that," Sara said. "Want to take a walk in the woods until they leave?"

Daniel looked out at the crowd at Gwen. He didn't actually want to go, but he told his sister he would. He started to follow her through the back of the cemetery toward the trees. He looked back at Gwen one last time and pointed to his watch to indicate that he would see her later. She seemed to understand and nodded.

Luca was watching them from between two adults in the crowd. As they disappeared into the trees, he backed up into the crowd and was gone.

Chapter 20

They didn't say much once they were away from the noise of the crowd. They simply walked with each absorbed in their own thoughts.

The forest was cool and peaceful. The afternoon sun filtered through the trees giving plenty of light. They also provided an abundance of shade.

Before long they came across a small creek. The water flowed across the rocky bed with a soothing bubbling sound. They stood for a moment on the bank and just listened to the sounds of nature.

Sara gazed thoughtfully at the water.

"Did you see what happened to Thomas?" She asked her brother.

"No," Daniel said.

"You were standing there in front of the diner. You had to see it," Sara said and began to walk along the stream again.

"I heard him call to you, and I saw him," Daniel said as he followed her. "I went back in the diner to tell Mom that he was back. When we came back out, you were both lying by the fountain."

"You didn't see us in the water?"

"No."

She sat down on a log and picked up a small rock. Daniel continued to stand for a few moments, and then when he realized that she was going to sit for a while, he sat down next to her.

It was a few minutes before either of them spoke. "There was a thing in the water, just like the Fire Djinn, except it was made of water. It pulled Thomas in, so I went in after him."

Daniel just listened and watched Sara scrape dirt from the rock with her fingernail.

"I tried to save him, but I couldn't." She continued after a moment. "I almost died too. I might have died, I'm not sure."

"What do you mean?" Daniel asked.

"I blacked out, I think. Then I heard a voice talking to me," she said.

"A voice?" Daniel asked.

"Yes, a woman's voice."

"What did she say?"

"If I don't get something for her, she'll kill all of us."

Daniel was silent for a few moments. "Are you sure it wasn't just a hallucination?"

"I'm sure."

"You might have hit your head, like the Sheriff said."

"I didn't hit my head. We were pulled under by a Water Djinn."

Daniel stared at the ground. He picked up a stick and started to peel the bark off of it.

"You don't believe me," Sara said.

"I didn't see it."

"So you think it was all my imagination?"

"I don't know," Daniel said. He finished peeling the bark from the stick and started scraping at the ground with it.

"What about the Fire Djinn that attacked us?"

"I didn't see that either," Daniel said in a low voice, still avoiding looking at Sara.

Sara stood up abruptly and grabbed the stick away from him. He looked up at her.

"Do you think my imagination killed Thomas and burned down our house?"

"No," he said quietly. "There has to be a more logical explanation, though."

She felt like hitting him with the stick. Instead, she threw it into the stream.

"Just go back home," she told him. Her voice was filled with both anger and sadness. "I want to be alone."

She crossed the stream and continued along a path through the forest, leaving her brother there sitting on the log.

After she had walked for a while, she heard the sound of an explosion ahead of her. She started hurrying toward it.

She came to a clearing and stopped. In the center was a hill. It was a low hill on one side and rose up on the other until it was more than twenty feet above the field that surrounded it.

On the higher end, there was a cave that looked like an old gold mine with smoke billowing out. Scattered around the field near the cave were various digging tools, an old wooden table, a folding chair and a pile of boards.

It was the noise she heard issuing from the cave that stopped her in her tracks. It was a high pitched whooping sound punctuated with fits of coughing that indicated that someone was inside either celebrating or choking to death.

She hurried across the field to the hill to find out which. As she approached the cave, a figure burst out. It was tall and thin and covered with dirt and dust. He almost jumped when he saw her and then began another coughing fit. It was the man she met the night before, Peter Jacobs.

"Are you alright?" Sara asked.

The man's coughs died down, and after a minute, he was able to talk. "What are you doing out here?" he asked.

"I went for a walk to get away from everybody from town. It was my brother's funeral today," she told him.

"Oh, yes. I was so terribly sorry to hear about your loss."

"Did you find something?" she asked him.

He looked back at the cave and then shook his head. "No. Absolutely nothing."

"You sounded as if you were celebrating."

"No. Not celebrating," he said glancing back at the cave. "No. I just," he paused. "I just blew up a large rock that was in my way. Now I can get some more digging done."

"Well, I guess I'll be going then. Good luck with your digging," Sara said.

"My digging, yes. Thank you," Peter said.

Sara turned to go. Then, she suddenly turned back to him. "You said that you're the curator for all Kask's museum pieces, right?"

"That's right."

"I read once about a box that he had in one of his museums. I can't remember what it was called. It was a wooden box. It had metal straps and seemed like it didn't have a latch or hinges. In the top was a cross-shaped slot. Have you come across anything like that?" she asked him.

"A wooden box, you say?" He thought a moment. "There are some wooden boxes but nothing with a cross in the top."

"Oh, OK," she said, disappointed. She went on her way.

Peter stood and watched until Sara left the clearing. Once she was out of sight, he rushed back into the opening with a shovel. About eighteen feet into the well shored-up mine shaft, it came to an end at what appeared to be a smooth rock surface.

Peter smiled and took a step back. He held the shovel like a baseball bat and swung it flat against the rock face. There was a loud metallic clang as the metal of the shovel banged against the metal surface of something buried in the hill.

Peter had finally found something.

When she returned to the mansion, Sara found Franklin trimming the hedges on the outside of the hedge maze.

"Hello," she yelled over the noise of the hedge cutter.

Franklin glanced over at her and turned the cutter off. "What can I do for you?"

"I have a question for you," Sara said.

"I see," he motioned her over to a nearby bench. She sat down at one end of the bench. He sat down at the other end. Sara sniffed.

"Do you like mint?" she asked, sniffing again.

"That's what you wanted to ask me?" Franklin asked, amused.

"No, it's just when I ran into you at the carnival, I could smell mint, and now I smell it again."

"Yes," he said. "Mint has a strong odor. Stronger than the smell of decomposition."

"Oh," Sara said, slightly embarrassed. "Sorry."

"No matter," Franklin told her.

"I wanted to ask you about the Fire Djinn. Are there other kinds, besides fire?"

Franklin narrowed his eyes at her. "Have you seen other kinds?"

"I think so," Sara told him. "Something made of water killed my brother, Thomas."

"Water?" Franklin adjusted the gloves on his hands. "Yes, there are four kinds of Djinns; Earth, Fire, Water and Air."

"Do you know who's sending them?"

"I don't know who specifically. I do know it is a Wielder."

"A Wielder?" Sara asked.

"Yes. This place is full of power. A Wielder is someone who knows how to use that power."

"What's full of power? The Mansion?"

"The Mansion. Shadow Bluffs. This whole area," Franklin told her.

"Is that why you're," Sara stopped.

"Why I'm," Franklin lowered his voice. "Undead?" He said in an eerie tone.

"Don't do that. I'm serious," Sara said.

"It is responsible, indirectly," he said. "The Wielders used the power to curse the old cemetery so that anyone buried there will not rest."

"How many undead are there?"

"I don't know for sure," Franklin said. "And we aren't the undead. We are just the Dead."

"Sorry."

Just then, Daniel came out onto the patio.

"Sara, we're supposed to help get ready for the Social tonight," he called.

"I'll be there in a minute," she called back. Then to Franklin, she said, "Thank you."

"Anytime," Franklin said.

Sara hurried off to help get ready.

Chapter 21

Shadow Bluffs enjoyed about a mile of shoreline on Lake Superior. Fishing and lumber were two important industries in the area, and the lake played a vital part in both. In its early years, the only way in and out of the small town was by boat during the summer and by sled across the lake in the winter.

Boats were still important to the town, and half the shoreline was given to the docks and piers necessary to service those boats. The harbor was even deep enough in a few places that a smaller ship or two could be accommodated.

The other half of the shoreline was set aside as a public park. And that night, Grimm Park was ablaze with lights. There were old-fashioned street lamps that were originally gas lamps, but had been eventually converted to electric lights. And there were paper lanterns strung along the pathways through the park that cast colorful light throughout.

Daniel and Sara helped Bramwell unload a number of hot dishes, salads and desserts prepared by Cook especially for the Social. They added them to all the other foods that lined the tables set up around the statue of one Alphonse Grimm for whom the park had been named.

Sara knew that Daniel wanted to go to the Social and, even though she didn't, she agreed to go because she felt responsible for him. Plus, maybe she would run into that boy, Luca again.

As Daniel placed a towering chocolate cake on the dessert table, a familiar voice welcomed him to the Social. He turned to find Gwen smiling at him. Before he could say anything, she gave him a quick hug.

"I didn't get a chance to tell you at the service this afternoon how sorry I am about your brother," she told him.

"Thank you," he said. And then to lighten the mood, he added, "So, what's there to do at this Social?"

"Oh, people generally spend the evening strolling, eating and talking."

"That's all?"

"Well, there's also dancing over at the gazebo there," she pointed to a large white gazebo where a small orchestra was playing.

"We'll have to keep that in mind," he said. "How about a stroll on the beach to start?"

"Why not?" she asked. They walked off toward the narrow sandy beach by the lake.

Sara stayed by the food tables. She didn't know anyone, and although there were a number of people milling about the tables, she ended up staying to herself.

After a while, she noticed a girl a little older than herself standing off to the side. Every time she would look over at her, the girl would be looking back, and then would quickly look away.

"Hi. My name is Sara Cross," she said to the girl. She noticed the strong smell of mint.

"I know your name," the girl replied.

"You do?"

"Yes, you are the talk of the town," she said. "My name is Lucinda." She held out a gloved hand to Sara. Sara looked at the glove. "Sorry, I burned my hands when I was younger. I have to protect them."

"Nice to meet you," Sara said, carefully shaking Lucinda's hand. She noticed that Lucinda's skin was graying and that her eyes had dark circles under them.

"So, everyone is talking about us, huh?" Sara asked.

"Oh, yes. You are all members of the Kask family. There aren't many of them left, you know."

"I know," Sara said quietly.

"Oh, no. I didn't mean it like that. I am sorry about your brother."

"Thank you. So what do you do when you're not partying like this?"

Lucinda laughed. "I help people out when they need it."

"What do you mean?"

"Cleaning and cooking mainly. Sometimes there are other jobs people need done. Jobs they don't want to do themselves."

"Have you ever been up to the mansion?"

"Once. They don't usually need my kind of help. They have their own people for that." Lucinda's voice trailed off.

A tall, elderly black woman came up to the table nearby to look over the food. A young, Asian girl followed closely behind her. The woman looked up at Lucinda and Sara.

"Hello, Lucinda," the old woman said.

"Hello, Piri. Asami," Lucinda quietly greeted them. Asami just stared at her without saying a word.

"And who is this?" Piri asked, looking at Sara.

"This is Sara Cross. She is visiting her great grandfather at the mansion."

"I see," Piri said and without another word the old woman and the young girl turned and walked away from them.

"Who were they?" Sara asked Lucinda.

"Piri and Asami Moira. Their family was one of the first families to move to the area. They made a lot of money in lumber, and now they think they own the town."

"Do they? Own the town, I mean."

"They own a lot of things but not the town. Not yet, at least."

Sara watched them as they walked away. Just before the path curved behind a small grove of trees, the little girl turned back and looked at Sara.

After they disappeared behind the trees, Sara saw a familiar face looking out from the trees. It was the boy they saw in the square when they arrived.

She told Lucinda that she needed to catch someone and hurried over to the trees. When she got there, he had disappeared back into them. She pushed her way into the trees looking for the boy.

"Luca," she called. "Luca, I saw you in here."

She stopped and listened to hear the boy moving around. She couldn't hear any movement.

"Luca," she called again. "I just want to talk to you."

"About what?" a small voice behind her asked.

She turned around to find the boy standing a few feet away.

"You're a tough one to pin down," Sara told him.

Luca looked at her curiously. "What does that mean?"

"Nothing," Sara said. "I wanted to ask you about last night."

"What about it?" Luca asked, his voice trembled a little.

"You aren't in trouble," she told him. "I just wanted to ask you about that woman you saw."

He backed up a step.

"Don't go," Sara said. "Please. Do you know who she is?"

"Yes," Luca said.

"Who?"

"I can't tell you," Luca said and took another step back.

"Why?"

"Because she'd be mad if I told you," Luca said in a low voice.

"Did she make the fountain kill my brother?" Sara asked him.

"Yes."

"Then, I have to know who she is, Luca. Please tell me."

He thought for a moment and glanced around, then he said, "Her name is Dior. She's one of the Moira Sisters."

Just then, there was the sound of someone coming into the trees.

"Sara," a woman called. "Sara, are you in here?"

Sara turned to see Lucinda approaching. She looked back and found that Luca was gone.

"Sara, there you are," Lucinda said. "What are you doing in here?"

"I was looking for someone."

"Who?"

"Someone I thought I knew. But, I guess he wasn't here."

"Let's get out of here," Lucinda said and they started pushing their way through the trees.

When they reached the path, Sara asked, "The Moira Sisters. Are there only two?"

Lucinda looked at her strangely. "No," she said. "There are three. Why?"

"Just wondering," she said. "What is the name of the other sister?"

"Dior," Lucinda told her.

Sara nodded and walked back to the food tables. Lucinda followed behind her.

Daniel found some sliced apples and a little caramel for Gwen and him to share. They sat on a bench and looked out at the dark lake. The little bit of light from the moon that filtered through the clouds glittered off the moving water.

"Are you staying with your great grandfather long?" Gwen asked him.

"I don't know. For a while, I guess. It's kind of complicated," Daniel said.

"Life is full of complications," Gwen said looking out at the lake.

"Are you from here?"

"I've lived here my whole life. My father came here when he was a boy with his parents, and they just decided to stay."

"Was he a fisherman or something?" Daniel asked.

"He was part of a circus," she told him.

"A circus? Cool. What did he do?"

"He was part of," She hesitated, "an animal act."

"Why did they come here?" Daniel asked.

"The circus came here as part of its tour. There was an accident and the circus just closed down. All of the performers were stranded. Most eventually left. Some, like my grandfather, just stayed."

"What kind of accident?"

"An animal got loose and killed one of its handlers. It almost killed a deputy too before he managed to put it down."

"So it just closed?" Daniel asked.

"Yeah. The owners just packed up and left. They never even took down the tents. They're still in a field south of town. They're tattered, but they're still standing."

"It's too bad they had to kill it. What was it, a lion?"

"It was a bear. My dad and grandfather never talked about it much."

"It probably wasn't the animal's fault. The conditions in some circuses were miserable, especially back then," he stopped and glanced at Gwen. "I don't mean to say that your family was cruel to the animals."

"It's OK. They didn't like how the animals were treated either," she said.

They heard a man calling Gwen's name. A large man standing down the beach toward the parking lot was calling to her.

"That's my dad," she said. "Maybe I can stop by the mansion to see you." Daniel wasn't sure the last was a statement or a question.

"That would be awesome," Daniel told her. She hurried off to her dad. He watched her until she disappeared from sight.

"That would be so awesome. Wouldn't that be awesome, Mason," a voice behind him asked.

"Yeah, Vincent. That would be awesome," another voice laughed.

Vincent and Mason were standing right behind him. Vincent

moved in closer as Daniel stood up from the bench. Their noses were just inches apart.

"What did we tell you about staying away from my sister?" Vincent asked between clenched teeth.

"What did Gwen tell you about staying out of her business?" Daniel asked him.

Mason grabbed Daniel by the shirt and pulled him toward him. "None of it is your business so just keep away from my girl. She doesn't need to be hanging around with your kind," he said.

"My kind?" Daniel asked. "You said that before. What do you mean 'my kind'?"

"What's going on here?" a man behind them asked. The three of them turned to find a police officer looking at them intently. Daniel recognized Jason Wells, the police officer from Wakina.

"Who are you?" Mason asked, letting Daniel go. Vincent jabbed him with his elbow.

"What he means to say, Officer, is you aren't from around here, are you?" Vincent asked.

"No, I'm not. I can recognize harassment and possible assault when I see it, though," Jason told him.

"No, Officer, we were just having a discussion with our friend here."

"Well, I think the discussion is over," Jason told them.

"I agree with you completely. We are done with our discussion." Vincent turned to Daniel. "For now." Then he added quietly, "I don't know how much longer I can keep Mason on a leash."

"Maybe you should add a muzzle," Daniel told him. He could see Mason turn red and clench his fists.

Vincent grabbed Mason's arm and pulled him along with him as he walked away.

"Are you OK, Daniel?" Jason asked.

"I didn't need your help," Daniel told him.

"I could see that. I just thought a little backup never hurt."

"What are you doing here?"

"I came to tell your mom the results of the investigation into the fire. We tried calling, but we couldn't get through."

"Cell phones don't work here."

"Where is your mom then?" Jason asked.

"She's not here. Let's go find Sara," Daniel said and led him back toward the food tables.

Sara sat down at one of the picnic tables and looked up at the statue towering above her. The plaque simply read Alphonse Grimm, Founder.

Lucinda left the Social a while earlier to meet up with her family at home. So, Sara found herself alone again. She decided just to sit and wait until Daniel was ready to go.

"Are you new here?" a woman asked her.

Sara turned to find a woman in her twenties sitting at a nearby table looking over at her.

"Yes, I am," Sara said.

"So am I," she said. "Mind if I join you?"

"I don't mind."

The woman sat down across from her. She held out her hand. "My name is Francesca."

Sara shook her hand and introduced herself. She noticed that the woman had a handkerchief clutched in her other hand. "Something wrong?"

Francesca looked confused for a moment and then realized what she was asking. "Oh, no. It's just that I have allergies," she used it to dab at her eyes.

"I see," Sara said. "How long have you been here?"

"A few days. I came up to visit my grandmother for a week."

Just then there was a metallic popping sound. Sara looked up at the statue. It was behind Francesca, so she had to look over her shoulder to see it.

"That was weird," Sara said.

As they looked at the statue, there was the sound of metal ripping and the statue started to fall toward them.

Sara was about to jump out of the way when she noticed the other girl was just sitting there watching it fall. She jumped up on the bench and then she dove across the table.

She grabbed the girl and pulled her off the bench onto the ground just as the statue crashed onto the picnic table. The table disintegrated under the crushing weight of the statue, and it continued falling smashing down onto the ground with the two women beneath it.

Chapter 22

Jason and Daniel pushed their way through the crowd that had gathered around the statue. Many in the crowd were sobbing or holding their hands over their mouths in horror at the legs that were sticking out. Jason flattened himself on the ground to look under it.

"Daniel. Quick. Down here," he called frantically. Daniel joined him on the ground.

Daniel saw that the statue was actually teetering on its base above the girls, but it hadn't actually fallen on them. The weight of the statue should have brought it down right on top of them. It was almost as if it were hovering over them. He looked at Jason, and it was obvious that Jason didn't understand what had happened either.

"Help me pull them out," Jason said and grabbed the legs of the nearest girl. They slid her out from under the metal figure of Alphonse Grimm and carried her a few feet away. It was the girl that had been sitting with Sara. Daniel noticed that even though she was lying unconscious, her hands were clenched into fists by her sides. She didn't have any injuries that either one of them could see.

They ran back to get Sara. Since the other girl had been pulled out, Daniel could see Sara clearly. Her eyes were open and staring up at the statue. Her hands were held flat as if she were trying to hold it up even though they were several inches from the iron figure. They reached under to pull her out.

As they started to pull on her, the statue began to teeter. They ducked as it rocked closer to the ground. It almost touched Sara's hands before it reversed and rose up again.

"Hurry," Jason said, "Get her out of there."

They yanked on her arms and pulled her out onto the grass beside the other girl. They looked back at the statue and saw that the teetering stopped.

Jason checked the other girl while Daniel looked at Sara.

"Sara," Daniel called to her. She didn't respond. He took hold of her arm and shook her a little. "Sara," He called again. Her muscles seemed to be straining.

He looked over at Jason and the other girl. She had regained consciousness and was sitting up, clutching one of her wrists. She was telling Jason that she must have broken it.

Sara was still staring straight up. Daniel leaned into her line of view and took hold of her stiff hands. "Sara. What's wrong?" He asked her and shook her arms.

She blinked, and her body relaxed. Her eyes focused on him, and she was about to say something when the statue suddenly rocked forward again and fell heavily onto the place where the two girls had been lying.

"Are you alright?" Daniel asked her.

She sat up and checked herself. "Nothing broken," she said.

"You were lucky that thing didn't kill you," Daniel told her.

"I thought it was going to," Sara said. Daniel just looked at her curiously. She decided to change the subject. "How's the other girl?"

"The other girl is fine," a woman's voice said. "Except for my wrist. My name is Francesca, remember?"

"Is it broken?" she asked, standing up.

"Probably. I'm going to head over to the hospital to get it looked at," Francesca said. "I just wanted thank you. It would have been much worse if it weren't for you."

"I just did what anyone would have done," Sara told her.

"Well, I didn't see anyone else doing it," she glanced over Sara's shoulder at the parking lot. "My sister's looking for me. She can take me to the hospital. Thank you again, Sara."

As Francesca hurried toward the parking lot, Sara turned back to Daniel.

"I didn't take you for the hero type," Daniel said without a trace of humor.

"I surprised myself too. I saw it start to fall, and before I knew what I was doing, we were on the ground," she told him. "Next thing I knew, you were shaking me."

"You don't remember when you were under the statue?" Daniel asked her.

She thought a moment. "Not at all." She hugged him. "Thank you for getting me out of there."

Daniel returned the hug. Then he said, "I wasn't the only one." He pulled away and turned toward the man who was examining the statue. She recognized Jason right away and went to him. She wrapped her arms around him. For several moments, everyone was silent.

Finally, she released him. "What are you doing here, Jason?" she asked.

"Helping get you out from under the statue, I guess," he joked. "I'm just glad you're alright."

"It was a miracle that it didn't crush you," Daniel said.

"Yes, a miracle," Jason said quietly to himself looking at the wrenched metal on the statue's base.

"You're pretty far from home," Sara said.

"Well, we couldn't reach you by phone, so I volunteered to come tell you the results of the fire investigation," he told them. "Daniel said your mom wasn't here."

"She's not doing very well," Sara told him. "Thomas died yesterday."

"Thomas?" He asked. "How?"

"He drowned," Sara said.

Jason stared at her. "I can't believe it."

"Neither can we," Daniel said.

"I'm sorry," Jason told them. "I can see that would be quite a shock. I'll wait until tomorrow then. Maybe I can stop by in the morning. Where are you staying?" Jason asked.

They pointed at the house on the bluff.

"That's my great grandfather's house," Sara said. "We're staying with him."

"I'll stop by in the morning. Is nine o'clock, OK?"

"You're not driving back to Wakina tonight, are you?" Sara asked.

"No, I'll just find a motel."

"You can't stay down here, Jason," Sara told him in a low voice. "This is not Wakina. You should stay up at the house with us."

"That's very generous, but I can't," Jason said.

"I agree with Sara," Daniel said. "It's better that you stay at the house."

They weren't going to let him refuse, so he agreed.

After they returned to the mansion and Bramwell was off showing Jason to his room, Matthew insisted that both Sara and Daniel head off to their rooms also.

"You need to get some rest after the excitement tonight," he told them.

Although Sara knew that she wasn't going to be able to sleep, she and Daniel agreed to head off to bed.

Sara didn't even think about going to sleep. She just sat in her room thinking about the day's events. After a while, there was a knock on the door. She opened it to find Jason standing there.

"We have to talk," he told her.

She let him in and he sat down on one of the armchairs. Sara closed the door and looked at him.

"Can't this wait until tomorrow?" she asked.

"Is there something going on?" Jason asked.

"What do you mean?"

"The statue."

"What about the statue?"

"That statue should have killed you. It should have killed both you and that other girl," Jason said. "It didn't. Why?"

"I don't know why. We were lucky, I guess," she turned away from Jason and walked over to the curtains. She knew he was right. It should have killed them.

"You weren't lucky, Sara. It didn't kill you because you didn't let it."

Sara turned toward him suddenly. "Because I didn't let it?" she asked. "You think I can lift bronze statues now?"

"Well," he said. "As a matter of fact, yes."

"What?"

"Maybe not physically, you weren't even touching the status. However, you were in some sort of trance, Sara. You were awake, and every fiber of your body was intent on keeping that statue off the ground until Daniel shook you out of it."

"I was probably in shock. You'd be in shock if something were going to crush you," she told him.

"Yes, but it didn't crush you. It would have. It should have," he corrected himself. "But it didn't. It didn't fall the rest of the way until

Daniel disturbed your concentration."

"You think I have some sort of psychic powers or something?" she asked with a laugh.

"Maybe. I don't know what it is. You have to admit, weird things are happening," he said.

"Just because a statue didn't kill me?"

"That and the Sheriff."

"What about the Sheriff?"

"Daniel told me that after Thomas had died, you were mad at the Sheriff," he said.

"He didn't believe me. Of course, I was mad," she said.

"And when you reached for him, he suddenly went flying down the street."

"He just fell."

"Daniel said that it was as if he were blown off his feet."

"So bench pressing a statue wasn't enough. Now, I'm throwing people around on the street." She laughed. "Do you think I'm some sort of freak?"

"Of course not—"

"You're being ridiculous, Jason," she cut him off. "Please, I'm tired. Just go to bed." She opened the door.

After trying to think of something to say, he shrugged his shoulders and left her alone in her room.

Sara tried to sleep. What little sleep she got was punctuated with disturbing dreams.

Chapter 23

When Sara got up for breakfast then next day, she found that Jason was not there. Bramwell told her that he was up extremely early and went into town.

After having breakfast with Daniel, her mother, Matthew and Peter, she decided to head into town herself. Not to find out where Jason went, she decided. Just to do some investigation herself.

She drove down to the park by the lake and parked in a spot where she could see the statue. When she arrived, there was a lot of activity around it as several men were trying to load it up onto a large flatbed truck.

She got out and walked around, staying well away from it. She wasn't there to see the statue, she was there looking for someone.

She found the small grove of trees where she had seen Luca and looked around in it. She called Luca's name several times. There was no sign of him in the trees. It was a long shot, she thought. She left the trees and started to follow the path back to her car.

"Looking for me?" a voice asked from behind her.

She turned to find the boy standing there with a large brown and white dog.

"There you are," Sara said. "Yes, I was looking for you. I didn't know how to find you, so I came back down here."

"Pounce and I play here a lot," Luca told her.

"I'd like to ask you a question."

"What?" he asked, rubbing Pounce's ear.

"Do you know what Wielders are?"

Luca stopped and looked around. "You shouldn't talk about them," he said.

"Why? Can they hear us?" Sara asked him.

"Maybe," he whispered. He took her hand and pulled her back toward the trees.

"What about the Moira Sisters? Are they Wielders?"

"Shh," he hissed. He looked around again and then disappeared into the trees. Pounce followed him.

Sara looked around and pushed through into the trees too.

"Where do they live?" she called to him.

"You don't want to go there," his voice came from somewhere in front of her.

"I want to know," she said, looking around for the boy.

"Above the Golden Lamp Pawnshop," his voice drifted to her from far away.

"Where are you?" she called. There was no answer. She continued to search around for him in the trees, but there was no sign of him.

When she got back out of the trees and on the path through the park, she noticed that the statue and the men were gone.

The Golden Lamp Pawnshop, she said to herself and headed for her car.

She stopped at the square to ask where the pawnshop was, and within a quarter of an hour, she was parked across the street from it. She got out and looked up at the windows above the shop. The curtains were closed.

She decided to wait. She saw two of the sisters at the Social the night before. She wanted to see what the third sister looked like.

Sara had watched the door that led up to the apartment for almost an hour when she was startled to hear her name.

"Sara," a woman called. "Sara Cross, is that you?"

Sara turned to see Francesca coming down the street toward her.

"It is you," the woman said. "I'm so glad to see you."

Sara just smiled at Francesca. She wasn't quite happy to see her. She just wanted to watch for Dior, but she didn't want to be rude.

Francesca showed Sara her cast. It almost seemed as if she felt it was a badge of honor.

"It hurt like the dickens when they adjusted it. It doesn't hurt now," she said. "Of course, I can't move it at all."

Sara saw that the cast started around the middle of her forearm and encased all but her thumb and first two fingers of her left hand.

"I'm just glad you didn't have anything more serious," Sara said.

"I can't imagine what condition I would have been in if you hadn't risked your life."

"Seems like it's becoming a habit with me," Sara said thinking about the events of the last few days.

"What do you mean?" Francesca asked her. She leaned against the side of the car.

"Nothing important," Sara said and wiped some of the dust off the driver's side mirror.

"Well, if there is anything I can do for you, just let me know," Francesca said.

"Nothing that I can think of," Sara said. "Unless you know anything about a chest with cross-shaped slot in the top." Sara added.

Francesca tried to think. "I don't think so," she said.

"I didn't really think that you would." Sara looked across at the pawn shop.

"Your great-grandfather would know where it is," another woman's voice said.

Francesca and Sara turned to find Lucinda standing in front of a nearby shop.

"How do you know?" Sara asked her.

"Because he had it in one of his museums a long time ago," Lucinda said joining them by Sara's car. She leaned on the car between the two with her back to Francesca.

"My Uncle Matthew won't let me talk to him yet," Sara said. "Do you know what it is?"

"I can tell you what it is supposed to be," Lucinda told her.

"What?"

"The Box of Anesidora or, as it is more commonly known, Pandora's Box," Lucinda said.

"Pandora's Box?" Francesca asked, laughing, "That's a fairy tale."

"You mean a myth," Lucinda said over her shoulder. "Fairy tales are children's stories."

"Fine, a myth then," Francesca said, annoyed. "Either way, it isn't real."

"I didn't say it was actually Pandora's Box. I said that is what it was supposed to be. At least, that was how your great-grandfather advertised it."

"And you think he would still have it?" Sara asked her.

"I don't know. Nobody knows what happened to everything when he closed his museums. Some people say there is a vast vault under his mansion."

"Do you think that's true?" Sara asked.

"I doubt it," Lucinda said. "You'd have to ask him, though."

"Well then, you should ask him," Francesca said. She moved so that she faced both Sara and Lucinda. She didn't want to be left out of the conversation.

"That's the thing. They won't let me see him."

"It's probably for the best. You shouldn't have anything to do with the artifacts from his museums. He didn't call them Museums of Terror for nothing," she paused for a moment looking at Sara. "Why do you want to know where it is?"

"What does it matter to you?" Francesca jumped in. "If Sara wants to know, she should just go to her great-grandfather and ask him, no matter what her uncle says. She has a right to know."

"Does she?" Lucinda asked.

"She's his great granddaughter," Francesca said. "If it were me, I'd sneak in to see him."

Lucinda shook her head in disapproval.

"That might not be a bad idea," Sara said, thoughtfully.

Chapter 24

Bramwell stepped back into the hallway. He had the silver tray containing what was left of C.J. Kask's dinner balanced in his hand as he closed the door to the master bedroom behind him. A moment later, he disappeared down the hall and was on his way downstairs and back to the kitchen.

The hallway was empty and silent for several minutes before a face peeked out from behind a large black and gold urn in a narrow alcove just past the door. Sara made sure that Bramwell was long gone before she slid out of her hiding place behind the urn and approached the door.

She turned the knob and found that it was not locked, so she knocked lightly on it and, after one last look down the hallway, pushed her way into the room where her great-grandfather was recuperating.

The room was unusually warm and dark and the strong smell of antiseptic stung her nose. She could see that much of the furnishings in the room were like the ones in her own in the east wing. The room itself was much larger and was dominated by an enormous four-poster bed facing the windows. Curtains had been drawn around the bed.

She closed the door behind her. It clicked loudly as the door latched and Sara winced at the noise.

As her eyes adjusted from the light in the hallway, She found that the room wasn't as dark as she had thought when she looked in. There was a dim lamp on in one corner. It was a floor lamp with a heavy navy blue shade that cast the room in a dim bluish hue.

The only sound in the room came from several machines next to the bed that seemed to be monitoring the old man's vital signs. His condition must be worse than she thought.

She moved around the bed to the other side, away from the machines. She could hear his low, raspy breathing behind the curtains. Yet, she could still see nothing of the person in the bed.

"Great Grandfather?" she asked in a quiet voice. "I'm Sara Cross." She listened for a moment for any response from the old man and then added, "I'm Mary's daughter."

She reached out for the edge of the curtain to draw it back so that she could see the man. "Great Grandfather?" she repeated.

A hand grasped her wrist. She cried out and pulled away, backing into a side table and knocking things over onto the floor, making all sorts of loud noises.

"Sara. It's me," the man holding her arm said. "It's Bramwell. Please, we must let your great grandfather rest."

She stopped struggling and looked up at the tall, balding man. He let her arm go. "Please Sara."

"I have to talk to him," she insisted, her eyes filling with tears.

"You've made that clear. Unfortunately, he isn't in any condition to talk to you right now."

"You need to tell me about the chest," she said loudly so that the old man in the bed could hear her. "Please," she sobbed.

"He can't hear you, Sara," Bramwell said trying to soothe her. "I'm sorry. As soon as he is able to, you will be allowed to talk to him as much as you like." He attempted to guide her to the door.

"They killed Thomas," she yelled to the curtained bed. "They'll kill all of us if we don't give it to them."

Bramwell stopped. "Who killed Thomas?" he asked.

"I don't know," she said trying to wipe the tears away. "When I was underwater with Thomas, I heard a woman's voice. I think it was Dior, Dior Moira"

Bramwell led her to a chair near the door. "What did she say?" he asked. He took a box of tissues from a table nearby and held it out to her.

"She killed Thomas because he refused to get the chest," she told him, wiping her eyes with a tissue. "She said that they will kill me if I don't get it for them."

"This chest. What does it look like?" Bramwell asked, his voice urgent.

The door opened abruptly, and Matthew strode in.

"What's going on here?" he demanded.

"She came to see her great grandfather," Bramwell said.

"Impossible. He can't see anyone right now," Matthew said.

"Perhaps it is time for them to know him for what he is," Bramwell said.

Matthew appeared flustered for a moment. Then his face hardened.

"Absolutely not," he told Bramwell and then turned to Sara. "You will see him when I say you can see him and not before. Do you understand?"

"No, I don't," she said standing up to face him.

"It doesn't matter if you understand or not. You will leave this—" Matthew was not able to finish what he was saying.

Sara had taken a step toward him. She had wanted to shake some sense into him. Instead, she was going to try and make him listen to her. She tried to grab his arms. Then she stopped and just stared in disbelief.

Her Great Uncle suddenly flipped backward over a chair and landed face down on the carpet.

She and Bramwell gaped at Matthew lying on the floor. Bramwell looked at Sara who broke into tears and rushed from the room. Bramwell just watched her leave, deep in thought, before Matthew's groans interrupted his thoughts and he turned to help Matthew stand up.

"Her power is growing," Matthew said straightening his clothes.

"She doesn't know how to control it yet," Bramwell told him. "She's scared, too. Thomas was killed, and she's been threatened. They should be told the truth."

"Maybe," Matthew said. "They might not like the truth."

"They aren't going to like you killing off the old man," Bramwell told him.

Matthew glanced at the bed and then left the room, and Bramwell followed him. Matthew closed the door and locked it.

Sara returned to her room and quickly locked the door. She waited, listening to see if Bramwell or Matthew had followed her. She couldn't hear anything out in the hallway above the sound of her own breathing.

What was happening to her? She began pacing about the room. Was Jason correct? Was she able to knock people off their feet and levitate statues?

Why is all this happening? They had their problems back home in Wakina. At least it was a normal life. Now their house was gone. Thomas was gone. And strange things were happening.

She sat down on the edge of the bed. Why were these things happening to her? She pulled a pillow into her lap and hugged it.

First, Franklin said the Fire Djinn was looking for her. Then, the Water Djinn attacked them in the fountain.

And she was the one that knocked the Sheriff down, wasn't she?

She pushed the pillow away. That's ridiculous. Jason was just letting his imagination run away with him. That's the kind of thing that happens in movies, not real life.

Or does it? Didn't she want the Sheriff to agree with her? Didn't she want to knock some sense into him? She pulled the pillow back into her lap. Could she have wanted to push him down?

She didn't push him. She didn't even touch him. How could she have done it without touching him? She'd never heard of anyone else with psychic powers like that. How could she have them?

Except, it didn't happen just that one time. It happened with the statue. It happened with Matthew. She was the only one there all three times.

No. She thought. She was letting Jason's imagination get to her. She wasn't doing it. She wasn't. She threw the pillow across the room, hitting a side table. A lamp and clock slid toward the edge of the table. Luckily, they didn't fall off. A candlestick, however, fell over, and the candle broke in half.

She looked at the candlestick and thought for a moment. OK. She thought. If she were the one doing it and if she could push people over and lift heavy statues, then she should be able to make a candlestick move. Shouldn't she?

She went over to the table and set the candlestick up in the center of it. She pushed several books away from it toward the other edge.

She looked at the candlestick and concentrated on it. Move, she thought. Nothing happened. Move, she thought more urgently. The candlestick stayed where it was.

She got up and paced again. How could she have pushed grown men down when she couldn't even get a candle to move an inch? Was she missing something?

She thought back on her conversations with the Sheriff and her uncle. What did she do that caused it? Neither one would listen to her.

She wanted them to listen. They just wouldn't. She wanted to grab them. She wanted to shake them until—

Grab them, She thought. She reached out trying to grab them. She hurried back to the table and looked at the candle again.

"Move," she said under her breath, pushing her hands toward it. The candle didn't move.

"I said, move," her voice was louder now, the frustration started to return. The candle sat there ignoring her.

She paced around. Why wasn't it working?

She closed her eyes. It wasn't her. She didn't have any powers. They killed Thomas, and she didn't have the power to stop them. They'll probably kill her too and what is she going to do about that?

And what will happen then? It won't be over if they kill her. A pang of fear touched at the edge of her thoughts. They'll try to kill Daniel and her mother, that's what they'll do. The fear grew. And she won't be able to do anything about it because she'll be dead.

And then, the fear changed. She's not dead yet, she thought. Her fear and frustration turned into anger at her unseen enemies. As long as she's alive, she'll fight them. She won't let them take Daniel, and her mother from her like they had Thomas.

Her hands were balled into fists at her sides the rage boiling throughout her. She won't let them. She opened her eyes and focused her emotions on the candlestick.

Everything on the table flew away from her and smashed against the walls in an arc of destruction around the room. She just stood there for several minutes, in shock, her anger evaporating, until a pounding on her door interrupted her astonishment.

"Sara, are you all right?" Jason asked through the door.

"I'm fine."

"I thought I heard something break."

"I dropped a tray," Sara lied, quickly trying to clean up the mess. She found the crumpled candlestick embedded in the side of a desk.

"You aren't hurt?"

"No. I'll be down for supper in a few minutes." She pried the candlestick out and found that it had been totally flattened.

"OK," Jason said, hesitantly.

Sara waited until she heard him go back down the hallway. She took one last look at the silver lump and then dropped it back on the table. She smiled and then went to join the others downstairs.

She was relieved to hear that the fire department found that the cause of the fire was broken wiring in the upstairs hallway light. That would stop any further questions into the fire.

She was also glad that Jason agreed to stay another night before returning to Wakina, even though she wouldn't admit it to anyone. Although they all enjoyed the quiet evening at the mansion, everyone could tell that Sara seemed distracted.

When they asked her about it, she simply said that she was just tired and when the clock chimed nine o'clock, she bid them a good night early. She went back to her room and locked herself in.

Chapter 25

Sara spent the night tossing and turning. When she was awake, her mind was filled with images of the objects on the table flying across the room and trying to figure out why this was happening to her. When she was asleep, she had disturbing dreams.

She dreamed that she was looking into the fountain at the square, but there was no water. The only thing in the fountain was a coffin. She slowly approached it. She didn't want to. She couldn't stop herself, though. She opened the lid. Inside, Thomas was lying just as she had seen him at his funeral. She looked down at the book her mother had given him. Most of the title had disappeared. All that was left was 'Tom Saw.' When she looked back at his face, his eyes were open and staring at her. She woke up in a panic.

She sat up on the edge of the bed and waited for her racing heart to slow down. It was still dark, and the clock beside her bed showed that it was 3:48 am. She felt like she couldn't breathe, so she unlocked the balcony door and stepped out into the cool night air.

The yard was dark, and she couldn't see lights in any of the windows along that side of the house. She was probably the only one up at that hour, she thought.

Then she saw something that made her blood freeze. There was light emanating from the windows of the mausoleum. At first, she thought that maybe the lights were left on after Thomas' service. When she saw shadows moving about inside, she knew that was not the case. She quickly backed into her room and closed the balcony door. She peered through the drapes. There were clearly people inside the mausoleum.

She dressed quickly, unlocked her door and hurried down the hall to Daniel's bedroom door and knocked on it softly. She couldn't hear any noise inside, so she knocked louder. Finally, there was the creak of the floor as Daniel crossed to the door.

"What do you want?" he asked. He wasn't happy that Sara had disturbed his sleep.

Sara pushed past him into the room and went to his balcony door. When she looked out, she could see the light was still there.

"Look," she told him. "In the mausoleum." She opened the door and went out on the balcony. Daniel sleepily joined her.

"What is it?" he demanded and then, he too saw it. "Who'd be down there at this hour?"

"I don't know, but I'm going to go find out," she told him.

"I'm coming with," Daniel said.

By the time they reached the patio that bordered the back lawn, the light in the mausoleum had been extinguished. They glanced around the yard. They saw no sign of anyone and the only sounds they heard were the gentle lapping of waves below the hill and the wind blowing in from the lake.

They hurried across the yard toward the little cemetery. Sara held her cell phone ready in her hand. Even though it was useless for making phone calls, it could be used as a flashlight when the time came. She decided to keep it off though until they got closer.

The gate to the cemetery stood partially open. They paused to listen again. They could hear nothing coming from the mausoleum. Daniel slipped through the gate and, after a moment's hesitation, Sara followed him.

Daniel pointed toward the lake end and whispered, "You head around that side. I'll go around this way."

Sara thought they should stick together. Before she could protest, Daniel hurried away and then darted toward the back where the cemetery and forest met.

Sara made her way across the front and followed the fence as it turned along the edge of the cliff that plunged down to the lake below.

She suddenly ducked down and turned to look back toward the mausoleum and the mansion. She thought she'd heard a cry, but she wasn't sure because the sound of the waves below her was far louder there at the edge. Could it have been Daniel? Or someone else?

She made her way toward the mausoleum, moving from one large headstone to another. Once she got close enough, she paused and checked for any movement or noise. Everything was quiet. "Where was Daniel?" she wondered.

After another glance around, Sara hurried up the steps and flattened herself against the wall of the mausoleum next to the metal outer doors that were closed. She waited a moment. There was still no sign of Daniel.

She moved to the doors and pulled on the handles. They wouldn't budge. She looked at the handles to see if there were a lock. She couldn't see one. She was about to try again when she heard a noise behind her.

She nearly had a heart attack when she saw a figure dash up the steps toward her. She took a step back and was about to raise her arms to ward off an attack when she saw that it was Daniel.

"Where were you?" Sara demanded.

"I was at the back gate, by the forest. It was open."

"You closed it after the funeral."

"I know. It's open now," Daniel said. "For a second, I thought I saw a light in the trees, but then it was gone. I could have been just seeing things. I'm not sure."

"Whoever it was down here seems to be gone."

"What were they doing in there?" Daniel asked.

"Let's find out," Sara pulled on the door. They didn't move. "Are they locked?" She asked aloud.

"I noticed this yesterday," Daniel said. He took the handles and twisted them. There was a loud clunk sound as the bolts retracted from the floor and door header. He then pulled them open to reveal the dark interior of the mausoleum.

Sara turned on her phone and launched a flashlight app. The screen lit up with a bright white light. She shined it into the entrance, and they saw that the inside gates were open as they had been the last time they were there. They could see part of the marble table where Thomas' casket had lain earlier. The rest of the interior was still shadowy. They cautiously moved forward.

Just when they reached the edge of the central room, Daniel suddenly hissed, "Look!"

Sara shined the phone at the wall behind one of the gates where Daniel was pointing. There was something there. However, she had to move the light to see it better. It was an old-fashioned push button light switch.

Daniel reached through the bars of the gate and pushed one of the buttons. A dim, yellow light hanging from the ceiling above the center table turned on, illuminating the interior room of the mausoleum.

Sara turned off the flashlight on her phone as they looked around, their eyes adjusting to the sudden light. Immediately, they saw that something was horribly wrong.

Nineteen of the vaults were as they had seen them last; eight with blank marble fronts and eleven with brass plates etched with names and dates. The twentieth vault, in stark contrast to the others, was open. The front enclosure had been smashed and lay broken on the floor in front of it. The brass inside plate was also removed and discarded on the floor.

They both instantly knew that it was the vault where their brother, Thomas had been placed the day before. They dashed over to it and looked inside. It was empty. Thomas and his casket were both gone.

Chapter 26

By the time the sun had risen, a small crowd of people had been milling around in the mausoleum. Daniel had immediately gone to wake up Matthew and Jason. And Bramwell had summoned the Sheriff. Jason and the Sheriff both went to work examining the inside and outside of the mausoleum.

Sara looked at what was left of the front of the vault where Thomas had been laid to rest. She picked up the plate that had his name and the years of his birth and death. Whatever they had used to bludgeon open the vault had bent the plate and distorted the etched words.

"Why would someone steal his body?" Sara asked Daniel. "What would they want with it?"

"Maybe they want to hold it for ransom," Daniel suggested.

"I don't think so. If they wanted to hold someone for ransom, they'd grab someone who's alive, not someone who's dead."

As the Sheriff and Jason were finishing up their investigations at the Mausoleum, Daniel noticed Gwen standing at the edge of the forest. She had stopped by to see if he wanted to take an early morning walk with her. Daniel told her about the situation.

"Can we meet a little later?" Daniel asked.

"Sure. Just follow the path," she pointed to a spot on the edge of the forest where a dirt path led into the trees. "Take care of yourself." She added.

Daniel assured her that he would try. When he went back to the patio where Matthew and Sara were waiting to hear any news about Thomas' disappearance, he found an extremely pale young woman wearing white gloves along with her jeans and t-shirt.

Sara introduced Lucinda to Daniel.

"As I was telling your sister. I heard about your brother and just wanted to tell you that if there's anything I can do to help, don't hesitate to ask."

"How did you hear about it so fast?" Sara asked.

"Rumors fly fast when it comes to this family," Matthew told her.

"It's true," Lucinda agreed. "It's a small town and news travels fast. Everyone in town is talking about your brother's disappearance."

"It's creepy that everyone is talking about us," Daniel said.

"Have they discovered what happened?" Lucinda asked.

"I think we're about to find out," Matthew said.

The Sheriff had walked around the house and was crossing the patio toward them. Jason was a few paces behind him.

The Sheriff told them the results of his initial investigation. There were tracks of a truck that parked just off the driveway where it entered the forest. The thieves carried Thomas and his casket to the truck and drove off from there. Once the truck reached the road, it turned toward town.

"I was hoping to follow it into town and see where it turned off," He told them. "When I got as far as the old cemetery, there was a funeral procession just leaving it, and any possible tracks were lost."

"Not much to go on," Matthew said with a sigh.

"I have a few things to check out," the Sheriff said. "I'll let you know if I find out anything more."

They thanked him, and he took his leave.

"I think I'll head out too," Lucinda said. She said her goodbyes and went around the house the same way the Sheriff did.

Jason watched her leave. When she rounded the corner, he said, "Her shoes and pant cuffs were covered with dirt."

Daniel shrugged. "Maybe she's a gardener," he suggested.

"Maybe," Jason said.

Sara looked at Jason curiously.

Chapter 27

Daniel found Gwen resting against a fallen tree just inside the forest. She smiled when she saw him. He helped her to her feet, and without letting go of his hand, she gently pulled him deeper into the forest and away from the mansion.

"Sorry it took so long," he said.

"I understand," she told him. "Any news about your brother?"

"Not yet."

"It's OK if you need to be with your family today," she said.

"I had to get out of there for a while. It will be nice to take a little walk," he told her.

There was a little bit of a breeze blowing through the trees as the two of them made their way along a path. The sounds of life at the mansion faded behind them as they walked through the forest. The only sounds they could hear were insects, the waves of the lake in the distance and their own padding footsteps.

Daniel liked having a forest right by the house.

At one point, they came across a small trickle of a creek running down a coulee toward the stream that ran through the forest. It wasn't big enough for any fish to live in. Other creatures found it habitable, though. Daniel crouched down and dipped his fingers in the water. He spotted a toad perched on a rock that split the creek in half.

He looked up to Gwen and held a finger up to his lips. He pointed to the toad. Gwen crouched down beside him and watched with him. The amphibian sat on the stone pretending it was just another rock. Then, suddenly, it jerked a couple of times before jumping off the rock and hopping up the bank on the other side.

Daniel smiled and glanced at Gwen who wasn't watching the toad. She was watching Daniel. And she was smiling too. Daniel became self-conscious and quickly stood up.

"Which way to your house?" he asked.

"It's not as much a house as it is a cabin," she told him.

"A cabin, like a lake cabin?"

"Sort of. We have electricity, running water and bathrooms. All the luxuries of a regular house. It's just in the woods, that's all," she said.

"Why not live in town?"

"Dad isn't the most sociable person. He decided to live out here because he doesn't actually like too many people." She saw Daniel's worried look. "I'm sure he'll like you."

They heard something rustling around in the underbrush. Daniel stopped and looked around. It became quiet again. The only sound he heard was the splashing of the water as it worked its way down the gully. Another rustling sounded from his left.

"What's that?" he asked.

"I don't know," Gwen said.

He heard a sound from behind him. He spun around toward it. Before he could do anything, the attack came. The weight of the attacker as it jumped up against him pushed him backward onto the ground. Quickly, the animal was on top of him licking his face.

"Stop it," he said, laughing.

"Pounce," she called to the dog. "Pounce, get off him."

The dog backed off as Daniel got to his feet again. It just stood there with its tongue hanging out one side of his mouth and his tail wagging, looking at Daniel. Daniel had to smile at the ruffian.

"Does he belong to you?" Daniel asked.

"No," Gwen said, "He doesn't belong to anybody. He's a family friend."

Daniel looked at her curiously. The dog wasn't wearing a collar, and she didn't seem to be joking.

"Hello, Pounce," Daniel said. He knelt down and greeted his new four-legged friend.

The three of them stepped across the stream and passed the toad who was still hopping along the path.

As they entered the small clearing where the cabin stood, Pounce ran ahead announcing their arrival to anyone who happened to be in the house. It was a typical log structure reminiscent of those built by the settlers who came to the area hundreds of years before. A shed stood apart from the cabin with a small woodpile next to it.

A plume of smoke rose out of the stone chimney that was built up on one end of the cabin. That and the fact that a green Jeep Wrangler was parked by the shed indicated that someone was at home. Pounce jumped up on the door and glanced back as the two of them crossed the yard.

"Home, sweet home," Gwen said climbing the two steps up to the door. An old-fashioned red bicycle with a pair of rear baskets was leaning against the cabin next to the door.

"Who's bike?" Daniel asked.

"It's mine," Gwen said without a glance at it.

"Kind of retro. I like it," Daniel said. Gwen scratched at Pounce's ear as he dropped back down on all four legs.

"It gets me to town and back," she said. She opened the door, and they went in.

Inside was a small room with several pieces of rustic furniture. A large worn rug covered the most of the floor with the exception of a mat in front of the door and a stone hearth in front of the large fireplace where a small fire was burning.

A grate was set in the fire with a large pot of something apparently boiling on top of it. He didn't see a kitchen, so he wasn't sure whether that was their only means of cooking.

Gwen saw his questioning glance at the fireplace. "We do have a stove and oven," she said, laughing, "And a microwave. Dad just likes his stew cooked over a fire."

"Is he home?" Daniel asked.

"He should be around somewhere," Gwen told him and then she became more serious. "I have something I wanted to show you."

She went to a bookshelf and pulled a large bundle from the bottom shelf partially hidden behind a chair. She motioned for him to sit on a low couch and placed the bundle on something like a coffee table in front of it. The table, like most of the furniture in the room, was made of sticks.

Gwen sat down beside Daniel and opened the bundle. Pounce laid down in front of the couch and rested his head on Daniel's feet.

The bundle appeared to be a scrapbook with newspaper clippings, notepaper and photos sticking out from every page. She set about to organize the loose memorabilia stuffed in the front cover.

"I thought you might like to see this," she told him. "It's everything I could get from my dad and granddad about the circus."

"What are you looking at that stuff for?" a gruff voice asked. A man, who looked remarkably much like a lumberjack and was dressed for the part, was standing in a doorway looking at the two of them. His thick, dark hair looked like it hadn't been combed in several months and his tanned face gave the two of them a deeply disapproving look.

"I told him a little about you and Granddad," she said, and her dad raised an eyebrow. "About how you worked with the animals in the circus."

The man's eyebrow returned to its normal place as he moved to a large chair and settled his bulk into it.

"This is my dad, Gus," she told Daniel.

"This is a friend of mine, Daniel," she told her dad.

"Nice to meet you," Daniel said.

"Yeah," her dad grunted. "You don't need to bore him with that rot."

"It doesn't bore me," Daniel said. "I think it is cool that you and your dad took care of animals at a circus."

"The circus life is not all that 'cool'," Gus said. "And we weren't treated all that well."

Daniel carefully paged through the scrapbook with Gwen. The first several pages contained a number of flyers for the circus, Cirque D'Arque. Each flyer was a different color and featured a different location in the Midwest.

"Did you like traveling?" Daniel asked him.

"It's OK when you're young and on your own. Once you have a family, it's nice to have a place to call home," he looked around the room. "Even if it's a dump."

"I like this place," Gwen told him.

"It's not the same without your mother," Gus said. He picked at the arm of his chair and didn't say anything more.

Daniel looked from Gus to Gwen. He wanted to ask about her mother, but it didn't seem to be a subject that Gwen's dad would want to talk about. Gwen looked down at the scrapbook for a moment and then glanced up at Daniel. She seemed to know what he was thinking.

"My mother died when I was young," she told him. "For as long as I can remember, it has just been my dad, my brother and me."

"I'm sorry," Daniel told her. Gwen gave him a weak smile. He looked at her dad sitting across the room. "I'm sorry." He repeated to him.

Gus glanced up at him and nodded his acknowledgment. He swished the ice around in his glass.

"Want anything to drink?" He asked.

"I'm fine," Daniel said.

"No thank you, Dad," Gwen told him.

Gus got up and left the room. Daniel and Gwen looked through the scrapbook for a while without saying anything more. There were many pages with pictures of aerialists, clowns and the myriad of other acts that were part of Cirque D'Arque.

As Gwen paged through the scrapbook, Daniel realized that it had been organized into sections and the next section she opened had all the pictures relating to the animals. Cirque D'Arque apparently had four animal acts and Gwen even had those grouped into their own sections by act.

The first one showed a group of elephants. Gwen told him that there were normally four in the act; one male and three female elephants. Sometimes when one of the females would give birth to a baby elephant, the baby would eventually be trained to be part of the act for a time. Once the baby was a certain age, the owner would sell it off to another circus.

The next section in the scrapbook had pictures of the big cats. The circus had an impressive group of cats; two tigers, three lions and a dark gray panther. Gwen pointed to one picture where the panther was jumping through a hoop of fire.

"Grandfather hated that stunt. Most circuses would have fire around most of the ring, but not on the bottom section. The animals were scared of fire and wouldn't jump through if there were fire on the bottom," she told him. "Anton D'Arque wanted a complete ring of fire."

"How did they get them to jump through it?" Daniel asked.

"Anton D'Arque was a brutal man. You did what he wanted or," Gwen stopped.

"Or what?"

"Or you were punished."

"Who? People or animals?" Daniel asked.

"Both."

They both looked down at the pages of pictures without really seeing them. Anton D'Arque was the real animal, Daniel thought.

"Didn't the animals get burned?" Daniel asked, looking at a picture of the panther jumping through the hoop.

"Many times," Gwen told him.

"Did your grandfather work with the cats?" Daniel asked.

"No. He did tend the cats sometimes after the show," Gwen said and turned the page to the next section.

The next several pages had pictures of a bear act. Most of the bears appeared to be small black and brown bears. In one picture, an enormous bear was standing full height on his hind legs on a small platform in the center of the ring.

"That one's pretty big," Daniel said pointing at the picture.

"That was Titan. He was a Grizzly bear and the star of the act, until," Gwen stopped and looked down, kicking at the edge of the carpet with her foot.

"Until what?" Daniel asked.

"He was the reason the circus closed," Gwen told him.

Daniel looked at the picture and imagined Titan running loose through the tent, people running everywhere trying to get out, children screaming in terror.

Gwen turned the page and a new section began.

"Are they dogs?" Daniel asked, looking at the pictures closely.

"No. They're wolves," Gwen said.

"I've never heard of a wolf act," Daniel said in amazement.

"This is the only one that I've ever heard of," Gwen agreed.

She turned several pages showing pictures that had the wolves climbing, jumping and navigating a dangerous obstacle course with several death-defying stunts. Some of the stunts were similar to the ones the big cats performed. Except while the cats would do them one cat at a time, several wolves would perform stunts either at the same time or in quick succession.

As Gwen turned the last page, there was a picture that made her stop. It showed all of the four animal acts together in one ring. Each animal was either standing or sitting, and they all appeared to be looking right at the camera. It was almost as if they were posing.

Daniel wondered if that were part of the act. Then, he realized that the stands in the background were empty. They must have taken it before or after the show. In fact, Daniel didn't see anybody in the picture except for the animals. Where were the handlers?

"How did they do that?" Daniel asked.

Gwen didn't say anything. She just gazed at the picture. She touched a corner of it where the big cats were gathered. In front of the cats were a young wolf and a young panther. Both were sitting with their heads cocked to one side.

Daniel looked at the picture and then at Gwen. She looked at the picture for a moment longer and then looked up at Daniel.

"What is it?" Daniel asked.

She opened her mouth to say something and then stopped. She looked into Daniel's eyes, and he saw that she was what? Afraid? He thought.

"There is something about my family," she started slowly. "About my family and the circus."

"I think that there has been enough circus talk," her dad said. They glanced over to the doorway. Gus was standing there holding his drink. He was glaring at Gwen.

Daniel guessed that his welcome was wearing out. "That's OK. I have to get back home anyway."

Gus didn't say anything. Gwen just said, weakly, "OK." Daniel got up off the couch. Gwen and Pounce followed him to the door.

"It was nice meeting you," he called to her dad as they walked out into the yard. He didn't hear him say anything back.

Gwen walked with Daniel back to the path into the forest. Pounce jumped up on him, and he scratched the dog's neck. After the dog had jumped down again, he turned to Gwen.

Gwen gave him a quick kiss on the cheek. "I'll see you later?" She asked.

"Definitely," Daniel said. She smiled at him and turned back to the cabin. He stood at the edge of the clearing until she got to the door. She turned back just before going in, and he waved to her. She waved back and closed the cabin door.

Daniel smiled to himself. He headed into the forest and back to the house.

Just as Daniel was disappearing into the forest, Vincent and Mason stepped out from where they were standing just behind the shed. They watched Daniel leave then looked at each other. Neither was happy with Daniel's visit.

Chapter 28

Mason and Vincent sat across from each other in a booth at Carson's Diner eating their usual lunch of double bacon cheeseburgers, chili fries and Cokes.

"What're we going to do about him?" Mason said despite the fact that his mouth was full of burger. Little bits of food showered the table as he spoke.

"Not much we can do," Vincent told him after a swig of Coke.

Mason took another bite of his burger and glowered at the table.

"I don't like the idea of him dating my sister any more than you do," Vincent continued. "But what are we going to do? She likes him."

"I ain't going to sit around and watch my girlfriend go out with the likes of Daniel Cross," Mason said. Mason glanced over to the counter where Gwen was taking a man's order.

"What are you going to do about it?" Vincent asked.

"Maybe we can scare him," Mason suggested. "Chase him through the woods so he'll never come back." Mason smiled at the thought.

"That won't do you any good," a woman's voice said from behind Mason. The boys looked over at the next booth to find an elderly black woman and a young Asian girl having an iced tea and lemonade.

"Why?" Vincent asked, suspiciously.

The older woman threw down some cash on the bill and got up out of the booth with the aid of her cane. The young girl followed her to the boys' table.

"Scaring him will just make things worse," she told them. Her severe look was rather unpleasant.

"How would it be worse?" Mason asked.

"The girl will feel sorry for him and will be angry with you for scaring him," the woman said.

The young girl nodded in agreement.

"What should I do?" Mason asked.

"Make sure he goes away for good," she said with a smile that made her look even more unpleasant.

"How do we do that?" Vincent asked.

"I don't know. I'm sure that two boys with your particular talents can figure out something permanent," she said patting each one on the shoulder.

The old woman gave them a brief wave goodbye and walked out of the diner with the young girl behind her.

Mason sat thinking while Vincent finished up his chili fries.

"Gwen works until nine o'clock tonight, right?" Mason said.

"Yeah, why?"

Mason looked at Vincent. "The old woman was right," he said. "I'll just use my talent." He flashed Vincent a broad grin.

Vincent hesitantly smiled back at him.

Although the table in the dining room was set for six, only four people were present. Mary and Daniel sat on one side of the table. Sara and Jason sat on the other. The other places, set for Matthew and Peter, were vacant.

A young man in proper serving attire brought them their salads and, when they were done, their soups. Cook had created a garden vegetable soup which almost everyone enjoyed. Daniel pushed the carrots around as he tried to eat everything that wasn't one.

The young man announced that the main course was to be Lemon Chicken. Before he could serve it though, Bramwell entered carrying a small envelope. He handed it to Daniel.

"This was left for you sometime this afternoon," Bramwell told him.

Daniel turned the envelope over. Other than his name scribbled on the front, there was no other writing on it.

"Who left it?" He asked.

"I don't know. I found it stuck in the front door. The person apparently didn't want to wait," Bramwell said and left the room.

He opened the envelope and inside was a half sheet of white paper with a short note.

Dear Daniel,

Please meet me at my father's cabin at 6:00. There is something I need to tell you.

Gwen

Daniel checked his watch. It was already 5:45.

"I'm sorry. I have to meet someone at 6:00," he announced and got up to leave.

"Who is it from?" Sara asked.

Daniel reddened slightly. "Gwen," he told her.

"Where are you going?" Sara asked him.

"To her cabin."

"Her cabin?"

"Yeah. She lives with her dad and brother in a cabin in the woods just north of here."

"I don't think you should be going out in the middle of nowhere. We have to be careful, remember?" Sara asked.

"It's OK. I've been there before."

"When?"

"Earlier today. We went out there this morning. I'll be ok."

"Don't stay out late then. Be back before dark," Sara insisted.

"You aren't my mom," Daniel said and quickly left the room.

After dinner, Sara helped her mother back to her room to rest. Along the way, Sara chatted with her about the delicious dinner and the beautiful warm weather. Mary said nothing. She simply smiled once in a while and clutched Sara's arm as they walked.

Once she had her mother tucked into bed, Sara sat on the edge of the bed and looked at her mother.

"Where are you, Mom?" She asked as she took her mother's hand.

Her mother just looked at her.

"I know things have happened," Sara said. "Bad things. But, Daniel and I need you."

Mary smiled at Sara and closed her eyes.

"We need you to come back to us," She said softly.

She watched her mother until she heard the soft, steady breaths that signaled Mary was asleep. She squeezed her mother's hand and laid it down on the bed.

She detected the faint smell of mint and turned to find Franklin standing in the doorway.

"What is it?" Sara asked him.

"I came to visit your mother," Franklin said.

"Come in then," Sara said, standing up.

Franklin walked over to the bed and gazed down at Mary.

"Did you know my mother very well?" Sara asked.

"Yes," he said. "It was always a pleasure when she came to visit as a little girl. She always brought life into this old house."

"She doesn't talk about her childhood much," Sara told him.

Franklin walked over to a table where some daisies were set in a vase. "She loved flowers and plants."

"I know," Sara said noticing the flowers for the first time.

"She would spend hours in the conservatory with the gardener." Franklin turned back to Sara. "Did you ever notice how plants would thrive under her care?"

"She had a green thumb," Sara said. "At least until my dad left."

"It was more than a green thumb. She has a talent."

"I suppose," Sara said. She thought Franklin was acting a little odd, even for a dead person.

"Were you ever sick as a child?" he asked, tilting his head to the side.

"What?"

"Were you ever sick where you had to miss school because of it?"

"Well, no," she said, thinking back. "There were times I didn't feel well, but I usually recovered fast."

"What would happen when you were sick?" he asked, stepping closer to her.

"She would put me to bed and hold me until I fell asleep."

"And when you awoke?"

"I usually felt better."

"Your mother has a talent."

"What do you mean? She can heal people?"

"She can fortify life. She can help plants grow healthy and strong, and she did the same thing with you and your brothers."

Sara thought about her childhood, trying to think of something to disprove what he said.

"I understand she was with Thomas at the end."

"Yes," Sara said, barely audible.

"I'm sure she tried to help him, to bring him back. She couldn't though."

Sara looked at her mother sleeping peacefully. She nodded.

Franklin went to the bed and gazed down at Mary again. "She gave everything until she had no more to give," He told her. "Now she is the one that needs healing."

"How?" Sara asked. "How can we heal her?"

"I don't know," Franklin said. "We have to find a way." He turned away from the bed and went to the doorway.

"Sometimes, I feel so helpless," Sara said looking at her mother.

"You're not helpless," Franklin said. "You have a talent too."

She turned to him, but he was gone.

Chapter 29

It was almost ten after when Daniel arrived at the cabin. Gwen was not waiting for him outside so he hurried to the door and knocked. He glanced around the yard and noticed that the Jeep and Gwen's bike were not there. He knocked again.

"Hello?" he called. It seemed there was nobody home.

He thought that maybe she was late getting there as well, so he sat down on the steps to wait.

Sara and Jason sat on the front porch after dinner. It was the first chance that they had to be alone that day. Jason rocked slowly in an old walnut rocker. He kept glancing at Sara and then away again.

"What is it, Jason?" she asked.

"What?" Jason looked at her. He seemed startled.

"Is there something bothering you?"

He stared into the distance and didn't say anything for a moment. And then he looked back at Sara.

"I have to go back to Wakina tomorrow," he said.

"I know. I'm glad you were able to stay a couple of days."

"So am I. I'm worried, though."

"About what?" she asked.

"About you," he said and then quickly added. "And about your Mom and Daniel too."

"Yes. Of course," Sara said with a little laugh.

"I don't know what's going on. But I know you're in danger here," he said.

Sara didn't say anything. She couldn't even look at Jason.

"Strange things are going on," he continued. "I can't put my finger on what it is."

Sara didn't want to talk about any of the strange things, so she tried to divert the conversation. "I'm flattered that you're worried about me."

Jason blushed slightly. Before he could figure out what to say, they heard a car approaching.

A small, red Acura drove up and parked at the bottom of the porch steps. Francesca got out and waved to them. Sara waved back.

"Sara," she called, rushing up the steps. "Sara. I just heard about your poor brother. What a horrible thing." She gave Sara a smothering hug. Sara patted her on the back and looked at Jason wide-eyed.

"You must be devastated," Francesca released her and sat down on a chair next to her. "What can I do to help? Just name it."

"Everything has been taken care of," Sara told her.

"What? They found your brother's body?" Francesca asked surprised.

"No. They haven't. There's nothing more that we can do right now."

"I understand." She looked at Sara with a pitying expression.

The three of them sat in awkward silence for several minutes. Francesca obviously wanted to say something more and kept glancing at Jason.

"What is it, Francesca?" Sara asked.

"I just wanted to find out what happened with," she lowered her voice and leaned toward Sara. "With that other thing we talked about."

"That other thing?" Sara whispered back.

"You know," Francesca said, glancing alarmed in Jason's direction. She mouthed the words, "The chest."

"Oh," Sara said. Jason almost laughed out loud at her attempt to keep him in the dark. Sara's face became serious.

"I didn't find out anything," Sara told her.

"Why not?" Francesca asked.

"I'd rather not talk about it right now," Sara told her.

"You need to find it, don't you?"

Jason spoke up, "She said, she didn't want to talk about it."

"I don't see what this has to do with you," Francesca told him.

"I'm her friend," Jason said.

"Well, so am I."

Sara was trying to ignore the two of them. She looked out at the front lawn and noticed someone on a bicycle riding up to the mansion.

"As a friend, then, you should respect her wishes," Jason was saying.

"You don't even know what we were talking about," Francesca told him.

Sara got up and walked to the steps. They stopped arguing and just watched her go. She stopped at the top step just as Gwen got off her bike.

"Hi, Sara," Gwen said as she climbed the stairs. "I got off work early and was wondering if Daniel is around."

"No," Sara said staring at her. "He's supposed to be with you."

"With me?" Gwen asked.

"He got a note from you telling him to meet you at your house," Sara told her.

"A note?" Gwen asked, confused. "I never sent a note."

"You never asked him to meet you tonight?" Sara asked, tension rising in her voice.

"No," Gwen said.

Sara looked at Francesca.

"Drive us to Gwen's place," She told her. It came out more like an order than a request. Francesca nodded.

"Daniel's in trouble. Show us where you live," Sara told Gwen. All four of them piled into Francesca's car, and they quickly drove off.

Chapter 30

Daniel stood and stretched. Where was Gwen? He had been waiting for almost an hour, and there was no sign of her. He pulled the note from his pocket and read it again. He had the right place, and he was only ten minutes late. It wasn't even his fault. He had gotten there as fast as he could have after he got the note. She would have waited, wouldn't she have?

The woods, under the canopy of leaves, were starting to get dark. Even though the sun wouldn't set for a while still, it was dipping below the tops of the trees to the west, and the shadows were starting to grow.

Daniel paced back and forth from the forest to the cabin steps. He kicked the bottom step. That's it, he thought. He'd give her another ten minutes. If she weren't there by then, he'd head back home.

He was just walking back toward the path again when he heard the sound of movement in the forest. He peered into the trees. He didn't see anything. Just a squirrel, he thought. No, it couldn't be. Whatever made the sound he heard was much larger than a squirrel. It could have been a deer, he thought.

There was more movement and that time, Daniel could also see that whoever it was had a flashlight. He couldn't see the person. He could see only the light bouncing along as the person walked.

"Gwen?" he called. The movement stopped, and the light shined toward him.

He hurried toward the light. Rather than following the path, which ambled off to his right, he cut into the underbrush and headed straight to where he saw her shadowy form standing. He was almost there when the flashlight was turned off, and he lost sight of her in the shadows.

Daniel reached the spot where he thought she had been and stopped.

"Gwen?" he asked again.

There was no response. He didn't see her, and there were no sounds of anyone nearby. He called her name several times and looked among the trees to see where she went. His foot kicked something, something made of metal by the sound of it.

He stopped and picked it up. It was the flashlight. He was confused. Why would Gwen drop the flashlight and hide from him?

Then he heard some low moaning coming from a short distance away. He shined the flashlight toward the noise and saw a disturbance in some bushes off to his right. Before he could investigate, another moaning sound came from his left, and he swung the light around to see someone moving behind a couple of close set trees.

"Gwen?" he called again. "Vincent?" He was starting to get uneasy about being in the woods when he heard something from his right that sent a cold chill through him.

It was a sound like someone cracking their knuckles. Except that it was more like several dozen people cracking their knuckles one right after another. As soon as those faded out, the same kind of sound started up on his left.

He turned and started running back to the path. After running several dozen yards or so, he still hadn't come across the path. He stopped and searched for a landmark he could use to orient himself. Nothing looked familiar.

Behind him, he heard a growl. He turned and raised the light in the direction of the sound. The light was reflected back from the eyes of what appeared to be a large wolf. It's gray-white fur gleamed in the light as it started to circle to his left. It growled at him and bared its teeth.

Daniel turned and continued in his original direction. The wolf didn't attack him. Rather, it ran past him and tried to block him. He felt the creature's fur as it brushed by him.

He stopped as the beast faced him again. Its ears were flat against its head, which was lowered as if he were ready to leap onto him. The fangs were showing, and drool was dripping from its mouth onto the dirt and leaves below it.

As they stood facing each other, he heard the deep growling of something else. It echoed through the trees, and he wasn't sure what direction it came from. He needed to make a break for it and ran to his left as fast as he could run.

As he ran, he didn't hear movement behind him. The sound of movement came from his right running parallel to him. After about twenty or thirty feet, he broke out onto the path. He quickly looked both directions. Which way? He thought.

A moment later, his decision was made for him. The wolf burst out of the brush to his right and blocked his way on the path. He heard the deep growling again. It was something large. And, this time, it was much closer. Too close. He thought.

Was the wolf just trying to hold him here until something else arrived? He had to get out of the woods before it could get there.

The small animal's ears popped up, and the snarl disappeared for a moment. It glanced back behind it on the path. Then, Daniel heard it too. Voices. There were several voices, and they were calling his name.

"I'm here," he yelled.

A growl from the wolf was the only warning Daniel got of the attack. It was enough. He ducked down and rolled forward into a somersault. He felt the fur and air movement as the wolf leapt at where he had been standing and passed above him. When he came back up to his feet, he turned and shined the flashlight into the face of the wolf as it turned back toward him.

Daniel backed away along the path. He wasn't moving fast, but at least he was moving toward the others. The wolf stopped growling and stood still. Daniel wasn't sure what that meant. He hoped that the wolf didn't like that people were on their way. He decided that he needed to take advantage of the moment and run.

When he turned, he stopped in his tracks and looked up at a hulking beast standing on its back legs towering over him just inches away. He didn't even have time to move when a massive paw slammed into the side of his head knocking him sprawling into the bushes just off the path.

He laid there dazed for a second, and then felt the side of his head. His hand came away covered with blood. He had just rolled onto his side to get up when the creature ran into him. It knocked him flat onto his back. It's claws dug into his leg and side. He looked up at the beast, but he couldn't get his eyes to focus.

The giant head leaned down toward his face, and his nostrils were filled with its hot, fetid breath. It opened its mouth and almost deafened Daniel with its terrifying wail. When he tried to move, he found that he couldn't budge under its weight. It turned its head and bit into his shoulder. Daniel screamed.

Daniel's head began to swim. He heard people yelling and felt the creature let go of his shoulder. Then a voice broke through the haze. A voice that Daniel thought he recognized. Gwen? He tried to clear his head. Just staying conscious was an effort for him. It had to be Gwen, he thought.

"Get away from him," the voice shouted. The pressure of the creature's weight was lifted from his body. He was able to get a little more air, although breathing was difficult because of the pain.

"Get away," she repeated and then suddenly hands were clutching at him, human hands. He could see blurry figures above him.

"Daniel? Can you hear me?" He thought that was someone else. Not Gwen. Sara? He tried to say something. He couldn't.

He felt something being pressed against the side of his face and other hands were pressing on his shoulder. He heard a voice high above him.

"He's losing a lot of blood," the voice said. He thought he heard someone crying.

The effort to keep his eyes open seemed to take all his strength. He was tired. He just wanted to sleep. He let his eyes close.

"Daniel," he heard someone call to him. "Daniel, stay with us."

Daniel couldn't stay with them. He was just too tired. The noises drifted away from him as he felt himself falling into darkness. And then he was gone.

Chapter 31

Daniel heard a beep in the darkness. And then another. More sounds started to drift toward him, but he wasn't able to identify them. He tried to open his eyes. The light around him was just too bright.

He tried to move his arms. They seemed heavy. His left arm moved just a little. He couldn't move his right arm at all. Something was holding it down. The creature in the forest?

"Daniel?" a voice asked out of the darkness.

He opened his eyes again and squinted against the light. He wasn't in the forest anymore. He was in a room with fluorescent lights and a tile ceiling. A girl leaned over him. He tried to focus on her face.

"Sara?" his voice came out weak and scratchy.

"I'm here," the girl said. His eyes were finally able to focus on his sister's face. She was smiling and crying at the same time.

"Where am I?" Daniel croaked out.

"A hospital of sorts," Sara said looking around at the room. She looked back at him. "We were so worried about you."

He tried to turn his head to see who else was in the room, but his head wouldn't move. He looked questioningly at his sister.

"They don't want you to move your head for a while until your neck heals a little," Sara told him.

Jason moved closer to his bed so that Daniel could see him.

"How are you feeling?" Jason asked.

"Not bad all things considered," he joked feebly.

Sara smiled at him.

"How did I get here?" Daniel asked.

"We knew you were in trouble and went looking for you," Sara said. "We didn't get to you in time. We found you lying in the forest, almost dead."

"Did you see it?" Daniel asked her. "Did you see what it was?"

"No," Jason told him. "It was gone when we got there."

Daniel tried to move his right arm again. "What's with my arm?"

"You have a cast," Sara told him. "Your arm and shoulder were badly injured. They've tried to repair the damage as best as they can. Your head and arm have been immobilized to help protect the wounds."

Daniel tried to process what she was telling him. His thinking was a little sluggish from the medication they were giving him. He didn't know what she meant by 'as best as they can.' He took a breath

"Are they worried about it? I mean, saving it?" He asked.

"They are watching it," Sara said. "And waiting."

He remembered that it bit into his shoulder. He remembered the pain and winced at the thought. Did it almost bite his arm off? The pain from that arm started to throb. He thought that maybe he should think about other things. More pleasant things.

"Is Gwen here?" Daniel asked.

Sara and Jason looked at each other.

"What? Did something happen to her?"

"No," she told him.

"What is it then?" Daniel asked them. Sara looked at Jason again. "Jason?"

"Nothing happened to Gwen," Jason assured him. "It's just…"

"Just what?" Daniel asked him.

"She knows more about what happened to you than she's telling us."

"What do you mean?" Daniel insisted.

"Try not to get upset, Daniel," Sara told him.

"What do you mean?" Daniel repeated. His voice projected the calm they wanted. However, the tense muscles of his uncovered arm and face betrayed his real emotions.

"Gwen was the one that found you. We heard her yelling at something. Telling whatever it was to get away from you. By the time we got there, it was gone."

"So?" Daniel asked.

"So, she won't say what it was. And why," Sara stopped. She looked at Jason again. Jason shook his head at her.

"What?" Daniel asked her.

Sara looked down at his arm sealed in the cast and said nothing.

"Tell me," Daniel said.

"Why would something that did this to you be scared away by her?"

"Is she here?"

"She was in the waiting room when I came in this morning," Jason said. "I don't know if she's still there."

"Could you check, please," Daniel asked him.

When Jason had gone, Daniel asked Sara. "Do you think she has something to do with the attack?"

"I think she knows something about it."

"Do you think she had a part in it."

"Well, she," Sara trailed off and stared toward the door. Daniel was able to see that Gwen was standing at the door with Jason behind her. Tears streaked Gwen's face.

"No," Sara said. "I don't think she had a part in it."

Gwen moved cautiously to the side of his bed. She looked at Daniel and smiled weakly.

"How are you?" she asked in a quiet voice.

"Holding together, I guess," Daniel said. "At least that's what they're hoping."

"I'm sorry, Daniel," she said. "I wish we could have gotten there sooner."

"Gwen," Daniel said softly. "Did you see it?"

"What?"

"Did you see what attacked me?" He studied her face. The color drained out of her, and she glanced up at Sara as she chose her words.

"Only shadows and from a distance. By the time I reached you, they were gone."

Daniel nodded slightly which is as much of a movement as he could make with his head.

"Somebody wrote that note," he said.

A nurse entered and announced that she needed to examine and clean some of Daniels wounds. She also suggested that it was probably time to let Daniel rest for a while.

After some quick goodbyes, they all went down the hallway to the family lounge to wait.

They hadn't been in there for too long when Sara announced that she wanted to go for a walk and get some fresh air.

"Would you go with me?" she asked Jason. He didn't need a second invitation.

A few moments later and they were standing on the sidewalk outside the small hospital building in the bright sunshine.

Sara didn't really pay attention to where she was walking. She simply started down the street and Jason followed along.

"I'm glad Daniel is doing better," Jason told her.

"Me too," Sara said. "I don't know what we would do if we lost him too."

"I'm glad you didn't have to find out," Jason said.

"Not this time, no," Sara said. "Will we be as lucky next time?" She suddenly stopped.

"What is it?" Jason asked. Then he realized that they had stopped next to the fountain where Thomas had died.

"First, Thomas. And now, Daniel," she said gazing into the blue water.

"You act as if they have something to do with each other," Jason said.

"Don't they?" Sara asked quietly. "I wish they didn't. I wish that there wasn't someone out there trying to hurt us."

"Sara," Jason said turning to her. He took her hands and looked into her eyes. "Whatever it is that's going on, you don't need to face it by yourself. You have people around you who care about you and can help you."

"No, I don't," Sara told him. "Thomas is gone. Daniel was almost killed. And my mom…" She looked away, trying to hold back tears. "She can't even help herself."

"What about me?" Jason asked her.

"You?" Sara asked. "You care about me?"

"Yes," he said. "And I can help you."

"No, you can't." Sara broke away from him and walked away. "You can't be a part of this."

"Why not?" Jason asked, trying to keep up with her.

She turned on him and stopped. She took his hand gently. "Because if I let you get involved. They'll try to kill you too."

"Who will?"

"I don't know for sure. They killed Thomas right here in this fountain. They tried to kill me and now, I think they tried to kill Daniel.

Everyone I care about is in danger. Don't you see why I can't let you get involved?"

Jason pulled her into his arms. She looked up into his eyes.

"The problem is," Jason said. "I'm already involved." And he kissed her.

For a moment, nothing existed outside of Jason, the kiss and her. She was unaware of anything except his arms around her, his lips on hers. And then the moment was gone.

She pulled away from him. "No. I can't make you a part of this." She turned away and started back toward the hospital. He stood there staring after her and then he hurried to catch up.

"I want to be part of this," he said. "I am a part of this."

Sara stopped and turned to him again.

"You have to leave here. You have to forget about me," she told him.

"Sara," he began.

"No, Jason," she said, "Go home. Go back to Wakina." She turned away from him and went back into the hospital leaving Jason standing there in the street.

Chapter 32

In the afternoon, everyone returned to the mansion so that Daniel could rest. Sara went into the back parlor and closed the door. She wanted to have some time to herself, and she wanted to think about what she needed to do next.

She had just sat down in one of the chairs when she heard a light tapping on the door.

"I want to be alone, Jason," she called out.

"It's Bramwell," the old butler said from the hall.

"What do you want?" Sara asked with a sigh.

"May I come in? I have a message for you," Bramwell said.

"Sure," Sara said.

Bramwell let himself in. After a quick look back out into the front hall, he turned to Sara and closed the door behind him.

"A message?" Sara asked. "Sounds mysterious."

"Your great grandfather would like to speak with you."

Sara was on her feet in a moment. "I'll go up and get my mom," she said.

"No, just you."

Sara didn't know what to say. "Why did he just want to see her?" she wondered. "Did he hear her the other night and decide to help her?" Her mind was swimming with questions. Questions that she hoped would be answered shortly.

She followed Bramwell upstairs to the west wing. Bramwell paused at the door to C.J. Kask's bedroom.

"He has agreed to speak with you, but he is still weak though. He is susceptible to infection so you must wear this mask and not approach too close." Bramwell produced a face mask sealed in plastic.

Sara ripped open the plastic and pulled the thin paper mask out. She pulled the elastic over her head and positioned it over her nose and mouth. Bramwell did the same with another mask.

Bramwell nodded his head in approval and opened the door.

The room was as it was the last time she was there. The blue lamp was on, and the curtains were closed around the bed. Bramwell led her to a spot several feet from the end of the bed where she could stand or sit as she desired.

She could not see the centenarian in the bed through the curtains and for several moments the only sound in the room was the beeping of the medical equipment. The mask was uncomfortable, and she pinched the wire over the nose to make it fit better. The only good thing about the mask was that she couldn't smell the hospital-like odors in the room.

"So you are Mary's daughter, Sara," a low voice rasped from behind the curtains. She heard a sharp intake of breath after the statement.

"Yes," Sara said. "And you are my great grandfather."

"Yes," he said.

Sara tried to see the old man through the curtains. It was too dark. She felt odd talking to someone she couldn't see. He apparently understood what she was feeling.

"I'm sorry about the curtains," he said slowly. "My doctor feels that it is necessary for my health, such as it is."

"It's OK."

"I would have had all of you in," he said, taking a breath between every sentence. "However, I understand that there is something that we need to talk about first. Something that you feel is important enough to break into an old man's sick room for."

"I've been told that you have a box. A box without hinges but with a cross-like slot in the top."

"Do you know what the box is?" the raspy voice asked her.

Sara hesitated and swallowed, her throat was dry. "Somebody said that it is Pandora's Box."

"Why are you interested in this box?"

"You do have it, then?" she asked excitedly.

"I have a box like what you described," he said.

"Someone killed my brother, Thomas," Sara told him.

"I was told of that," he said quietly. He was barely audible to Sara.

"Daniel is in the hospital after something attacked him. I was almost killed too."

"How does this relate to the box?"

"The person who killed Thomas told me that if I don't give her the box, she will kill Daniel, my mom and me."

"I see," the old man said and then was silent for several minutes.

"Can you tell me where the box is?" Sara asked.

"No. I can't."

"You said you had it."

"I do have it. I have it someplace safe where the people who are hungry for its power can't get to it. It has to stay there."

"They'll kill us if we don't give it to them," Sara pleaded.

"Everyone will die if we do," the old man said, his voice a little more powerful.

"What do you mean?"

"It is an ancient thing. It has been many places in the world over the last several millennia. And many of those places were destroyed because of the men, and women, who tried to bend the power to their will. It will be the same here if I let them have it."

"I can't just let my family die," Sara told him sharply.

"I know. We have to find a different way." His voice trailed off into a fit of coughing.

As it subsided, Bramwell approached Sara again.

"We must let him rest now," he told her and put a hand on her arm to guide her to the door.

"You're just going to lie there and let them kill us?" Sara asked angrily as she was led to the door.

"No. However, the box is not the way to save them," he said in a hoarse whisper that she barely heard.

"Please." Tears came to Sara's eyes. There was no reply from the hidden figure in the bed.

In the hallway, she pulled off the mask and turned to Bramwell as he locked the door again.

"Please, help me," She said.

Bramwell looked down at her tear streaked face.

"I will help you all I can," he told her. "But not with the box. Mr. Kask is right. The box contains nothing except destruction."

Sara turned away from him and ran down the hallway, leaving Bramwell standing outside C.J. Kask's room. He looked down at the floor and wiped a tear from his eye.

When Sara got to the top of the stairs, she saw the housekeeper, a thin, middle-aged woman named Mrs. Baskin overseeing two of the maids sweeping the grand foyer floor. A track of dirt extended from the front door past the stairs and disappeared through a doorway to the back of the house.

As she descended the stairs, Sara heard Mrs. Baskin muttering angrily to herself.

"What happened?" Sara asked, quickly wiping the tears from her eyes.

Mrs. Baskin threw up her hands. "What happened?" she almost shouted. "What happened? He happened. That's what happened."

"He?" Sara asked.

"That Jacobs person," she said. She pointed out a spot that one of the girls missed. "I rue the day he moved in here."

Sara smiled to herself and went back to the back parlor. As she got to the door, she had an idea. Peter Jacobs, she thought. She turned back to Mrs. Baskin.

"Do you know where Mr. Jacobs is?" she asked.

Mrs. Baskin looked at Sara as if she had lost her mind. Then she pointed to the trail of dirt leading to the back of the house.

"You can't miss him," she said and returned to overseeing the cleaning.

The trail led to a stairway to the basement. She followed the steps down where the amount of dirt increased. The trail ended at an old, wooden door.

A crude sign was taped to the door that read, "Do not disturb" in block letters. Scrawled underneath were the words, "do not clean." Sara smiled at that and looked back along the hall. By the looks of things, no one had ever cleaned down there.

Sara could hear someone moving around in the room and banging things together. She knocked on the door and instantly the room was silent.

"Mr. Jacobs?" Sara called, knocking on the door again. "It's me, Sara."

She listened. There was no response. She waited a moment longer and was about to knock again when she heard the door unlock. She took a step back as the door creaked open and Peter Jacobs appeared in the doorway.

Behind the man, Sara could see counters lining most of the walls of the room and several tables filling the center area. It reminded her of the physics room at Wakina High School.

Various pieces of a dark-colored metal were lined up in rows across every available surface. However, the thing that got her attention was an empty gurney set up at one end of the room next to a large metal door.

"Yes?" he asked, tapping his foot and closing the door a little which blocked her view of the room.

"I was wondering if we can talk about some of the things my great grandfather had in his museums years ago," she said.

"Well," he hesitated. "I can't right now. I'm in the middle of something."

"Later, maybe?" Sara asked.

"Yes," he said, "Later. We can talk about it later." He began to close the door.

"When?" she asked abruptly.

"What?" he asked.

"When can we talk?"

"Tomorrow," he said and started to close the door again. He stopped suddenly and swung the door open again. "No, not tomorrow," he practically shouted. "The next day."

"I'll come back then," Sara promised.

"Yes," he said aloud to himself. "The next day." And he shut the door. After a moment, the banging sounds began again.

"The next day," Sara repeated to herself and retraced her way back up the steps to the main floor.

Franklin was just coming into the mansion from the patio when Sara reached the top of the stairs. He nodded a greeting to her and was about to head toward the front rooms.

"Franklin, could I talk to you?"

He paused. "Certainly," he said and followed Sara to the back parlor just off the grand foyer. As she closed the door, he stood and waited.

"You know a lot about goes on around here," Sara began.

Franklin made no response. He just continued to look at her.

"I'm in trouble."

"In what way?"

"Somebody killed Thomas, a wielder I think," she told him. "I think she attacked Daniel too."

"And you think that this wielder will come after you next?"

"I know she will. She told me that she would kill me. Unless I can find something for her," Sara said.

"What is this something?"

Sara hesitated a moment and went over to a chair. "Pandora's Box," she said, sitting down.

He looked away and gazed off into space, thinking.

"My great grandfather has it," she said.

"I know."

"He said that we can't let her have it."

Franklin walked over to Sara's chair and stood, looking down at her.

"Your great grandfather is a smart man."

"Why can't we give it to her? What is it?" Sara asked.

Franklin sat down on the edge of a chair next to hers.

"The Greek legend says that Pandora was given a box by the gods. Except, she was never to open it. Her curiosity got the better of her and she had to open it. When she did, it is said that all the evils of the world spilled out."

"Are there more evils inside?" she asked. "Is that why we can't give it to her?"

"The box is not a container as the legend says. It is a portal. The evils that spilled out were not things like hate, sickness and poverty. The evils were living creatures from other worlds."

"Those creatures were evil?" Sara asked.

"Most of them, yes. Not all of them though."

"So we can't let her have it because more of these creatures could come out."

"That is one reason," Franklin told her. "More importantly, the box radiates power."

"Power?"

"Yes. That's why the area around the Mansion is different from the outside world. The power from the box changes things. That's where the Wielders get their power. And why the Dead don't rest."

"Just having the box gives you power?" Sara asked.

"The closer you are to the box, the stronger the power is. If you have the ability to use the power as the Wielders do, you will be more powerful. You will be able to do more evil."

"What if you use it to do good?"

"The power is too much. It corrupts," Franklin said.

"What if we found someone who could use it for good? So we can save my mom and brother?"

"No. It cannot be used for good."

"Well, I'm going to try."

"If you do, I will try to stop you," Franklin said, leaning forward. His dark eyes became even darker. "All of the Dead will try to stop you. We will not let the box cause any more evil than it already has."

Sara suddenly became afraid of Franklin. And afraid of all of the Dead.

"OK," was all she could manage to say.

He stood up. "I hope so," he said. He went to the door and opened it. "Your great grandfather swore an oath to keep the box safe." He paused. "Help him keep that oath."

Sara sank back in her chair after he left. "Can she protect her family without the box?" she wondered.

Chapter 33

Sara went to visit Daniel again. Jason didn't go with her. He told her that he needed to pack for his return to Wakina.

When Daniel's dinner was brought to his room, Sara took one look at the grilled cheese sandwich and tomato soup and decided that she was hungry too. While he ate his dinner, Sara went over to the diner and had a quick bite to eat herself.

When she returned, Daniel was napping, so Sara sat down to wait. It wasn't long until she was bored. There were a few paperbacks on his bedside table, so she looked through them.

The first book was a Sudoku puzzle book. The second was a swords and sorcery novel called Seabane. The last one was a horror novel called Grave Deeds. Although she had already read the two novels and enjoyed them and wasn't averse to reading them again, she didn't feel like a novel right then. She decided to do a Sudoku puzzle instead.

Quickly, Sara discovered that she couldn't concentrate on the puzzle. Her problems intruded into her thoughts and distracted her. Her life seemed to be falling apart. Daniel was almost killed. Her great grandfather wouldn't let her have the box. And she was sending the only person she can trust home to Wakina.

It was almost 8:00 pm when Sara finally gave up on trying to solve the puzzles. The room was uncomfortably warm, so she opened a window slightly. The light breeze felt good. She was just going to sit back down again when something out on the street attracted her attention.

There was a man standing across the street in the shadows of a closed shop. A man dressed in black pants and a black hoodie with the hood pulled up over his head, hiding his face in darkness.

She backed away from the window and turned off the lights in the room. Then she went back and peered out from the edge of the window. The man was still standing there in the shadows.

She wasn't sure that the man was actually watching the room and was debating whether to call the Sheriff when she saw a woman walking toward him on the far side of the street. When she got closer, Sara recognized the woman. It was Lucinda.

Sara watched her walk past the spot where the man was standing. She didn't acknowledge the man or give any kind of indication that she even saw him. She continued down the block and then turned at a narrow walkway between two buildings and disappeared.

When Sara looked back to the man's hiding place, she saw that he was on the move. He followed Lucinda's path, and when he arrived at the walkway, he paused and looked into the gap. After a quick glance up and down the street, the man disappeared into the walkway too.

Sara was afraid that Lucinda was in trouble. She looked at Daniel. He was still sleeping. With the amount of medication they were giving him, he was probably out for the night. Still, he should be safe there in the hospital. She looked back out to the street and then made up her mind.

She quickly left Daniel's room and headed for the stairs down to the main floor of the hospital. She took those two steps at a time and was soon out on the street and running for the narrow walkway where Lucinda and the man who was pursuing her had entered.

She peeked around the corner expecting to see the man accosting Lucinda. The walkway was empty. It was no more than five feet wide and led between the two buildings to an alley behind them and then continued between the two buildings behind that.

She hurried down the walkway as fast as she could go without making too much noise. As she approached the alley, she could hear low voices coming from it. She wasn't sure whether one of them was Lucinda, but there obviously wasn't a struggle going on.

She carefully looked around the corner. A rear light over the back door of what appeared to be a bar illuminated two people talking in the alley. One was Lucinda. The other was the man dressed in black.

She still couldn't quite hear what they were saying. She glanced around to see if she could get any closer.

There was a dumpster just around the corner from her, and it appeared to be just far enough from the wall of the building that she could slip behind it and move to within a few feet of the two people.

She ducked down and slid around the corner shielded by the dumpster. Slowly, she moved along the wall behind it until she was at the other end of the metal container.

She carefully looked out. The two of them were still there talking. Lucinda was sideways to Sara. The man in black was very close to her almost whispering with his gravelly voice.

Just then, she heard a small sound below her. When she looked down, she saw a large rat with gray, mottled fur. Startled, she tried to move her foot away from it and lost her balance.

One of her feet slipped and accidentally kicked a soda can noisily out into the alley. It was followed by an equally startled rat. Her other leg folded up under her, popping her knee. She clenched her teeth trying to bear the pain without making any other noise.

She heard Lucinda exclaim and then she said, "Damn rats."

Sara pushed herself back up into a crouch and looked out into the alley again. They were apparently satisfied that the can had been the work of the rat and were continuing their conversation.

"You said that Sara saw you," Lucinda was saying.

"Maybe. It doesn't matter though," the dark man said in a low, raspy voice.

"Do you think she'll be able to find the box?"

"I don't know," the dark man told her. "You stay close to her."

"What about you?"

"I'll check on the Sisters and make sure their plans haven't changed."

"And what happens if she finds the box," Lucinda asked.

"When that time comes," the dark man said, "I'll take care of her. Now go."

Lucinda hurried past Sara's hiding place, and she listened until her footsteps faded away. She listened for the dark man's footsteps too, but she didn't hear them. "Was he just standing there waiting?" she wondered. "Did he know she was there?"

Her legs were getting cramped, and she was just thinking that he must have gone another way when he silently walked past the end of the dumpster back to the walkway. It was so sudden that she almost cried out in surprise.

He stopped just at the corner. He didn't look behind the dumpster where he certainly would have seen Sara. He stood looking into the walkway with his face hidden.

"It was very foolish of you to follow us," he said quietly and then he was gone.

It was several minutes before she got up the courage to crawl out from behind the dumpster. She peered into the walkway. She didn't see anyone. She hurried back out onto the street and got into her car. She immediately locked the doors, started it up and sped back up the hill to the mansion.

When Sara arrived back at the mansion, she hurried into the house and closed the front door. She leaned against it and breathed a sigh of relief.

Without turning on lights, she went into the front parlor and peeked out the front windows. There was no sign that she had been followed. She turned a chair toward the window and collapsed into it.

She thought about what she had overheard. Was Lucinda working with the Sisters? Or was the woman she heard in the fountain Lucinda and not one of the Sisters? The voice was distant and wispy. She could have easily disguised her voice. And she was under water after all.

"And why did they want that box?" she wondered." Was her great grandfather correct? Would her family be in more danger if they handed the box over to Lucinda and the dark man?"

The only person left that she could turn to for help was Franklin. With Daniel in the hospital and Jason gone, there was no one else that she trusted.

She wished that Jason was still there. If only she hadn't gotten defensive with him. He didn't deserve that. Besides, he was only trying to help, and she certainly needed his help right now.

She was just about to head up to her room and get some sleep, when the light of a flashlight swept across the front porch. She ducked down. When she peeked over the window sill, she saw that someone was standing on the porch.

Her breath caught in her throat. Did the dark man follow her after all? She watched him go to the front door. She hurried across to the doorway to get a better angle into the grand foyer.

With a click of the lock, the front door opened. The man didn't go in. Instead, it sounded like he went back down the porch steps, leaving the door wide open.

She thought about running across the grand foyer and throwing the door shut. Maybe she could lock it before he could get back to it.

Then she realized that it had been locked before he opened it. He had a key to the house. That thought sent a chill down her spine.

And then he reappeared at the door. This time he was dragging a large object. As he brought it through the doorway, it was obvious the way he struggled with it that it was unusually heavy.

Once he had wrestled the object into the hallway, the man closed and locked the door again. As he turned back, she heard something clatter to the floor. The man had dropped something.

He turned the flashlight on again and swept it around the floor until it shone on a strange piece of dark metal. He picked it up and examined it in the light.

Sara saw his face in the light of the flashlight. It was Peter Jacobs. "Why was he sneaking around late at night like this?" she wondered.

She didn't think about that for long because Peter started to drag the object across the grand foyer toward the hallway that led to the back of the house. He must be dragging it to his workroom in the basement. She thought.

She backed away from the doorway and flattened herself against the wall and waited for him to go by the room.

He dragged his bundle straight through the doorway and toward the basement stairs.

She went into the grand foyer and peered through the back hallway until she saw the glow of the stairway lights come on and she heard the thump, thump, thump of the object dropping down one stair at a time.

She moved quietly to the stairs and looked down into the light. She could see the object clearly now. It was a large, black plastic bag with a zipper down the length of it. Sara suddenly couldn't breathe.

It was a body bag. And there was a body in it.

Chapter 34

Peter stared up the steps into the shadows of the main floor. Dragging the body downstairs made a lot of noise. However, he was sure he had heard something else. "Could someone else be up at that hour?" he wondered?

He stepped over the body and quickly ascended the stairs. The back entry was empty. He glanced down the hall toward the front of the house and went into the next room along the back. Both were empty.

Then he remembered a small closet near the back door. He crept up to it and put his hand on the door handle. He paused and then yanked open the door. There was nothing in it except brooms, mops and other cleaning supplies.

He closed the door and after one last look around, went downstairs.

When he first pulled the body out of its resting place, he didn't think that it weighed all that much. It wasn't even too heavy when he'd dragged it from there to a hiding place until he could get it in the house.

It seemed to be gaining weight as he dragged it from there through the house and then into the basement. He grabbed its legs and pulled it down the passage toward his workroom.

He unlocked the door and turned on the light. The room was as he had left it. Taking a hold of the bag one more time he pulled it through the door and across the room to the gurney.

To get it on the gurney, he grabbed it under its arms and lifted it with all his might. It took him a number of tries to lift the body enough that he could lean it onto the gurney. He made a mental note to start a strength training routine.

He maneuvered the legs up and flipped the body over so that the zipper was on top. That meant that the body inside was lying on its back.

He turned his head suddenly toward the door. It was open just as he had left it. Was there something else? He went to the door and looked out. The hallway outside was empty in both directions.

He closed the door and went back to the gurney. He unzipped the bag and pulled it open to see the face inside. It wasn't pretty, he thought. He zipped it up again, opened the metal door near it and rolled the gurney into the room beyond.

The temperature in the room was brisk. He wasn't sure what they used a walk-in cooler for before he got there. It was perfect for his purposes, though. He closed the body in the cooler and went to the outer door.

Tomorrow, I start to experiment, he thought. He smiled and turned off the light. Tomorrow, he said to himself and shut the door.

There was no sound in the room after Peter locked the door and his footstep faded away down the hall. There was a tiny bit of light left in the room spilling under the door from the hallway. Even that disappeared when Peter turned off the lights when he reached the top of the stairs.

The room was pitch black and silent, except for Sara's slight breathing. She sat hidden behind one of the lab tables in the dark. It didn't matter whether her eyes were open or closed, she couldn't see a thing.

Sara continued to wait until she was sure that Peter was not coming back. After more than a quarter of an hour, she stood and made her way along the table and then across and along a side counter until she was near the door. She looked for a light switch.

The room flooded with light, and she took a moment to adjust to it.

The room was just as she had seen it through the door way. There were metallic objects lining every counter surface. They were nothing like she had ever seen before. They were various shapes and sizes.

Some looked something like television remotes with larger buttons and strange symbols etched into them. Others were like short tubes with a grip on one end and odd fluting on the other.

Sara wasn't sure whether these were artifacts from the Kask museums or whether Peter had found them in the barrow where he was digging. Either way, while they were interesting, they were not what Sara had sneaked down there for.

She went to the cooler door and opened it. She pulled the gurney out and brought the bag into the light. She placed it directly under one of the lights hanging from the ceiling and paused to calm her nerves.

She stood next to the upper part of the body and took a hold of the zipper. "Had Peter stolen Thomas' body?" she wondered. "It had to be him. If it weren't Thomas, who else could it be?"

She pulled the zipper down halfway. The edges of the opening dipped toward each other keeping the body inside hidden. She took a side in each hand and, after a breath, pulled it open.

She looked down at the face inside with horror. Whatever it was in the bag, it was not Thomas. It wasn't anyone. At least not anyone human.

The skin was a mottled gray with thin white whisker-like hairs. The face was longer and thinner than a human and while there was a short trunk-like nose that extended several inches out of its face. The rest of the face was so wrinkly that she wasn't sure if it had any of the other features that corresponded with a human face.

She was starting to feel physically ill from looking at it. She quickly zipped up the bag again and pushed it back into the cooler. She backed away from it, half expecting it to rise off the gurney.

She closed the door and turned, running right into Peter Jacobs. She screamed.

"What are you doing here?" he demanded.

"I, I," she fought to get her thoughts together, "I thought it was Thomas."

"Why would you think that?" he asked.

"I don't know," she said and ran around him toward the door. She ran as fast as she could run through the passage and up the stairs. She didn't stop running until she got to her room and locked the door behind her.

She threw herself on the bed and cried. She cried out of fear, out of horror, out of sadness for Thomas. She cried until she couldn't cry anymore. And then she slept.

Chapter 35

aniel stood outside of Gwen's house. The sun was shining brightly. However, he was aware of shadowy figures standing just inside the forest all around the clearing. There was whispering, but he couldn't make out what they were saying.

"Who are you?" he shouted at them.

The whispering continued as if he hadn't made a sound. He looked back at the house, and the front door was open. He was sure that he was supposed to go in and, at the same time, he was sure that he didn't want to.

He glanced at the figures in the forest and realized that they had stopped whispering. They were just watching. Waiting for him to enter the house.

"What do you want from me?" he shouted. There was no response.

He climbed the steps to the door and went into the house. The living room was empty except for a fire burning in the fireplace. There was nothing on the grate cooking, just a small fire that made the room pleasant and warm.

"Gwen?" he called. "Anyone home?" No one answered.

He sat down on the couch because he felt that he was supposed to wait. "Wait for what?" he wondered. "Or who?" He didn't know.

He noticed a large red and black striped cat curled up in one of the chairs with its back toward Daniel. He didn't remember them having a cat. It was familiar somehow, though.

The cat stood up and stretched. Daniel was amazed at how big of a cat it was. It turned to look at Daniel, and he realized where he had seen it before. It wasn't a house cat, it was the bobcat he'd seen on the road when they first came to the mansion.

He slowly stood up trying not to startle it or make it nervous. It just sat down and looked at him. He moved to the door and backed down the steps. When he got to the bottom, he turned and ran toward the forest.

He looked back and saw the bobcat standing in the doorway watching him, its tail lazily darting back and forth behind it. He ran faster. Just before he got to the edge of the forest, he turned back again, and Gwen was standing there. Her red and black hair was shining in the sunlight.

Just as he entered the forest, a stabbing pain throughout his body brought him to his knees. He heard a popping sound all around him and realized that it was the joints in his body expanding and twisting. Pain wracked his body as he saw his arms grow thicker, ripping his shirt. The fingers on his hands shortened, and his finger nails transformed into two inch claws. He felt his nose and mouth stretch out, and his teeth grow. His whole body grew a coat of dark brown hair.

He rolled onto his back. He tried to call out. The only sound that came out was deep growling roar. He saw Gwen standing over him.

"Daniel?" a voice asked. It sounded like it came from Gwen, except it wasn't her voice.

"Daniel?" the voiced asked again.

Daniel closed his eyes. "What was happening to him?" he wondered. When he opened his eyes again, he was looking at fluorescent lights and ceiling tiles.

"Daniel?" the nurse repeated. He looked at her and didn't say anything. His heart was pounding wildly. The monitor was beeping in time with it.

"Were you having a bad dream?" she asked.

He looked around the room as best he could. Everything looked normal. The beeping slowed down.

"I guess," he said.

"The doctor is here to check your injuries," she told him as an older man in a white lab coat walked around the bed to his right side. Daniel recognized him as the doctor who tried to save Thomas. He was also the coroner.

"Well, let's see how we're doing," the doctor said turning back the sheet and lifting the side of Daniel's hospital gown.

"How are you feeling?" he asked as he began to remove the bandage over a wound in his side.

"I'm feeling pretty good." Daniel told him.

"Any pain?" the doctor asked, pulling the bandage away.

"No. I'm good," Daniel replied.

The doctor paused. "Nurse, hand me his chart," he ordered gruffly.

The nurse did as she was told. The doctor flipped through the chart and then checked Daniel's side again.

"Something wrong, Doctor?" the nurse asked.

"I'm not sure what's going on?" the doctor told her. He went on to check other places on Daniel's body where Daniel knew that he had lesser injuries.

"How is that possible, doctor?" the nurse asked.

"I don't know," he said covering Daniel up with the sheet again. Daniel saw him gazing at the cast, deep in thought.

"What is it?" Daniel asked. The doctor ignored his question.

"Let's get an x-ray of his arm," the doctor told the nurse. "Right away."

An orderly was summoned, and Daniel was transported down to the basement of the hospital where an x-ray was taken of his arm and shoulder. In less than an hour and with no further explanation, he was back in his room again.

The doctor and nurse huddled around the computer checking the x-ray results on the screen. Daniel couldn't see the monitor.

"Are those correct?" the nurse asked.

"How can they be?" the doctor wondered out loud.

"What's going on?" Daniel asked.

"Get me the saw." the doctor said. "We'll take it off and see what's what."

"Doctor?" Daniel asked.

"We're going to take off your cast and see how the healing is coming," the doctor told him.

"Is there something wrong?"

"No. Nothing wrong. Just curious."

The nurse returned with a small electric saw. They set about removing the cast around Daniel's shoulder and arm. The process was quieter than Daniel thought it would be. It sounded almost as if his cast were being vacuumed off. Before long, Daniel was free of his cast. He looked at his right arm.

He stared at it. The doctor examined every inch of the arm and his shoulder. He had Daniel bend it and move his shoulder. Daniel threw back the sheet and checked where the doctor had removed the bandage earlier. No one could think of anything to say.

There was no sign of any injury on his body. Not even a scar.

Chapter 36

Sara didn't wake until almost noon. She dressed even though she didn't intent to leave her room. She would have been hungry, but one thought of that thing Peter Jacobs had in the basement was enough to rid her of her appetite.

She was sitting in one of the chairs just staring into the cold, dark fireplace when there was a light knock on her door. She didn't move. She just ignored it.

The knock came again, and this time it was followed by someone speaking her name. And it was that someone that startled her out of her thoughts.

"Sara," Lucinda called.

Sara stared at the door. "What was she doing there?" Sara wondered. "She's there to check on me," she decided. "To make sure I'd find the box for them."

"Sara, it's me, Lucinda," she said again after yet another knock.

Sara stood up stiffly. She went to the door and opened it.

"There you are," Lucinda said with a smile. Sara just looked at her stone-faced. "Can I come in?" she asked.

Sara just stepped back out of the way. Lucinda took that as a yes and went in.

"I heard the news about Daniel. I think it's great," Lucinda told her.

"What about Daniel?" Sara asked.

"Didn't you hear? I stopped by the hospital to see if you were visiting him. The nurse told me. He's getting out of the hospital today."

Sara's eyes narrowed. How could Daniel be getting out of the hospital? He was barely holding it together last time she visited him.

She looked at Lucinda. She didn't trust her. "But why would she lie about that?" she wondered. She easily could check on it.

"I'm glad," Sara told her evenly. "I suppose I should go with my uncle to get him."

"Of course," Lucinda said. "Before you go, though. I was wondering about something."

Here it comes, Sara thought. "About what?" She said aloud.

"You were talking the other day about that box," Lucinda started.

"That box?" Sara decided to play dumb.

"Pandora's Box. You know, the one with the cross keyhole in the top," Lucinda reminded her.

"It's a keyhole?" Sara asked.

"Well, yes," Lucinda said, confused. "Isn't that what you told us?"

"I said there was a slot in the shape of a cross on top. I didn't know that it was a keyhole."

"I must have just assumed," Lucinda said.

"What about the box?" Sara asked her.

"I was just wondering if you got anywhere with your great grandfather. Did he tell you where it was?"

"Why do you want to know where it is?"

"Why do I," she stammered. "I don't want to know where it is. I just know that it seemed important to you to find out."

"And you know why it is important for me, don't you," Sara pressed.

"Why?" Lucinda asked, taking a step back from her.

"You want me to find it. Both you and that man I saw you talking with last night in the alley."

Lucinda's eyes widened. "How do you know about—"

"I heard you, you and that man. You're just keeping me around until I can get the box for you. You tried to kill Francesca and me, didn't you?" Sara accused her.

"What?" Lucinda asked.

"And Daniel," Sara shouted.

"No."

"And Thomas. You killed my brother."

"No, Sara," Lucinda insisted. "I would never hurt Thomas."

"Don't even say his name," Sara spat her words at Lucinda.

"There's something you don't know about your brother," Lucinda said. "Thomas is—"

Sara exploded. She raised her arms, and Lucinda flew up and was slammed against the ceiling, cracking the plaster. She fell heavily onto the floor. She sat up and tried to stand. Sara stood over her, the disgust she felt for Lucinda reflected in her face.

Lucinda tried to speak again. Before she could say anything, Sara gestured sideways with her hands and Lucinda was flung against a wall, smashing a lamp with her body and then crashing down on it as she fell to the floor.

She sat up and looked at the shards of the light bulb in her arm. She picked them out one at a time. A large piece had cut deep into her forearm. She plucked it out, tossed it to the side and looked up at Sara.

Sara was just staring at her. The rage was gone, and a mix of horror and amazement was on her face.

"You're not bleeding," Sara said quietly.

"You're a Wielder," Lucinda said looking at her with surprise. She stood up and straightened her clothes.

"You're one of the Dead," Sara said. "Why would you be helping the Sisters?"

Lucinda ignored her question and walked over to Sara. "I didn't kill your brother," she said.

Sara was staring at Lucinda's arm. She reached out to touch it. Lucinda pulled away.

"And I'm not trying to kill you or Daniel," she said as she went to the door.

Sara stood and watched her leave. Lucinda pulled open the door to find Bramwell standing there.

"We were trying to protect you from the Sisters," Lucinda told her and pushed past the old butler.

Bramwell looked at Sara with a questioning look. Sara just stared back at him.

"It fell," she said simply, gesturing toward the lamp.

Bramwell nodded. "Your great uncle was going to pick up Daniel from the hospital. He was wondering if you wanted to go with."

"Tell him to go ahead," Sara said. "I'll drive down shortly."

Chapter 37

It was late afternoon by the time they were able to get Daniel released from the hospital. Matthew, Bramwell, and Sara were there to bring him home.

Sara tried to help Daniel down the steps to the front door of the hospital. He shrugged out of her grasp.

"I can do it," he said. "There's nothing wrong with me."

"That's what I don't understand," Matthew said.

"Me neither," Sara told him. "Yesterday you were almost dead and today, not a mark on you."

"I don't understand it either," Daniel told them. "I've got a lot of unanswered questions." He looked between Matthew and his sister.

Gwen was standing at the bottom of the stairs.

"And, if I'm not mistaken, here are the answers."

"I heard you were getting out of the hospital," she said nervously as they reached the bottom of the stairs.

"Yes. They couldn't believe how fast I recovered," he said.

She looked from Sara to Matthew and then back at Daniel.

"Could we talk?" she asked him. "Privately?"

Both Sara and Matthew looked at Daniel. He nodded to them, and they left the two of them and went outside to get the cars. Daniel and Gwen moved to an empty waiting room near the front doors.

Daniel sat down. "Do you want to sit?" Daniel asked, indicating the chair next to him.

"Sure." Gwen said. "I should have told you before," she started. "I was going to tell you that day at my house. My father stopped me."

"Tell me what?" Daniel asked softly.

She hesitated and looked down as she wrung her hands in her lap.

"You can tell me," Daniel said, putting his hand on hers. She looked up at his face, his green eyes.

"The animals that came here with the circus," she said. "They weren't regular animals."

"What do you mean?" Daniel asked.

"They were shape shifters."

"Shape shifters?"

"People who can transform themselves into animals," she said.

"Really? You actually believe that?" Daniel asked.

"It's true," she said. "As a Shifter, it's hard to live normal lives and settle down somewhere. When people find out, they are treated like freaks. And people always find out."

"And I supposed villagers with torches drove them out."

"Pretty much. But it isn't a joke," she said. "It was easier for them to band together and move from place to place. The circus gave them that kind of life."

"And your grandfather?" Daniel asked. "He's one of them."

"He is a Wolf Shifter."

"A Wolf Shifter?" Daniel asked.

"Someone who can shape shift into a wolf?"

"The young wolf and panther in the picture."

"They were my parents. My father is a Wolf Shifter, and my mother was a Panther Shifter."

"And you?" Daniel asked, his voice barely audible.

"I inherited their ability. I can shift into a bobcat," Gwen said. She watched Daniel carefully.

"You inherited it," Daniel said. He leaned forward with his elbows on his knees, suddenly interested in his finger nails.

"Yes," she said quietly.

They were quiet for a few minutes. Daniel stared at the floor. Gwen sat very still, watching him out of the corner of her eye.

"Can you only change into one thing?" Daniel asked, finally breaking the silence.

"Yes. It's part of a Shifter's DNA. It determines what you shift into."

"And the thing that attacked me. It was one of these Shifters?" Daniel asked.

"Yes."

"Vincent?" Daniel asked.

"No. Not Vincent," Gwen said quickly.

"Who then?"

Gwen just looked at the floor.

"Mason?" Daniel said.

Gwen nodded. "He was jealous. He's had a crush on me for years. Vincent thought they were just going to scare you."

"Vincent was the wolf?"

She hesitated and then nodded.

Daniel was quiet again as he tried to wrap his mind around the idea of werewolves.

"What do the police think happened?" Gwen asked.

"The Sheriff told us that he thinks it was just a wild animal."

"The Sheriff won't do much about it. Mason is his son."

"Do you think Mason will try to finish the job?" Daniel asked.

"I don't think so. Vincent and I have warned him against it."

"Do you think that's enough?"

"We don't want trouble. We just want to live in peace. He knows that," she said.

Daniel stood up. He looked down at Gwen and said, "Tell him, if he tries anything again, there will be villagers with torches. And I'll be leading them."

Without waiting for a response, Daniel turned away and left the hospital.

Sara leaned against her car. Bramwell and Matthew were in Matthew's Rolls Royce. According to Bramwell, it was a 1946 Silver Wraith. She was amazed that a car that old was still on the road. She had to admit that it looked good with its red and black paint job. Still, she preferred her 1971 red Mustang convertible.

Cars weren't the only thing on her mind. She still had no idea where the box was, and she was starting to wonder if she truly wanted to find it. Could she somehow save her family without giving up the box?

She was confused about Lucinda too. It sure sounded like she and the dark man were working with the Sisters. She said they were trying to protect her from them, but Sara found it hard to trust her.

She was suddenly aware of someone close by. She looked up to find Francesca standing several feet away from her.

"You were deep in thought," she said. "I didn't want to disturb you."

"It's OK," Sara said.

Francesca leaned against the car beside her.

"What are you thinking about?" Francesca asked. She started to play with a frayed edge of her cast by her thumb.

"Lucinda," Sara told her.

"What about her?"

"We talked earlier," Sara said. "I accused her of working with the Sisters." Sara told her.

Francesca stopped playing with her cast for a moment. "The Sisters?" Francesca asked.

"Yeah. They're the Wielders who have been threatening me and my family," Sara said.

"Wielders?" Francesca said. "Superstitious nonsense." Her fingers began working on the edge of the cast again.

"That's what I thought," Sara told her. "At first. What brings you out on this chilly evening?"

"I just wanted to apologize for fighting with your friend, Jason. And sticking my nose in your business," she said.

"No problem."

"My sister always tells me that I'm too direct with people and give my opinion when it's not wanted. And asking embarrassing questions."

Sara interrupted her. "I talked with my great grandfather about the box."

"Did you?" She turned to Sara, forgetting all about her cast.

"Yes. He told me that he couldn't tell me where it was."

"He doesn't know where it is?" Francesca asked.

"He does. He just won't tell me."

"Why not?"

"Because it has some sort of power and we can't let it fall into the wrong hands."

"Power?" Francesca looked puzzled. "Like magic?"

"Yeah. Like magic."

Francesca leaned back against the car again. Neither one spoke for a while.

"What if you found the box and used the power yourself?" Francesca asked.

"To do what?" a voice behind them asked.

They turned to find Lucinda standing on the other side of the

Mustang.

"What do you want?" Sara asked.

"You think that I want to hurt you and your family. That I'm working against you."

"That's what it sounded like," Sara said.

"Why don't you just go away?" Francesca asked.

"This is between Sara and me," Lucinda said. She came around the car and stopped in front of Sara.

"Well, I'm her friend. So you have to deal with me too," Francesca said standing up straighter.

"Really?" Lucinda said turning toward her.

Francesca cringed a little and took a step back.

"I thought so," Lucinda said turning back to Sara.

"Do you want to know who you can trust?" Lucinda asked.

"Yes," Sara said.

"Come with me, then," she said. She turned and headed toward the town square.

Francesca looked at Sara. "It's a trap," Francesca warned her.

"Maybe," Sara said and followed Lucinda. Francesca stared after them.

Chapter 38

Sara caught up to Lucinda at the square. Lucinda led her down a street leading toward the shoreline. The street was dark and seemed almost deserted. However, she became aware of dark figures huddling in the shadowy corners of buildings and doorways.

Lucinda stopped in front of a building that was home to a music shop. She could see the shapes of violins, trumpets and drums displayed in the windows.

However, she didn't stop in front of the door to the shop. She stopped at the top of an outside stairway down to a basement entrance. Above the stairwell, there was a neon sign for something called The Raven.

"What is this?" Sara asked.

"You can trust the people here," Lucinda told her. She started down the stairs.

Sara looked up and down the street. She wasn't sure she wanted to go in. However, she wanted to stay up on the street far less. She hurried down the stairs after her.

The Raven turned out to be a coffee shop. There was a corner with bookshelves and several people sitting in comfortable chairs reading. A coffee bar was along the back wall with a small line of customers. To one side was a lit stage area with a good sized audience gathered around it. A man was sitting on a stool reading what she thought was poetry, though she couldn't follow it very well.

One thing that Sara found odd was that rather than a strong coffee smell, the whole place smelled of peppermint.

Then, she realized who it was that Lucinda thought she could trust.

She glanced around at the people. The readers with their pale skin. The dark circles under the eyes of the performer and the various decayed states of the audience members.

They were the Dead.

Lucinda saw the realization in her face. "You are safe here," she told her. "Come with me."

Sara followed her toward the back of the coffee shop near the bar. A man behind the bar came over to her. He held what appeared to be an iced cappuccino with chocolate drizzled over the top.

"What's up, Luce?" He asked.

"Hi, Monte. Just taking her to see him."

He gave Sara a sideways glance. "You think she's ready?"

"We'll find out," Lucinda told him. She opened a door beside the bar and went in.

"That looks good," Sara said, pointing at the drink the man was holding. "Could I get one?"

"You don't want anything this place serves," Lucinda told her

"Why?" Sara asked

"The living generally find that our drinks don't agree with them," The man said. He smiled at Sara as she followed Lucinda through the door. He was missing several teeth.

When the door closed, the noise of the coffee shop almost disappeared. They were on a landing with a door to one side and a stairway down on the other.

Lucinda led her down the stairs and along a hallway until it ended at a double door. She paused before opening it.

"The council is in session, so when we go in, don't talk. Just listen," Lucinda warned her.

Sara nodded even though she really didn't understand what was going on.

Lucinda opened the door and went in. Sara followed her into the large, well lit room.

They were at the top of a central stairway that led down to what appeared to be courtroom with five people seated behind a curved desk having a discussion with a small man standing at a podium in front of them.

There were two men standing just behind the man at the podium and several tables to either side where various other people were seated including one that was dressed all in black with his hood pulled up over his head. "Was he the dark man?" Sara wondered.

Auditorium seats were on either side of the stairway where people could watch the proceedings. Most of the seats were full. Lucinda guided her to a pair of seats near the back of the auditorium.

Sara was starting to think that maybe following Lucinda was a mistake. With the exception of herself and the man at the podium, everyone else appeared to be one of the Dead.

The man seated at the center of the desk was speaking. His snow white hair made him look even paler than the rest of the Dead in the room.

"You are accused of destroying three of the Dead, and you do not intend to present a defense?" He asked the man at the podium.

"No," the man said in defiance.

"In light of the evidence presented against you and without any kind of rebuttal, I would have no choice, but to find you guilty," The white haired man told him.

"I will not present a defense since I am innocent. Instead, I claim the right to defend my honor against my accusers."

The audience erupted. There were shouts of "He's not one of us!" And "Hang him!" The white haired man stared at him impassively for several minutes and then picked up the gavel and began to pound it on the desk for order.

Slowly the crowd settled down back into their chairs. There was silence for another several minutes before the white haired man spoke again.

"It is true that you are not one of the Dead. However, if we are to apply some of our laws to you, then we must apply all of our laws. You may claim the right to defend your honor."

The audience erupted again. The white haired man signaled for order right away, and the roar died down quickly.

"As it was I who brought the charges of murder against you, Robert Powell, I am your accuser. What is your choice of weapons?"

"Lord Danville, I choose pistols," Powell said.

"Very well," Danville said. He turned and pointed to a man sitting next to the man in black. "Reynolds, you will be Mr. Powell's second." And then, to the man in black, he asked. "Would you do me the honor of being my second?"

The man in black nodded and with that, the area in front of the podium was cleared of both furniture and people. The four other people at the desk stayed where they were, and none of the audience moved.

"They're fighting a duel?" Sara asked Lucinda.

"Yes. That choice is available to all defendants."

"Isn't that illegal?"

"Not according to our laws," Lucinda told her. "The Dead have no rights under the laws of the living, so we have our own laws."

"It's not really fair, is it? I mean, the judge is already dead. The man can't kill him."

"It is still possible to destroy him, if the man shoots him in the right spot."

"Where's that?" Sara asked.

Lucinda ignored her question. "If Lord Danville is destroyed, then the defendant has proved his innocence. If Lord Danville destroys the defendant, then justice has prevailed," Lucinda told her.

Reynolds returned to the room with two cases and gave one to the man in black. Powell and Lord Danville took their positions at opposite ends of the room, and their seconds joined them.

The seconds opened the cases and allowed each man to choose one of the pistols inside. The seconds then placed the cases aside and loaded the chosen pistols and inspected them to make sure that they were ready.

Sara almost expected to see old-fashioned flintlock pistols that would fire just one bullet with a flash and puff of smoke. The pistols that they were using, however, were revolvers and the seconds loaded each with six shots.

Once the pistols were returned to the participants, the seconds stepped away. One of the other judges at the desk then spoke.

"Gentlemen, at the signal, you will aim and fire continuing until you are out of ammunition or your opponent has been destroyed. Are you ready?"

Both men nodded.

"Very well," the judge said. He raised his gavel and then rapped it loudly on the desk."

Powell immediately raised his pistol and shot at Danville. The bullet hit the man in his right shoulder. He neither flinched nor raised his pistol.

Powell started running at Danville firing as he went. One bullet took the man in the center of the chest and another apparently missed, ripping into a painting on the wall behind Danville. His fourth bullet cut into Danville's left arm just above the elbow.

Finally, Danville raised his pistol and just as Powell was about to fire his fifth bullet into him, he shot Powell straight through his eye. The back of the man's head exploded and he was immediately knocked backward off his feet onto the floor where he twitched violently for a moment and then laid motionless in a growing pool of blood.

Everyone was silent for a moment and then the crowd began to pound their fists on the arms of their chairs in a slow, solemn rhythm.

"That's a sign of their approval," Lucinda whispered to Sara.

Sara had looked away when the man was killed. She couldn't believe how little emotion they showed for someone's death, and a bloody one at that.

Lord Danville signaled for the guards to take away the body and announced to the crowd. "Justice has been done. The victims have been avenged. We are adjourned."

The crowd got to its feet and started to file out of the room back up to the coffee shop.

Lucinda put her hand up to indicate that Sara should stay where she was. Once the crowd was gone, Lucinda stood up and waited.

Lord Danville was shaking hands with the man in black, apparently thanking him for his services as his second. Afterward, he and the other judges filed out of the room through a door behind the desk.

The man in black glanced up toward Lucinda. She gestured toward Sara. He started up the stairs toward them.

Sara knew then that it was the dark man.

Sara stood and started to back away.

"You might not trust me, Sara," Lucinda said. "I'm sure you'll trust him."

"Why would I trust either of you?" She said. "He said that if I found the box, he'd kill me."

"That's not what I said," the dark man said quietly when he reached the top step.

"What did you say then?" Sara demanded.

"I said that when the time came, I would take care of you," the dark man said. He reached up and pulled his hood down revealing his face. "And I meant exactly that."

Sara stopped cold. The man standing there in front of her was her dead brother, Thomas.

Chapter 39

Sara stared at the man. He looked like her brother, but how was that possible? She saw him in his coffin. She saw him closed up in the mausoleum wall.

She sat down heavily in one of the chairs.

"You can't be my brother," she told him. "He's dead."

"I know it's hard to believe, Sara. It is me." He sat down in a chair near her.

"I'll let you two talk," Lucinda said and, after a nod from Thomas, she left the court room.

Sara leaned forward cautiously, frowning in concentration on his features. He had her brother's nose, his chin, the little scar by his left ear that he got when he fell down a slide when he was eight years old. And he had her brother's blue eyes.

"Is it really you?" She asked him in wonder.

"Yes, Tabby. It's me," he said, using her nickname from when she was a little girl. His voice was a little gruff, but it had the familiar sound that she knew well.

"How?" She moved to the chair next to him and touched his pale face. It felt cold. "You were dead."

"Yes," he said. "I am."

"What happened to you?" She asked.

"I'll explain everything. First, it's time that Mom and Daniel should be told too," he said. He stood up and held his hand out to help Sara to her feet.

"I missed you," Sara told him as she followed him from the room.

"I missed you too."

They went back up the stairs and through The Raven. As they passed through, all of the people in the place turned and stared at them. A hush fell over the crowd.

"What is it?" Sara asked. "Did I do something?"

"No," Thomas told her. "It isn't you."

They went out into the street. Thomas pulled his hood back up, and they headed to her car. They drove to the mansion in silence. Sara was unsure what to think about her Dead brother and Thomas was worried about the reactions of the rest of his family.

When they returned to the mansion, Sara and Thomas went to their mother's room first.

When he went into her room, he saw her sitting up in her bed staring off into space. He went to her and sat on the edge of the bed.

"I'm here, Mom," Thomas said in a quiet voice. The next few moments seemed like an eternity as he waited for her to look at him. She turned and at first, she didn't seem to recognize him.

"Thomas?" She said, puzzled. She slowly drifted back. "Is it you?"

"I'm back," he told her.

"Oh, Thomas," she said and covered her mouth with her hand. Her eyes filled with tears. She touched his arm. "My Thomas is back."

Thomas hugged his mother. He would have cried too if he were able to.

"I'll go get Daniel," Sara told them and went across the hallway.

"I tried to save you," Mary told him as she held him. "I tried, but I couldn't."

"It's OK," Thomas said. "There was nothing you could do."

Thomas let her lay back again.

She held his hand in hers. "You're chilled to the bone," she said, slowly. "Maybe Bramwell will get a fire going so you can warm up."

"Later, Mom. For now, just sit back and rest." He said.

He heard Sara and Daniel enter the room.

"Thomas?" Daniel just whispered.

Thomas stood up and faced his brother.

"Hey, Daniel," he said. "I heard about what happened to you. I'm glad you're OK."

"You were lying dead in a coffin," Daniel said, frowning. "I saw you sealed up in a wall."

"I know," Thomas said softly.

"What happened to you?" Sara asked.

"Well, I was apparently dead," he began. "And yet, three nights ago, I woke up. At first, I wasn't sure where I was. I just knew it was dark. It was a few minutes before I realized that I was in a coffin. I was terrified. I thought that I had survived drowning only to be buried alive."

"You weren't buried," Sara told him.

Thomas shook his head. "I pounded on the lid and yelled to someone to let me out. I'm not sure how long I went on pounding on that thing. After what seemed like hours, I heard something above me. It was the sound of a shovel digging into dirt."

"You were in a vault out in that mausoleum," She said, pointing toward the back of the house. "You weren't buried."

"Well, evidently, I was no longer in the mausoleum," he said. "After a while, the shovel hit the top of the casket, and after some scraping around the top, enough dirt was cleared to allow the lid to be opened. I found myself looking up into the light of a flashlight."

"Who was it?" Sara asked.

"It was a man named Angus," Thomas told her. "He told me that he was the caretaker of the cemetery where I was buried and happened to be out locking the gates for the night when he heard the pounding coming from my grave."

"Did you find out what cemetery you were in?" Matthew asked from the doorway.

Thomas looked up at Matthew curiously.

"This is our Great Uncle Matthew." Sara told him.

"Nice to meet you," Thomas said.

"It's very interesting to be meeting you." Matthew said. "All things considered."

"He told me that it was Elmwood Cemetery." Thomas told him. Thomas watched his reaction. Matthew simply nodded.

"You know what that means don't you?" Thomas asked him.

"Yes. I do."

"What?" Daniel asked. "What does it mean?"

"Elmwood hasn't been used for years," Matthew told him.

"Why not?" Daniel asked.

"Because people are afraid of that cemetery," he told them. "They're afraid of burying anyone in that land."

"What are they afraid of?" Daniel asked.

"The cemetery is cursed." Sara said.

"Cursed? What do you mean 'cursed'?" Mary asked. She appeared agitated.

"It's OK, Mom," Sara tried to soothe her.

"If you bury someone in that cemetery, they come back," Thomas said.

"How is that a curse? We have our Thomas back with us alive and well," Mary said smiling at her son.

"No, Mom," Thomas told her.

"What do you mean 'no'? You're sitting right here in front of us," Mary said.

"You're right. We have him back, that's all that matters," Sara said, heading off any further discussion of her brother's condition.

"You're right, Sara," Thomas said. He looked at the others. Matthew stood with one hand stroking his chin, staring at him, deep in thought. Daniel managed a weak smile.

He smiled back at them. Not as good as he hoped. Not as bad as he feared.

"Do you require sleep?" Matthew asked him.

"No." Thomas said. "If you have a spare room though, I will spend the night there so that I don't disturb anyone else."

Matthew nodded his approval and called for Bramwell.

Mary said goodnight to Thomas and gave him a hug. Then they all left her and went to their own rooms.

Sara hugged her brother warmly. She felt the chill of his body and began to cry.

"I'm sorry you died," she told him.

"Me too," Thomas said.

Daniel too gave him a tentative hug. "I'm glad you're back," he told him.

"Thanks."

They looked at him sadly and wished him a good night. Then they went into their rooms and locked themselves in.

Bramwell arrived and showed Thomas to his room.

"If there is anything you need, just let me know," Bramwell told him.

Thomas thanked him and closed his door for the night.

Chapter 40

Sara was up early the next morning. In the light of day, it was hard to believe that her brother's return was something other than a dream. She looked in on both Daniel and her mother. They were both still asleep.

She went to Thomas' room and found the door open. She tapped on the door as she went in and looked around. Thomas was not there. In fact, there was no sign that anyone had actually been in the room overnight.

She rushed downstairs and searched all the rooms around the grand foyer. Thomas was nowhere to be found. Then she went through to the back patio and looked around outside. She started to think that maybe the night before had been a dream.

On the way back into the house, she noticed there was a lot of activity in the kitchen. Cook and her assistants were busy preparing breakfast for the household. She noticed a girl, not much older than herself rolling out some dough for biscuits nearby.

"Excuse me, you're Katy, aren't you?" she asked the girl.

"Yes, ma'am," Katy said continuing to roll out the dough.

"Did you see somebody go through here earlier? A tall boy with dark clothes?"

"Nobody has been back here all morning," the girl replied.

Sara thanked her and was just turning away when the girl added, "When I was out in the dining room setting the table earlier, I saw a boy go out the front door. He was wearing a black hoodie."

"Oh, good," Sara said with relief. She knew it wasn't a dream.

Just then there was a rumbling sound.

"What is that?" The girl asked, looking around confused.

Then the rooms shook violently. Everyone in the kitchen grabbed a counter to steady themselves. The pots and pans hanging over an island in the center of the room rocked back and forth.

When the shaking ended, they all slowly went back to work talking excitedly about what had just happened. Except for an egg that had rolled off the counter and smashed on the floor, the breakfast preparations went on as planned.

Katy turned to ask Sara if she thought it had been an earthquake. She found that Sara was no longer there.

In fact, Sara had run back to the front of the house and was standing at the door to the back parlor. She glanced around the room. There was nobody there.

Then the rumbling started again. She had just grabbed onto the door jamb when the shaking started. She watched the room. As the shaking died away, it was still empty.

She had just closed the door to the room and was thinking about where else to look when she heard a woman scream and something crash onto the floor. It sounded as if it came from the direction of dining room.

She hurried across the grand foyer and found the dining room in disarray. A shattered serving platter was on the floor, and the piles of fruit that were on it were scattered all around. One of the girls from the kitchen, Sara didn't know her name, had her hands over her mouth and was backing away from a young man attempting to help clean up the mess.

"Matthew," Sara said.

The man straightened up at the sound of his name and glanced around the room until he saw Sara. He straightened his old-fashioned suit.

"You have me at a disadvantage, Miss," he said.

"What?" Sara asked him.

"I don't know your name," he told her.

"I'm Sara. You don't know me?"

"I'm afraid I don't."

Sara noticed that the girl was still standing there staring at them.

"It's OK," Sara told her. "I'm sorry he startled you."

Sara pulled Matthew out of the dining room and into the front parlor next door.

"My name is Sara. I'm a distant relative of yours."

"Really? I'm happy to meet you. My name is Matthew," he began. "Oh, wait. You already knew that."

"I don't mean to be rude. However, I have a feeling that we don't have a lot of time," Sara said.

Matthew looked at his watch. "No, I suppose we don't." When he looked back at her, he cocked his head to one side. "You've met me some other time. Haven't you?"

"Yes," she said. "Can you tell me what's happening to you?"

"Well, about a month ago, I guess, I," Matthew stopped. "What year is it?"

"2012," Sara said.

"Oh," Matthew paused. "More than fifty years ago, I was helping my father cataloging some of the artifacts that he had in storage. He didn't always let me help him. That time he did."

"Your father is C.J. Kask?" Sara asked.

"Yes. Everything was going well until I came across this small metal cube that had buttons everywhere. I asked my dad what it was. As I showed it to him, it started to move."

"What started to move?"

"There were circular panels on every side, and they were turning. I must have accidentally pressed a button and activated it."

"What happened then?" Sara prompted him.

"Well, it startled me so much that I let go of it, and it started to fall to the floor."

"Did it break?"

"Well, it didn't actually hit the floor. My reflexes are pretty good, so I was able to catch it just before it hit."

"That's good," Sara said.

"Not really. Because when I grabbed it, I must of pressed another button because it started to shake and then everything swirled around me. A moment later, I was in another part of the house."

"It was a teleporter?" Sara asked.

"A what?"

"Something that transports you from one place to another instantly," Sara explained.

"I thought that's what it did, at first. Then, I saw a calendar on a wall. The year on it said 1972. It was 1956 a moment before," he said.

"It was a time machine?"

"Evidently, it was."

"It was?" Sara asked. "You don't have it anymore?"

"No." He said in embarrassment. "When things started to shake again, I got nervous and as the room started to swirl around, I accidentally dropped it."

"Where were you when you dropped it?" Sara asked him.

"I think it's not a matter of where I dropped it, but when," he said.

"If you don't have it anymore, why are you still going from time to time?" she asked.

"I don't know. Maybe because I dropped it between times rather than putting it down while I wasn't traveling."

"So you need to find it again," Sara said.

"I think so. I never have much time in any one time or place though." He said.

Then Sara remembered something. She told Matthew to stay where he was. She would be right back.

"I'll do my best to stay right here," he said with a smile.

She ran up to her room and grabbed the letter opener that Matthew had given to her on his previous visit. She ran back to the front parlor. To her relief, Matthew was still standing there. He was looking at the portrait of Sadie.

"Is that your mother?" she asked him.

"Yes." He turned to see what she went to get. "A letter opener?"

"A letter opener. You are supposed to take it with you," she told him and held it out to him.

"Why?" he asked, taking it.

"I don't know," she said.

"How do you know I'm supposed to take it then?" he asked.

"Because you told me to give it to you," she told him.

He stared at her. "I told you."

Sara nodded. A rumbling began. Then the room started to shake. Several frames on the mantle under the portrait of Sadie started to shift. Sara tried to make sure they didn't fall. The shaking subsided.

Sara stared at one of the pictures. A portrait of a man in a gold-colored frame. She grabbed it and quickly turned to Matthew. She held out the picture for him to see just as the rumbling began again.

"Is this your father?" Sara asked him.

"What?" Matthew asked over the rumbling.

"Is this your father?" Sara yelled to him.

He looked at the portrait.

"Yes," he said as the room began to shake. "Why?"

Sara was not able to answer him. As the shaking stopped again, she just stared at where Matthew had been standing a moment before. He was gone.

Chapter 41

When Sara returned to the dining room a few minutes later, Daniel and Mary were just starting their breakfast. Bramwell was there too. Thomas, Peter, and Matthew were not.

"Have you seen Matthew this morning?" She asked Bramwell.

"No. I haven't. I understand that he left early this morning."

"Do you know when he'll be back?"

"He did not say," Bramwell told her.

Sara sat down to some Havarti and Bacon Quiche.

"Did you feel the earthquake this morning?" Daniel asked.

"Earthquake? Here? No," Sara lied.

"I didn't either. The girls in the kitchen told me about it," Daniel told her.

"Where's Thomas?" Mary asked her.

"He went out, I guess," Sara said.

"I hope he comes back soon," Mary said mostly to herself.

When Peter Jacobs entered the dining room, nobody even noticed at first. He cleared his throat to get their attention, which startled Mary.

"Pardon me, Mrs. Cross," He said. He turned to Sara, "Could I speak with you a moment."

Sara shrugged and followed him into the front parlor. He closed the door between the two rooms.

"I wanted to apologize for scaring you the other night," He told her.

"It's OK," Sara said.

"You thought it was your brother. I see can why after his body disappeared." Peter started pacing and talking excitedly. "It's just that I've been working here for a while now cataloging all of Mr. Kask's artifacts."

Sara sensed that it might be a long explanation, so she found a comfortable chair to sit down in.

"I was impressed by all of the amazing things he found," he continued. "So when I found there was something in that hill, I thought maybe I could discover something amazing too."

"I understand," Sara said.

"And then I found that thing frozen inside. Well, you can imagine how I felt," he said, his pacing never slowing. "It could be an alien, or a Sasquatch or some sort of missing link."

"Missing link?" Sara asked.

Peter ignored her question. "I was thinking I found this. Me. This could make me famous," he said. "And when I found you down there, I thought for a moment that you might try to take that away from me."

"That's not why—"

"I know. I know," Peter interrupted. "You were just looking for your brother. That's why I wanted to apologize. I jumped to the wrong conclusion."

"I understand," Sara said. "You don't know what that thing is?"

"No. I've been searching through area history in Mr. Kask's library. I haven't found anything relating to that hill though."

"You've been searching where?" Sara asked. She was excited now.

"Mr. Kask's library," Peter repeated.

"There's a library in this house?" Sara asked. "Where?"

"I'll show you," Peter said.

Peter led her into the main floor of the east wing to a set of doors that opened into her great grandfather's library.

It was a two story room with bookshelves along the walls from floor to ceiling. Two circular stairways in opposite corners led up to a narrow balcony the circled the room. In the center of the Oriental rug that covered most of the floor, was a desk with a computer. Around the desk were several large tables and chairs. There were also several overstuffed chairs and a couch that looked like comfortable reading spots.

Peter again apologized. However, Sara was no longer paying attention.

She mumbled, "No problem," again and began to look around the library.

Peter sensed that their conversation was done and left her there.

Sara sat down at the computer and powered it up. When the desktop appeared, she found that there were two icons in the center. One was for the book catalog. The other was for the Kask Collection.

She double-clicked the Kask Collection icon and waited for the software to start. A window appeared with Kask Collection as its title. The window was empty except for a search box.

Sara typed in "Pandora's Box" and hit enter. She held her breath and waited for several seconds. Then, the entry for Pandora's Box appeared. There was a picture of the box, and it looked exactly like what she had seen that night in the fountain.

She started reading about the box and its history. Farther down the page, there was a picture of a thin metal cross on the end of a short wooden dowel. The caption said that was the key to the box.

She read that the chest was not actually Pandora's Box. The real container that Pandora, who was also known as Anesidora, opened was found by knights returning from one of the Crusades.

They knew that Pandora's Box was an object of immense power and utter corruption, so they fashioned the chest and the cross key to keep Pandora's Box safe. Pandora's Box itself wasn't even a box. In reality, it was a—.

"It isn't something you should fool around with," a little boy's voice said, interrupting her reading. Luca was looking down at her from the balcony.

"How did you get in here?"

"It was easy," he told her. He went to the nearest stairway and quickly came down to the main level.

"You could get arrested for breaking in," Sara told him.

"I didn't break in," he said. "Besides, you wouldn't call the Sheriff on me."

"You don't think so."

He just smiled. Then the smile faded. "You really don't want to fool with it."

"What do you know about it?"

"A little," he said. "All it brings is misery."

There was a knock on the library door. Sara turned to see Bramwell poke his head in.

"Mr. Jacobs told me that I could find you here," he said. "There is a young woman to see you."

Sara looked back to Luca. He wasn't there. She stood up and glanced around the room. There was no sign of the little boy.

"What should I tell her?" Bramwell asked.

She clicked off the monitor. "I'll go see her now," she said.

When she entered the front parlor, she was greeted by the smiling face of Francesca.

"Hi, Sara. It's not a bad time, it is?" she asked.

"Well, I am right in the middle of something. Could we talk tomorrow?"

"I just wanted to find out if you've made any headway on finding the box?"

"Not really. Actually, some things have happened that I have to deal with first. The box will have to wait."

"Oh, OK," Francesca said. It was obvious to Sara that she was disappointed.

"Is tomorrow alright?" Sara asked again heading to the front door.

"Sure. That's fine," Francesca said. "See you tomorrow then." She went out onto the porch.

"Thanks," Sara said and abruptly closed the door.

Chapter 42

iri and Asami were just exiting the stairway from their apartment when a woman whose face was hidden behind a scarf blocked them.

"I just discovered that the little witch isn't even looking for the box anymore," she told them

"Calm down, Dior," Piri told her. "We should go back inside."

"Nothing is more important than that box," Dior said. "Maybe I need to remind her again. Maybe I should send some friends to pound some sense into her."

"Shh," Piri said and ushered Dior through the door and up the stairs.

Asami glanced around the street. There were a few Dead here and there. Nothing to worry about. She looked closely at the nearest one. He was sitting in a doorway at the shop next door bundled up from head to foot.

As she moved closer to him, he was mumbling something. She couldn't tell what he was saying. When she got a whiff of wintergreen, she relaxed. Always with the mint, she thought.

She returned to the stairway, closed the door and locked it.

After the women had gone back up to the apartment, the man stood up and pulled the hood of the jacket back. Jason glanced up at the covered windows upstairs.

The sun was setting when Thomas returned to the mansion. Sara was in the back parlor looking through photo albums when she heard him come in. She hurried to catch him.

She found him climbing the stairs. "Thomas," she called, "Where have you been?"

"I've been doing some checking around town," he told her.

"Checking about what?"

"I haven't told you yet about what happened the night I died," he said.

"I didn't think it was something we needed to talk about with mom there."

"I agree," Thomas said. "Let's go talk in my room now."

They had just reached her brother's door when the first scream echoed through the house. Sara immediately began running back along the hallway to the stairs.

Moments later, Daniel opened his door. He was about to say something when he and Thomas heard a second scream. It came to an abrupt end, and silence followed.

"Get back in your room," Thomas commanded.

"I can help," Daniel told him.

"Don't be foolish. Just get back in your room and lock the door," Thomas said and ran down the hallway.

Daniel started to close his door. As soon as Thomas was out of sight, he immediately pulled his door open and followed him down the hall.

Sara reached the top of the steps to find the front door hanging open with one of its hinges broken. A dozen or so dark figures were lumbering around the front hall. Off to one side, amid several of the massive creatures, one of the girls who worked at the mansion was lying face down on the floor. Sara didn't know whether she was unconscious or dead.

The creatures were human shaped. Except, their faces had no features and their hands had stubby fingers that were balled into fists. On a spot where their forehead would be, there was some sort of mark or design that reminded Sara of hieroglyphs or Chinese characters.

Thomas stopped beside her on the upstairs landing. He glanced around along the balcony and located a shield with two swords displayed on the wall. He rushed over to them and pulled them from the wall.

He handed the shield to Sara and tossed one sword aside. "Use this to protect yourself. Go back to your room and lock yourself in. I'll try to hold them off."

"What are those things?" Sara asked.

He was already halfway down the stairs. "I don't know," he yelled over his shoulder.

He swung the sword at the nearest creature catching it in the shoulder. The weapon gouged out part of its upper arm. It slowly turned toward him and swung one of its club-like arms at him. Thomas ducked backward, missing the force of the blow. The fingers caught his shirt and threw him to the side.

He sprawled on the floor and rolled into the feet of another one of the monsters.

He looked up to see that creature's foot about to stomp on him, so he rolled away from it just as the foot came down. He could feel the vibration of the floor from the impact. He grabbed the sword and jumped back up on his feet.

He swung the sword at another creature. It was low and caught it on the leg slicing right through. Thomas expected it to fall. However, the two pieces of leg seemed to seal back together again. The creature took a step toward Thomas, its leg was undamaged.

Thomas paused almost too long in his surprise. He ducked down just in time for another creature's arm to pass harmlessly above him.

Sara was amazed at how fast Thomas was moving. She saw that all the creatures in the room were aware of her brother, and they began to surge toward him. She tried to send those nearest to Thomas flying away. She couldn't seem to do more than put them off balance. At least that gave Thomas a little more time, she thought.

Daniel ran up beside her. "You shouldn't be here," she yelled at him as she headed down the steps.

"And you should be?" Daniel wondered. He grabbed the other sword from the floor and ran down the steps after Sara.

As Sara neared them, she found that she could push them more and more. By the time she reached the bottom, she was able push them backward a few steps and sometimes even knock them off their feet. She still wasn't able to send them flying as she did Lucinda. And she wasn't able to attack more than one at a time.

Thomas swung his weapon at the head of another creature. It leaned back to avoid the blow and the sword only sliced lightly across it's forehead disfiguring the mark that was etched there.

The creature exploded creating a cloud of sand that quickly dissipated leaving a coating of dust around it. Thomas took a step back in surprise.

"Hit them in the head," he yelled to Sara. "Destroy the mark."

Daniel came running down the stairs yelling at the top of his lungs. He waved the sword over his head and chopped at the first creature he met. The sword sliced into the torso of the creature and then became stuck. It was ripped from his hand as his momentum carried him past that creature and head first into the next. He fell backward and landed on his butt. He held his head, wincing in pain.

"I didn't say hit them with your head," Thomas yelled at Daniel. He sliced at the head of another one sending out a shower of sand and dust as it collapsed.

Daniel tried to stand up again. A number of creatures converged on him, and he disappeared under a pile of them as they pounded his body.

"Daniel." Sara yelled. She tried to push them out of her way so that she could get to him. They were just too powerful. They pushed in a group toward her, and it was all she could do just to hold them back. She found that she was being pushed back behind the stairs, and her only chance was to get through the doorway to the back of the house. Otherwise, they would crush her against the wall.

Thomas saw Daniel go down, and he grasped his weapon with both hands swinging it in an arc around him. He found that there were too many of them, and he had to fall back to the stairs. He backed up three steps and at that height, he had a good shot at the heads of the creatures below him. Soon the bottom of the stairs was covered in dust.

Daniel barely could breath. The creatures were practically lying on top of him pounding on him with their arms. He thought he couldn't last much longer as his air was running out and the pain from their blows overwhelmed him.

Then, another kind of pain flooded his awareness. Sharp pains stabbed into every joint. He thought they started to attack him with knives. He cried out. The sound was muffled under the weight of creatures that held him down. Suddenly, they started to fall away from him. He stood up on his hind legs, and a growl echoed through the room.

Thomas was stunned to see the pile, where Daniel had fallen, rise up. The creatures fell off the sides until a giant bear stood up and growled at them. Luckily, the creatures were just as surprised as he was and stopped attacking Thomas for a moment. He swung the sword and took out another one of them while they were distracted.

Daniel waded into the crowd. He whacked a few with his paws, sending them flying into the creatures behind them. Then he stood up part way and swiped at one of them with his claws, destroying the mark and reducing it to a pile of dust.

Sara made it to the doorway and immediately turned and ran down the hallway into the east wing. She was hoping that a number of them would follow her, and she could find a weapon to face them with.

Then she had an idea. Just before she reached a pair of tapestries facing each other in the hallway, she stopped and turned. The passage was filled with the large creatures. She held out her hands and prepared. The creatures in the front slammed into an invisible barrier several feet in front of Sara. Those behind slammed into the front ones until all of them were bunched up trying to get through.

She knew the next part would be tricky. She didn't think she would be able to hold them back and attack them at the same time, so she had to be fast.

She turned and directed her focus to the tapestries. The rods that held each one lifted up and after dumping the tapestries on the floor, levitated in the air barring anyone from going further down the hall without ducking under them. As she turned back to the creatures, the nearest one's fist caught her across the face knocking her backward on the ground. They quickly closed in on her.

The pile of dust at the bottom of the stairs was starting to get thick as the creatures tried to get to Thomas. One of the creatures fell onto Thomas knocking him back onto the steps and trapping the sword between them.

The creature attempted to crush him against the steps and alternately pounding him with one fist and then the other. He couldn't get out from under it. He looked at the sword blade between them. It was stuck under the creatures chin. If only he could move it, he thought.

He found that while he couldn't pull the sword out from between them, it was able to slide it a little as the creature rocked from side to side. He heard his ribs cracking on one side and knew he had to move fast. The next time the creature rolled toward his left, he slid the sword up as fast as it would go.

The sword cut up through the creatures jaw, through its head and burst out through the mark on its forehead. Thomas was enveloped in a cloud of sand and dust. And then the weight of the creature was gone.

Daniel was taking out his share. Although he received quite a beating from their fists, the power of his massive body was enough to knock them back and allow him to dig his claws into their foreheads, destroying them.

Soon there were only a few creatures left in the room and the two of them set about to destroy them all.

After Thomas had taken care of his last one and Daniel had chased his last one out the front door, Thomas checked the girl. It looked like she had just fainted.

"You'll be OK, I think," Thomas said to himself.

"Oh my word!" Mrs. Baskin exclaimed from the dining room doorway. She surveyed the dust covered room. "Where did all this mess come from?"

Sara shook her head to clear her thoughts. The creatures were on top of her. She looked up and saw that the rods were still suspended in the air. She made a quick motion toward them and the rods swept down the hallway taking off the top of the creatures' heads as they went.

In a moment, the only thing left of the creatures was a cloud of dust gently settling down in the hallway. Sara lay back and waited for her heart to slow down.

Thomas ran toward her from the grand foyer.

"Sara?" he yelled.

"I'm OK," she said, sitting up. "Did you get the rest?"

"Yes," he told her. "You should see the little surprise Daniel had up his sleeve."

Chapter 43

She sat there for a few minutes nursing the bruise on her face. Out of the corner of her eye she saw something familiar.

She stood up and looked down a short passageway that had been hidden behind one of the tapestries that now lay on the floor. She recognized the passageway that Matthew had gone into and disappeared.

She flipped on the light. The short hallway was empty. She looked around. The five tapestries that covered the five mirrors were there. Each of the mirrors was large enough to hide a door. She went from one to the next checking the frame around the edge looking for a latch.

When she got to the mirror at the opposite end of the hallway, she checked the frame and found something different from the rest. On either side of the mirror, there were two round disks carved into the frame, each with a different geometric design carved into it. On the left were a circle and a triangle. On the right were a square and a hexagon.

She looked closely at the four designs and noticed that the hexagon was more worn than the other three. She ran her fingers over it and found that it could move. She held her breath and pressed it.

She felt herself being pulled into the mirror. She tried to grab onto the sides. Her fingers just slipped off of the frame. She had a sensation of being on a roller coaster as it climbed and dropped again and again.

And then she fell on a cold stone floor in the dark.

She felt around herself. On one side, the floor seemed to disappear. In the other direction, she found a wall. She stood up next to the wall and searched for some light switch. In a moment, she found the switch and the room was filled with light.

It was an unusually small room, barely wider than the hallway that led to it. In the center of the room, a circular stairway led down into the floor. There was no railing and Sara realized that she was lucky she hadn't fallen over the edge when she tumbled into the room.

On one wall was a mirror that appeared to be a duplicate of the one she had been pulled into including the four disks with the four geometric figures.

She followed the stairway down. She lost count of the number of times the stairway went around. It seemed to go on forever though. At last, she reached the bottom. She checked along the wall and found a button rather than a switch. She pushed it, and old fluorescent lights flickered on.

The stairs were at one end of a short hallway. The other end opened up into a larger room. At one point in the hallway, she felt a cold draft. She couldn't tell where it was coming from.

In the massive room at the end of the hallway, there were display cases everywhere with strange things inside. These had to be some of the artifacts from her great grandfather's museums, Sara thought. She wandered through the maze of cases. There were many wondrous things to see. However, Sara barely noticed any of them. She was looking for something particular. Then, she stopped.

Recessed in one wall on an ornately carved wooden pedestal was a box. It was a wooden box with metal straps. It seemed to be made of one solid piece of wood with no latch or hinges. In the center of the top, there was a circular design with a slot in the shape of a cross.

It was the box she was shown when she was in the fountain. A plaque on the display said it was Pandora's Box.

She had found it.

Chapter 44

The apartment above the Golden Lamp Pawnshop was quiet. Piri sat in a wing-backed chair reading a book. The lamp next to it illuminated her worn copy of Macbeth.

She looked up and peered down the hallway. She had turned the chair so that she easily could see Dior's bedroom door. It was still closed.

Asami sat cross-legged on the floor. She placed a bowl on the floor in front of her, closed her eyes and flipped a playing card up into the air. The card would flutter down, flying this way and that until it landed in the bowl. She then would move the bowl again and flip another card. She wasn't trying to get the card into the bowl. She was placing the bowl where the card was going to land. It was her favorite game.

Piri glanced down the hall again.

"Not yet," Asami told her.

"What is she doing in there?" Piri asked.

"Things are not going as she planned," Asami said softly. "She needs to put more pressure on them."

"She has to stop playing with them." Piri slammed her book shut.

"She thinks she has things under control."

"Does she?"

Asami merely shrugged. "Too many possibilities are still in play." She closed her eyes and sat unmoving for a short time. "There is a good chance that she can still pull it off."

"I'm worried what will happen if she manages to get the box," Piri said. "I think she may be too young to be able to handle it."

"She is older than me."

"You're different. You can see things she can't"

Asami remained quiet. She moved the bowl on the floor again. This time, she balanced a book on a TV remote and placed a card on the book. She took a second book and placed it hanging off the edge of a table above the other. She sat back and waited.

"I hate when you do things like that," Piri said and reopened her book.

"We could prevent her from getting it," Asami said.

"I've thought about that too," Piri said. "The only way to do that—"

"Shh," Asami said. "She'll open the door," Asami paused and then added, "Now."

The bedroom door opened, and Dior's shadowy form moved through the hallway and into the living room.

"Did you have a good think?" Piri asked.

"I have everything under control," Dior assured them.

"Did I say that you didn't?" Piri said, annoyed.

Dior turned to go and sit in her chair. Her leg caught the table next to Asami, and she stumbled.

"Damn it, Asami. Why do you insist on doing that?" she yelled at her.

Asami watched the book tumble off the edge of the table and land on the higher end of the book on the floor. The card, propelled up into the air, fluttered down into the bowl. Asami ignored Dior's rebuke and simply smiled.

Dior swore again under her breath and sat down.

"Everything is as I wanted it to be," Dior said. "Sara is looking for the box so that she can save her family. She even thinks that her brother's attack was part of it." Dior smiled to herself in the shadows. "I'll have to thank the Sheriff's boy for that. He's dull-witted, but he can be of use sometimes."

Dior continued, "It's true that I didn't foresee her dead brother coming back. It's an amusing twist. I don't think it matters too much one way or the other. Still, that wasn't a failure on my part."

"The future is a maze of possibilities," Asami defended herself. "Just because the probability of something is low, doesn't mean it won't happen." She picked up the cards and bowl and stood behind Piri's chair.

"Are you sure that you are ready to wield that much power?" Piri asked.

Dior was silent for a moment. "You don't think I am?"

"There have been mistakes," Piri said.

Asami nodded her agreement. She wasn't looking at Dior. She was looking curiously at a light scarf hanging on a nearby coat rack. It was the one that Dior wore if she left the apartment at night.

Dior stood up. "I am ready to go home, and I won't stand being second guessed by anyone." The edge in her voice told Piri that she had crossed a line.

"Very well," Piri told her. "I hope you are right."

"I am," Dior said. The sense of tension in the room subsided. Dior sat back down in her chair. Piri absently flipped through the book in her lap.

Asami turned her attention to a birdcage where an ancient raven stood like a statue on a bar inside. She took two steps over to it and stuck a finger through the bars. The raven pecked at it, and she instantly pulled it back in pain. There was a drop of blood on the tip. She stuck her finger in her mouth and savored the blood on it.

"What is your next move then?" Piri asked.

"It's time to offer an exchange for the box," Dior said.

Asami went back to stand behind Piri's chair. She looked up to a shelf high above the chair and laid a card on the edge between the two potted plants that had called that shelf home for years.

"An exchange?" Piri asked.

Dior got up and went down the hallway toward the front door of the apartment. Asami circled around Piri's chair, handed the bowl to the old woman and sat on the floor again to watch.

Piri put her book on the table next to her and set the bowl on top of it. Just as she stood up, Dior came back in.

"An exchange?" Piri repeated.

"Yes. They give me the box, and I give them back," Dior paused. "One of them." She roughly pulled the scarf off the coat rack and turned to leave.

The force that she used caused the coat rack to rock violently. It spun a little and just as the front door shut behind Dior, it tipped over.

It fell against the bird cage breaking the cage door open. The raven inside made a break for it as both the coat rack and birdcage fell to the floor.

The raven flew up and circled the room several times before taking refuge on the shelf above Piri's chair. It flapped it's wings knocking the potted plants over. One fell and broke on the coat rack. The other fell knocking over the table where Piri had placed her book and the bowl.

Both the book and bowl went tumbling to the floor. The cards spilled out of the bowl, and it landed facing up as it spun to a stop.

The bird pecked a hole in the card beneath its feet getting its beak stuck for a moment. It shook it's head flinging the card away. The card tumbled down and landed in the bowl on the floor.

"I love kidnappings," Asami said with a smile.

"I hate when you do that," Piri said.

Chapter 45

Thomas dropped Daniel off at the diner to talk to Gwen. When she came over to his table to take his order, he asked if she could sit down for a minute. She yelled back to Willie that she was taking a break.

"Don't make it too long," Willie yelled back.

Gwen sat across from him. She didn't look directly at him.

"How many shifters are there?" he asked.

"I'm not quite sure. Close to two hundred, I think," she told him. "There's one more now." She said softly.

"Me. I know," Daniel said.

"Yes."

"How?" he asked.

"They say it's like an infection. If it enters the bloodstream, it starts infecting your cells. Changing them. Changing your DNA."

"What happens now?"

"At first, you can't control the shifting. It will happen because of stress or emotion. You'll need to learn to control it."

"Will you teach me?" Daniel asked her.

She looked at him. "You don't hate me?" she asked.

"No. I don't hate you," he told her. "I'm not too happy with Mason, though."

"Yes, I'll help you."

"How do I know when I'm going to change?" Daniel asked.

"You'll feel it. And when you do, get away from everybody. You don't know how they'll react."

"Anything else?"

"A side effect is that you heal fast," she told him.

He nodded. "I noticed."

They stood and hugged.

Daniel watched her for a few minutes as she went back to work. Then he met up with Thomas again, and they headed back to the mansion.

Thomas, Daniel, and Sara made their way to Sara's room. Sara sat on one of the chairs. Daniel sat on the floor and leaned back against the end of the bed. Thomas paced by the fireplace.

Daniel and Sara watched him. He had promised to tell them about what happened before he died and they were waiting impatiently for him to start.

"When Mom and I got to town," he began, "I went to try to find a phone because our cell phones didn't work."

Daniel nodded. "The Sheriff said the tower isn't working."

"It was late, and nobody was out on the street. I've never seen a town like this that completely closes in the evening."

Sara and Daniel looked at each other. They hadn't either.

"I finally found an old woman walking with what I thought was her granddaughter. The woman was friendly and offered to let me use their phone. She told me their apartment was just around the corner. So I went with them."

Thomas continued, "The whole way there, the little girl just stared at me. The old woman told me her name was Asami and that she was shy around strangers."

"Asami?" Sara asked. "Was the old woman a tall black woman with white hair?"

"Yes," Thomas said.

"And was Asami around 8 or 9 years old?" Sara asked.

"Yes,"

"Lucinda told me about them. She said they acted as if they own the town," Sara told him.

"Well, they might not own it. They do have a good deal of control."

"What do you mean?" Sara asked.

"Along with a third woman named Dior, they are known as the Sisters. They are probably the most powerful Wielders here," Thomas said. "I met the third sister as soon as I entered their apartment."

"What did they say?" Sara asked.

"They wanted me to find a box that great grandfather has. I told them that I didn't even know my great grandfather. Even if I did, I wouldn't steal from him."

"What did they do?"

"They threatened me if I didn't agree. So I lied and said that I would try. As soon as I was out on the street, I hurried back to the restaurant as fast as I could go."

"That's when I saw you." Sara said.

"They must not have believed me. So they sent that monster in the fountain to kill me."

"They'll kill all of us if we don't give them the box," Sara said.

"They aren't the only ones with an interest in the power in that box," Thomas said.

"There are others?"

"Yes, the Dead. They don't want the Wielders to get their hands on it," Thomas told her.

"Why?"

"The Wielders are the ones that cursed the cemetery. They are why the Dead exist. If we are not careful, we could ignite a war between the Wielders and the Dead."

"Did you learn all this from that Dead Lord?" Sara asked.

"Lord Danville? Yes," Thomas said.

"What do you think, Daniel?" she asked her brother.

Daniel had been quiet during the discussion. He looked up at Sara with a frown.

"I don't know what the answer is," he told her. "Thomas is right. We can't just give them the box."

"I'm not saying that we should give it to them," Sara objected.

"I know," Daniel said. "The Sisters said they will kill us if we don't. I'm just not sure that we can use the power that the box is supposed to have. We might not be able to control it. Or something worse than that can happen."

"Worse?" Thomas asked.

"We all could end up dead," Daniel told them. He looked at Thomas. "Or deader."

"What do you want to do, then?" Sara asked him.

"I just want them to leave us alone," Daniel said.

"We all do," Thomas told him. "We just can't use the box to do that."

"It's the only thing we have," Sara said impatiently.

"We have to find something else," Thomas' voice was stern.

"We don't have time," Sara shouted at him.

Thomas faced Sara. "Everybody will be against us if we try to use the power. I told you both the Sisters and the Dead will try to stop us."

"Stop it," Daniel told them.

Sara was on her feet. "It has nothing to do with the Dead."

"It has everything to do with them. It's the power that created them. Us," He corrected himself.

"They won't do anything to you either way. So it's not your choice," Sara yelled.

Daniel covered his ears. "Stop it!" he yelled.

"It is a family decision, and I still am part of this family," Thomas insisted.

"I have the power that can use it. And I'm going to do it," Sara told him a dark look coming over her face.

"I won't let you," Thomas told her.

"Really?" Sara asked. Before Thomas could react, he was lifted off his feet and was sent into the wall behind him. He slid down but remained on his feet. He took a step forward and was thrown back again. He remained against the wall unable to move.

Daniel leapt to his feet. "Stop it," He yelled. He was going to say something more. Suddenly he fell back down on the floor writhing in pain.

Sara turned to Daniel. "What's wrong?" She asked, kneeling beside him.

The force holding Thomas to the wall released, and he rushed over to Daniel.

Daniel rolled over. They knew instantly that he was changing and backed away quickly. They saw his body stretch and grow. They saw the hair appear, his face lengthen and his hands and feet turn into claws.

In moments, the brother they knew was gone and, in his place, a giant brown bear stared back at them.

"Daniel?" Sara asked. She didn't know if he still knew who he was or whether he would attack them.

The bear roared.

"Do you know us?" Sara asked him.

The bear looked at Sara and then at Thomas. It looked at Sara again, and its head bobbed up and down.

"Is that a yes?" Sara asked Thomas.

"I think so," Thomas replied.

There was a loud knocking at the door. Sara looked at Thomas in horror.

"Who is it?" Sara asked.

"Francesca," the girl said. "Your mother told me that you were up here."

"Go back downstairs," She said, a little desperation seeping into her voice. "I'll meet you in the front parlor in a couple of minutes."

"Oh," Francesca was taken aback. "OK."

Sara looked back at Daniel. The bear was apparently trying to hide behind the bed.

"You keep track of him," Sara told Thomas. "See if you can get him to turn back." She looked at what remained of his clothes shredded all over the floor. "You might want to get him something to wear, when he does."

She opened the door a crack to make sure Francesca had gone. The hallway was empty. She slipped out and heard the door lock behind her. She headed downstairs.

Thomas looked at the bear. "What are we going to do with you, Daniel?" he asked.

Sara caught up with Francesca in the grand foyer. She showed the girl into the front parlor and closed the door. Francesca eyed Sara suspiciously.

"What was going on up there?" Francesca asked her. "I heard strange noises in your room."

"Strange noises?" Sara asked.

"Yeah. Do you have a dog or something?"

"A dog? Oh, yeah. A dog," Sara was thinking fast. "That was just my brothers. They were fooling around. You know how brothers are."

"Not really," Francesca said.

"Well, they're not much different from animals sometimes," she told her. She decided that she should change the subject.

"I found the box," Sara told her in a hushed voice. She sat down on the couch. Francesca sat close to her.

"Did you?" Francesca said excitedly. "Where?"

"I stumbled into a storeroom where my great grandfather keeps some of the exhibits he had in his museums. And there it was."

"Where is it now?" Francesca asked.

"It's still down there."

"Why didn't you take it?"

Sara got up and walked over to the fireplace. "I wasn't sure what I was going to do with it."

"What do you mean?" Francesca asked.

"Well, the reason I wanted to find the box is that the people that killed Thomas threatened to kill me if I didn't get it for them."

"Really?" Francesca asked, horrified.

"So I could hand it over to them and hope they leave us alone, or," Sara paused.

"Or what?"

"I can use the box against them," Sara told her.

"Who are they?"

"The Sisters."

"The Sisters? The Moira Sisters?" Francesca asked. "They're harmless."

"Not according to what I've heard. They're Wielders," Sara told her.

"Wielders? Wielders don't exist. It's just something that parents tell little kids to make them behave. They're not real."

"Like Pandora's Box?" Sara asked. "A lot more things are real than I ever realized."

"Well, let's say they are wielders," Francesca said, not wanting to argue. "Why do you think you can defeat them?"

"Because, I'm a wielder too," Sara said.

"What? You're," Francesca hesitated then she laughed. "You must be joking."

Sara didn't smile. "I'm not."

"You can do magic?" Francesca asked. "I don't believe you."

"Do you want me to show you?" Sara asked.

"I, uh," Francesca didn't seem thrilled with the idea. Then she stood up and put her hands on her hips. "Yes. Prove it."

Sara smiled a humorless smile. She looked around the room and decided on a small round table across the room from the fireplace.

"Ready?" Sara asked her.

"Yes," Francesca said. Sara thought she heard a tiny bit of apprehension in her voice.

She concentrated on the table. It moved suddenly toward them.

The objects resting on it slid around the top a bit. In a moment, the table came to a stop between them.

Sara watched Francesca's expression as the table moved across the room. When it came to a rest, Francesca looked thoughtful.

"Well?" Sara prompted her.

"I don't believe it," Francesca said.

"You just saw me do it," Sara said.

"I know," she replied. "OK. Let's say wielders exist. And you're a wielder. If they were wielders as you said, that's still three to one."

"I'll have the element of surprise," Sara told her.

"You're just learning. If what you say is true, they are probably experts. You just can't do it."

A book that was lying on the table flew across the room and hit the back of the couch with a muffled thud.

"I'm going to," Sara told her solemnly.

Francesca stared at her for a minute. "I can't help you then," she told her.

"I don't need your help," Sara said.

Francesca just stared at her. She shook her head and went to the door. She looked back at Sara. Neither of them broke the silence. Francesca left them room.

Sara stood there until she heard the outside door close.

She returned to her room where she found Thomas waiting for her. Daniel had changed back and was in his room getting dressed.

"I was thinking. We should talk to Matthew. Tell him everything we know. Maybe he can help us," Thomas told her.

"I already talked to him. He won't help us."

"Maybe great grandfather, then. The box belongs to him."

"Yes," Sara said thoughtfully. "Not Matthew, Maybe great grandfather. Wait here for Daniel. I'll be right back," Sara told him and quickly left the room.

Chapter 46

Sara didn't knock before entering her great grandfather's room. The room was dark and quiet. The familiar beeping of medical machines was gone. The dim bluish light was gone. The only thing that remained was the faint odor of antiseptic.

She switched on the light. The machines still stood by the bed. However, they had been turned off. The curtains were still drawn around the bed. She approached it and pulled the curtains aside.

There was no one in the bed. The bed had been made neatly, and there was no sign that anyone had been recuperating there at all. She pulled the pillows away from the headboard. Nestled between the headboard and the mattress was a small tape player. She turned it on and listened for a minute to the sounds of someone sleeping. Then she turned it off and smiled to herself.

She turned off the light and left the room. She went back to the east wing to find her brothers. They weren't in their rooms. Her mother wasn't in her room either. She was just on her way downstairs when she met Bramwell coming up.

"There you are, Sara. Mr. Kask has asked that everyone gather in the front parlor," he told her.

"Have you seen the rest of my family?"

"Your mother and brothers are already down there." Bramwell turned and started back down. Sara followed him.

"Did he say why he wants to talk to us?" Sara asked.

"I believe he has some news to give everyone," he said.

Sara followed Bramwell down the stairs. "So do I," she said under her breath.

When they entered the front parlor, they found that a small crowd had gathered. Matthew was standing at the fireplace. Her brothers and mother were seated in chairs around it. Even Peter Jacobs was there, pacing near the front windows nervously.

All of the people who worked at the mansion were standing in a group by the door to the dining room except for Cook and Mrs. Baskin. They were seated on a couch in front of them.

Matthew turned as Sara and Bramwell entered.

"Good," he said. "We're all here."

Sara sat by her mother. Bramwell took a seat on the coach next to Mrs. Baskin.

"Thank you all for gathering in here today," Matthew told them. "I'm afraid that there is some news that concerns all of us."

"Late last night, my father had a relapse. As some of you know," he said looking toward the group seated on the couch, "I summoned Dr. Cameron to the mansion and he tended to my father for several hours in the night."

A number of the staff looked at each other and began whispering. Bramwell, Cook and Mrs. Baskin sat in stone-faced silence.

"How is he?" Mary asked.

"Unfortunately, it proved too much for him. C.J. Kask passed away early this morning," he told them.

Murmurs of shock rose up from the staff. Bramwell, Cook and Mrs. Baskin immediately stood and gave Matthew, Mary and her children their condolences. Sara stared at them. The three seemed remarkably composed for just receiving the news that their employer was dead.

Most of the staff were young and hadn't worked at the mansion for very long. Those three had probably worked for C.J. for upward of two or three decades. Wouldn't they show more emotion?

She looked over at Peter Jacobs. He was sitting by the window gazing out at the front lawn. Had he not heard the news or was he that unruffled by it?

Or maybe it was just that they knew what Sara knew.

"A service will be held for my father in a few days. I will keep you informed," he told the staff. They filed out. Bramwell, Mrs. Baskin, Cook and Peter followed them. Soon Matthew, Mary and the three kids were left alone in the front parlor.

Sara started to clap slowly.

Daniel and Thomas looked at her in alarm.

"Sara," her mother said sharply. "Stop that."

Instead, Sara stood up and faced Matthew with a smile.

"Very well done," Sara said. "Uncle Matthew." She pronounced the word, uncle as if something weren't quite right about it.

"You really should be in show business," she continued. "You put on a really convincing performance."

"Sara," Daniel said, grasping her by the shoulders. "What do you think you're doing?"

Sara just shrugged her brother off. She walked up to Matthew and stood looking up at his face. Matthew just stared at her, frowning.

"C.J. Kask is not dead," she said.

"What are you saying?" Mary asked her. "Are you saying Matthew is lying?"

Sara turned away from Matthew. He just watched her without saying a word.

"Ever since we arrived, I had wanted to see my great grandfather. He was always too sick to see us. That was disappointing, but not unbelievable." She told them as she walked around the room.

"A short time after we got here, I met a young man who was a little confused about what day it was. He also introduced himself as Matthew."

"Where did you see him?" Matthew asked abruptly.

"In the small parlor across the hall," she told him.

"It got me thinking about this Matthew here." She walked back to him. "He told us that he was my mother's uncle, Matthew."

"I have an uncle, Matthew," Mary told her. "And this is him."

"You only believe that because he said he was." Sara told her. "A woman at the diner in town told us that Matthew disappeared back in the 1950's. No one there disagreed with her."

"It wasn't until yesterday morning that I confirmed my suspicions." Sara said.

"How?" Mary asked.

"I saw the other Matthew again," she said.

"Where?" Matthew asked urgently.

"Right here in this room," Sara told him. "He told me an incredible story that I won't go into right now. He also told me two things."

"What?" Mary asked.

"That was his mother," She pointed to the portrait of Sadie Kask over the fireplace. She picked up the gold-framed picture off the mantle.

"And, that this is his father," she showed the picture to everyone in the room. The man in the picture was the man standing before them who called himself Matthew Kask.

"You aren't Matthew," Sara said softly. "You're C.J. Kask, my great grandfather."

"How could he be C.J.?" Mary asked. "He would be over a hundred years old."

"One hundred and six," the fake Matthew told her. "You're absolutely right, Sara. I am C.J. Kask."

"You look as if you could be in your sixties. How is that possible?" Mary asked.

"Magic, my dear. Pure magic," he said with a laugh.

"No, seriously," Mary insisted.

"I think he is being serious," Sara said looking at her great-grandfather.

"Why didn't you tell us who you were?" Mary asked.

"As you observed, I am over a hundred years old and yet, physically, I am much younger. Most people," He glanced at Sara, "do not believe that I could be C.J. anymore. So I decided that I needed a new identity. Since my son had disappeared and had not officially died, I took on his identity and have been working to have C.J. die of old age and leave everything to his son, Matthew. Me. Then I could continue my life without unanswerable questions."

"I guess I screwed that up," Sara said.

"I guess so," Kask said. "Your arrival was not the best timing for my plans. I couldn't turn you away though. You're my family."

Sara held out her hand. "I'm glad to meet you face-to-face, as my great grandfather."

Kask looked at her hand and tentatively took it. "I'm glad to find that I have such a clever great granddaughter. It is kind of nice to be me again. It's been a while."

Daniel, Thomas and Mary all joined in on getting reintroduced to the man they had known as Matthew.

"Can you tell us about the magic that's keeping you younger?" Daniel asked.

"That is a long story and one for another time. For now, I fear, this may have been too much for your mother."

Mary complained that she did have a slight headache and Kask helped her up to her room to rest.

After they had left, Thomas, Sara and Daniel started talking about their great-grandfather and speculating what was keeping him from aging.

Later, when the three of them went up to their rooms, they noticed that their mother's room was open, and the light was on. Sara went in to see her. Her mother was not there. Sara saw that her balcony door was slightly open, so she went out.

She frantically called to her brothers. When they reached the balcony door, they saw that part of the railing was gone as if it had been ripped away. Sara was looking over the edge toward the ground below.

"Mom?" Daniel said urgently and rushed to the railing and looked over. He expected to see their mother lying on the ground below. The piece of railing was lying on the grass, but their mother was not down there.

"Something is wrong," Sara said. She pushed past Thomas to get back into the room. "We have to find her."

They ran through the house calling for their mother, searching rooms as they went. There was no response. They found Kask and Bramwell downstairs and told them about the railing and their missing mother.

"We have to find her," Sara said.

"You disappoint me, Sara," a woman's voice said softly.

Sara looked around trying to find whoever said that.

"Did you hear that?" she asked.

"Hear what?" Thomas asked.

"Somebody said I disappointed them," Sara said. They all shook their heads.

"I told you to bring me the box and you decided to try to use it against me. Very disappointing," the voice said. It was indistinct like a wind through trees.

"Where's my mother?" Sara yelled looking around the room.

Everyone stared at her.

"She is with me. If you want to see her again, bring the box to me at midnight tonight in the mausoleum where Thomas was entombed."

"If I do, will you leave my family alone?" Sara asked.

"Sara, who are you talking to?" Daniel asked her.

"It's the person I heard in the fountain," Sara said still trying to see where the voice was coming from.

"I have no use for any of you. Once I have the box. I will give her back to you."

"Fine. Tonight at midnight," Sara said.

The voice laughed and then it was gone.

"What is it, Sara?" Kask asked her.

"They have my mom," Sara said.

"Who does?" Daniel asked.

"The Sisters," Thomas told them. Sara nodded.

Chapter 47

When Bramwell entered the front parlor, no one noticed. Kask was sitting on the couch with Sara questioning her about what she heard. Daniel and Thomas were quietly talking by the window. Bramwell cleared his throat.

"Excuse me, Sir. The staff has checked the house from top to bottom. Your grand-daughter is definitely not here," he said.

"Thank you, Bramwell," Kask said. "It was a long shot."

"Is there anything more you would like them to do?"

"No. There's nothing more that can be done right now," Kask told him. "Thank you."

"We have to do something," Daniel spoke up from the end of the room.

"What do you suggest?" Kask asked.

A knock on the front door interrupted them. Bramwell left the room to answer it.

The four of them stared at the open door into the grand foyer, waiting to hear who it was. There were low voices as Bramwell greeted the visitor and then footsteps as they crossed the hall to the front parlor.

Bramwell was the first to appear.

"Sheriff Marco is here, sir," Bramwell said as the Sheriff appeared in the doorway. His bulk filled the frame. Kask stood up to greet him.

"Good Evening, Sheriff," Kask said shaking his hand. "Thank you for coming out here."

The Sheriff greeted him and glanced around at everyone else in the room.

"My niece has been kidnapped," Kask told him.

"Kidnapped?" The Sheriff looked surprised. "Who would kidnap your niece?"

"The Moira Sisters," Thomas said. He stepped into the light at the center of the room.

The Sheriff's eyes widened. The white eye bulged out a bit and then his eyes narrowed again.

"Who are you?" The Sheriff asked him coldly.

"He's my brother," Sara told him.

"Then who was the guy in the fountain," He asked.

"That was me," Thomas said.

"He was dead."

"I recovered," Thomas told him.

"And you say that the Moira Sisters have kidnapped your mother," The Sheriff continued.

"They told me that they did," Sara said.

"When did they tell you that?"

"Tonight, here in this house."

"Who else heard them say they kidnapped your mother?" The Sheriff asked, looking around.

Nobody said anything. Sara spoke up, "Just me."

"Were you alone with them?"

"No. They were all with me," Sara said indicating the other three.

"So, they just waltzed in here and told you that they kidnapped your mother. And even though they were right there with you, no one else heard them. Did you see them whisper to her?" the Sheriff asked Daniel.

Daniel looked at the others nervously. "No," he told the Sheriff. "I didn't see them."

"I am the only one who heard them," Sara said. "They used magic to talk to me."

The Sheriff just looked at her. For a long moment, no one spoke.

"OK," the Sheriff said finally. "I see how it is. I think I'll just go back to my office, and we'll forget all about this little talk."

"They kidnapped my mom," Sara snapped at him.

"Yes, and I'm sure they are the ones that killed your brother there," he said.

"Yes, they did," Sara insisted.

"And yet, there he stands. I'm sure your mother will be back soon too," the Sheriff told her and turned to leave.

"Aren't you going to do something about it," Sara yelled at him.

"Sara," Kask said and put a hand on her arm.

"There's nothing to do," the Sheriff said.

"If you don't do something about it," Sara began.

The Sheriff whirled at her. He stepped toward her, and his face darkened. "What? You'll do one of your tricks?"

Sara stood facing him silently. She wanted to back away, but she willed herself to stand her ground.

"If you even try one of your tricks, I'll haul you in for assaulting an officer. And I'll throw in filing false police reports while I'm at it."

Sara couldn't stand it anymore. She broke down and ran from the room. The Sheriff watched her go.

As Sara's steps could be heard fading into the distance in the house, another knock was heard on the front door. Bramwell left to answer it.

"There's gonna be trouble if you don't get that one under control," the Sheriff grumbled at Kask. "I'm sorry about your niece. There's nothing I can do. I can't investigate magic."

"I know," Kask said.

Jason Wells rushed into the room with Bramwell behind him. He glanced around the room at all the people.

"Where's Sara?" he asked.

"She just ran out," Daniel told him. "I think she went up to her room."

"What are you doing here?" the Sheriff demanded. "I thought you left town."

"I stayed so I could look into what's going on," Jason said. "I couldn't just abandon Sara. I have to help her in whatever way I can." He narrowed his eyes at the Sheriff. "Why are you here?"

"My mom has been kidnapped," Daniel blurted out.

"Kidnapped?" Jason asked.

"Hold on. There's no evidence that any kidnapping has occurred. There's just the girl who said she heard voices," the Sheriff told him. "She's obviously delusional."

Jason looked at the Sheriff. "If Sara said that's what happened." He stepped closer to him and looked up into his white eye. "I believe her."

The Sheriff stared at him for a moment. "You can believe anything you like. I don't see any evidence of a kidnapping."

"What about the broken balcony railing in my mom's room?" Daniel asked.

"There could have been an accident. Maybe she fell and has been wandering around the woods. I can start a search for her if you want. It still isn't a kidnapping."

"Why don't you talk to the Moira Sisters?" Thomas asked.

"About what?" the Sheriff asked. "A girl says they talked to her using magic? I have no cause to go bother them about this."

"You don't have a right to search them," Jason said. "You can still question them."

"I'm not going to question any of the good citizens of Shadow Bluffs just because a little girl heard voices in her head."

"She's not a little girl," Jason said.

"Whatever," the Sheriff mumbled and headed toward the door.

"So you're not going to do anything?" Jason asked.

"That's right."

"Then I'll have to do something about it," Jason told him.

The Sheriff whirled on him. "You watch yourself, kid. You might have a toy badge back where you come from. Here, it doesn't mean a hill of beans."

"Are you threatening me?" Jason asked.

"Threatening? No, I'm not threatening you," the Sheriff said in a quieter voice. "If you start pestering folks around here though, I'll haul you in for," he thought for a moment. Then he continued, "for disturbing the peace."

Without another word, the Sheriff turned and strode out into the grand foyer. They all stood silently until they heard the front door slam shut.

Chapter 48

I need to talk to Sara," Jason told Kask. "You said she went up to her room?"

"I believe so," Kask said.

Jason hurried out of the room without another word.

"What are we going to do?" Daniel asked.

No one had an answer. They sat about the room in silence either wringing their hands or staring at the floor.

After several minutes, someone came down the stairs swiftly and dashed over to the door. Jason appeared in the doorway. He was short of breath.

"She's not in her room," he told them.

Kask jumped up. "We better find her before she gets herself into trouble," he said. "Daniel and Thomas, you look down here and outside." They hurried out of the room.

"Bramwell," he continued. "Get the staff to help look as well." Bramwell nodded and turned to leave.

Kask turned to Jason. "Come with me. We'll check the bedrooms upstairs again."

They returned to the east wing and started with Thomas' room. Kask waited in the hall to prevent Sara from escaping while Jason searched to see if she were in the room.

They continued systematically through Mary's room and Daniel's room.

When they were about to look in Sara's room again, Daniel called to them from the top of the stairs. Thomas was with him.

"No sign of her downstairs. We're going to check in the west wing."

He said, and they headed off that direction.

Kask followed Jason into Sara's room. However, like in the other rooms, there was no sign of her.

"Where would she have gone?" Jason asked.

Kask just shook his head. "I don't know."

They returned downstairs after checking the other bedrooms and met with the others to see if they had found her. No one had any idea where she was.

"Do you think she would have gone after the Moira Sisters?"

"I don't think so. She wouldn't go after them unless she had the," Kask stopped.

"The box?" Jason asked.

"Everybody keep looking," Kask told them. "Jason, you come with me." He hurried out of the room with Jason close behind.

Kask didn't want anyone to know the way to the secret room. At the same time, he knew that Jason would be his best bet to convince her not to try to use it.

The tapestry over the hidden hallway had been replaced. When they got there, Kask held the tapestry aside. The light was off, which he thought was a good sign that Sara had not been there. He switched it on and waved Jason into the hallway.

Kask went directly to the other end of the hallway and again, pulled the tapestry back.

"This mirror is original to the house. There are three other mirrors in other places around the mansion. By touching a button, you can pass through to one of the other mirrors like a door." Kask told him.

"Or an elevator," Jason said.

"Just push this button," Kask told him, indicating the disk with the hexagon.

Jason looked at him worriedly. "Are you sure?" he asked.

"Here hold this," Kask said handing him the tapestry. Jason took hold of it, and Kask pressed the button and disappeared.

Jason looked at the mirror, took a breath and then pressed the button, closing his eyes at the last second.

He stumbled to a stop and opened his eyes to find that he had left the hallway and entered a cool stone room. Kask was standing at the top of a circular stairway leading down into the floor.

"Down here," he said and started down the steps.

A large room that looked like a museum storeroom was at the end of a short hallway at the bottom of the steps.

"Keep an eye out for Sara," Kask told him. "She may already be here looking for it."

Jason followed Kask through a maze-like path between the displays. Jason thought that a person could get easily lost in the room. Kask seemed to know exactly where he was going.

After wandering through most of the room and searching for Sara, they stopped in front of a nook where a wooden chest was resting on an intricately carved pedestal. The display sign said, "Pandora's Box."

"Here it is," Kask said. "She hasn't taken it."

"Yet," Jason added.

"Yes. That means she's still somewhere in the house."

Jason examined the lid of the box. He traced the cross-like slot on the lid with his finger.

"Do you have the key that opens it?" he asked.

"I do," He said. "I have it hidden as well."

Jason simply nodded. He could tell Kask would not tell him where. Even so, he noticed that Kask couldn't help a quick glance at the pedestal under the box when the key was mentioned.

"Let's go back up and see if they've had better luck finding her," Kask said.

They made their way through the room and then back up to the main floor.

The room was pitch black when Kask turned off the lights. The sound of their feet on the steps bounced off the smooth stone surfaces and echoed through the room. Finally, after they had gone back through the mirror and let the tapestry fall back over it, the room fell into silence.

The room remained silent and dark for several more minutes until, suddenly, with a soft click, a flashlight app turned on and illuminated the floor behind one of the displays.

Sara stood up and glanced out from her hiding place. She swept the light from her phone around to make sure she was, in fact, alone in the room. Convinced that no one else was there, she stepped out into the aisle across from the box.

She made her way over to the box and shined the light over it. She smiled. They left it there for her. She lifted the box off the pedestal. It was the size of a large suitcase, and it was heavier than it looked.

She set it down on the floor with a dull thud. She stopped to listen and see if anyone, having heard the sound, would return to the room. No one came.

She shined the flashlight on the pedestal. Jason was not the only one who saw Kask glance at the pedestal when the key was mentioned. Sara had been watching them from her hiding place.

It was an old pedestal carved out of some type of wood that Sara did not recognize. Each side of the square pedestal had a carving of the sun shining down on an empty cross. The wood surface was dark. Whether it was from age or stained that way, Sara didn't know.

The crosses were symbols obviously used by the knights of the Crusade despite the fact that the object it held was of Greek mythology.

She touched the carving, running her fingers over the lines of light running from the sun down to the cross. She pressed on the sun. It seemed solid. She did the same to the cross. It didn't move either.

She looked at the carvings on the sides and noticed that the one on the left had much less detail than the one on the front. However, the one on the right had even more detail. She realized that the pedestal was actually turned sideways. The right side, with the most detail, was meant to be facing to the front where it could be seen. The left side, with very little detail was meant to be in the back where few would see it.

She turned the pedestal around to the right side and examined the carving. She pressed on the sun, and like the other side, it did not move. When she pressed on the cross, it sank into the surface, and she heard a click. When she had let go, the cross popped out. She took hold of the cross and pulled it out of the carving leaving a dark recess open behind it.

She looked at the cross in her hand. Two ends of the cross had a hooked edge toward the inside. Probably to keep it in place inside the pedestal, she thought. It was far too large to use as a key for the box, so she turned her attention to the recess behind it.

She laid the cross to the side and shined the flashlight into the hole. Inside was another cross, this one made of metal. She pulled the cross out and examined it. It was a thin cross on the end of a post.

She looked at the lid of the box. The cross appeared to be the right size. She took hold of the handle and held it above the slot. She held her breath and tried the key. It went smoothly into the slot. She turned it and with a satisfying clunk the lock released and the lid of the box came loose.

She lifted the lid off the box and set it aside. She then shined the light into the box and gaped at the contents.

Chapter 49

Daniel stared at the broken railing on the balcony of his mother's room. He had spent the last couple of hours searching the house for Sara. However, it wasn't until he stepped into this room that it hit him. His mother had been taken away from him. And she might not be coming back.

He stood in the middle of the room for a while almost as if he were trying to feel his mother's presence there. He couldn't. So he went out onto the balcony, probably the last place that his mother had been in the house. She was gone.

He heard voices. He didn't pay any attention to them. He looked down at the broken railing still lying on the lawn.

"Daniel," a woman's voice called to him.

He turned his head a little. "Was it her?" he wondered. "Was his mother back?" He hurried back into the room.

"Daniel," the voice called again from somewhere outside the room.

No, he realized. It was not his mother. She was still gone.

Gwen appeared at the doorway and looked in.

"Daniel," she said. "I've been looking everywhere for you. Are you all right?"

He just nodded.

She rushed over to him and pulled him into her arms. He laid his head on her shoulder.

Gwen just held him without saying anything. Daniel was quiet for several minutes before he said anything. And when he did, it was little more than a whisper at first.

"I miss my mother," he said.

"I know," Gwen told him.

"And I'm afraid."

"We all are."

Daniel pulled away from her. He walked over to the balcony door and looked out again.

"I haven't been nice to her," he said.

Gwen didn't say anything. She just waited for him to continue.

"I'm supposed to be growing up. I'm almost a man. I'm not supposed to need my mother."

"Everyone needs their mother," she assured him.

"Not in school. Not in front of my friends. Not in public."

"I'm sure she understands."

"What if we don't get her back? What if something happens?" He turned back to her. "What if I don't get to tell her," his voice trailed off.

Gwen went over to him and held him.

"She knows," she said.

"We need to get her back. I need to tell her," he said quietly. "Before it's too late."

"It's not too late," she told him.

"I don't know what to do," he said.

"You, Thomas and Sara, together you'll find a way to get her back."

"Sara's gone."

"What do you mean?"

"She ran away," Daniel told her.

"What?" Gwen asked.

"The Sheriff wouldn't believe her. She told him what they said. He won't help."

"What did they say?"

"They want some box that my great grandfather has. If they don't get it, they'll kill my mom."

"Why doesn't the Sheriff believe her?" Gwen asked.

"Because only Sara heard them," Daniel said.

Gwen thought for a moment.

"Do you believe Sara?" she asked.

"What do you mean?"

"Just what I said. Do you believe her?" she asked sternly.

"Yeah. I guess," he said.

"Don't guess. Do you believe her or not?"

He thought a moment. "Yes. I believe her."

"Then you need to find her and help her."

"We've been trying to find her."

"Try harder. She's out there by herself trying to find a way to get your mom back and she thinks no one will help her."

"Even if I find her, what can we do?" Daniel asked. He wasn't actually expecting an answer.

"I don't know. You need to find Thomas too. You may not be able to do it alone. The three of you together can defeat them."

He thought about that for a minute. "We're family. We need to stick together," Daniel said as he jumped up and hugged her again. "Thank you."

She returned his hug and then pushed him toward the door. "Now, get going," She commanded. Daniel smiled and quickly left the room.

Thomas was in the dining room. He had checked the kitchen for any sign that Sara had been there and had just come into the room through the swinging door when Daniel burst in from the grand foyer.

"Thomas," he almost shouted. "We have to find Sara."

"That's what we're trying to do," Thomas said flatly.

"No, we have to find her and help her."

"We have to stop her, not help her," Thomas told him.

"We have to find her, and she won't let you find her unless—"

"Unless what?" Thomas demanded.

"Unless you're willing to listen to her," Daniel said.

Thomas thought about that. "Fine, I'll listen," he said. "If we find her."

"I know where she'll be," Daniel said.

"Where?"

"Wherever the box is," he said.

"Where is that?" Thomas asked.

"I know where it is," a voice said from the doorway. Jason stood watching them from the grand foyer.

"If we go there and wait, she'll come to us," Daniel said. He looked at Thomas and Jason expectantly.

"I don't have any better ideas," Jason said. Thomas nodded.

They followed Jason to the secret hallway. Jason showed them the mirror and told them how to go through and when they hesitated, he stepped up to it, closed his eyes as he did earlier and pressed the button.

On the other side, he watched them as they each appeared in the room with him.

Jason turned on the lights as Daniel raced down the steps. Jason and Thomas followed him.

When they got down to the bottom, Jason found Daniel looking into the room at the end.

Thomas suggested that they check around and make sure Sara wasn't hiding anywhere.

Daniel set out to the right winding his way in and around the various strange artifacts, checking in any space that looked as if it could hide someone.

Jason did the same starting out to the left of the entrance.

Thomas headed down the path through the center of the room toward the other end checking along the path as he went.

The search took almost three quarters of an hour, and when they met up again, none of them had seen any sign of Sara in the room.

"I suppose we should sit down and wait then," Daniel said. "She won't go anywhere without the box, so she'll have to come down here for it."

"Not anymore," Jason said. The other two looked at him curiously. He nodded to a display a short distance from them.

It was a carved, wooden pedestal labeled with a sign that proclaimed it to be "Pandora's Box." There was nothing on the pedestal.

"She's already taken the box," Jason told them.

Chapter 50

They hurried out of the hidden hallway and to the back of the house. When they got to the back door, Thomas stopped the other two.

"She's going to try to get to the mausoleum. We have to find her first," he told them.

"Do you think she's already out there?" Jason asked.

"I think she'll hide out in the house until the last minute," Thomas said. "Check the rooms along the back of the house."

"What are you going to do?" Daniel asked.

"I'll check the mausoleum, just in case," Thomas said.

Daniel and Jason went on into the next room while Thomas slipped out the back door and hurried across the patio into the darkness.

Daniel watched him from the conservatory as Thomas disappeared around the corner toward the cemetery.

"I think he's hiding something," Daniel said.

"Maybe," Jason said pulling on the cabinet doors beneath a garden workbench. "All I know is that we need to find Sara," The doors wouldn't budge.

"I know," Daniel said. He went to the back of the room where a number of dead potted bushes created a small forest along the back wall. Jason joined him as they pulled the pots away from each other, and the wall hoping they'd find Sara hiding behind one of them.

Daniel sighed. "She could be anywhere."

"And she has the advantage," Jason agreed. "All she has to do is avoid us for as long as she can."

The door to the conservatory opened. Daniel and Jason whirled around to find Thomas standing in the doorway.

"She's not in the mausoleum," he told them.

"And she doesn't seem to be in here," Daniel said, kicking one of the dead bushes over.

"Let's go back and check the kitchen," Jason suggested. The other two agreed and soon they had left the conservatory behind.

As soon as she couldn't hear them anymore, Sara released the cabinet doors under the workbench and rolled out onto the floor.

She stretched her aching legs and softly groaned. She stood up and was about to get the chest out from under the workbench when she heard someone enter from outside.

She turned to the door as she pushed the cabinet doors shut.

"We've been looking for you," Franklin told her.

"I know," Sara said. "And now you've found me."

"Yes."

"What are you going to do?" Sara asked.

"I'm not going to try to stop you," he told her.

"How nice," Sara said.

"I will give you a warning."

"What kind of warning?"

He started toward her and stopped when she backed away.

"The Dead will stop you from using the power of the box," he said.

"What will they do?"

"Whatever they need to."

"Will they try to kill me?" Sara asked.

Franklin paused. "I hope that is not necessary."

"They would if they needed to?"

Franklin turned away from her and looked out the door onto the patio. "Yes," he said in a quiet voice.

"I'm going to do what I need to do to get my mom back," Sara told him.

"I know."

"If you aren't going to try to stop me. Leave me alone and let me do what I need to do."

He bowed his head and didn't say anything for a minute. And then, without turning to Sara, he said, "Goodbye, Sara. It is unlikely we will meet again." He opened the door again and was gone.

After watching him go, Sara stood a moment in thought and then grabbed the box from under the workbench. She set it down by the door out to the patio.

She had been moving around from hiding place to hiding place ever since she took the box from the storeroom. This time, she had been caught.

Listening to Jason and her brothers' conversation, she got a glimmer of hope. Thomas had checked the mausoleum and found that she wasn't there. Maybe they won't think of checking there again, she thought, at least not until it was too late to stop her.

She quietly opened the door to the patio. Although the moon was out, she thought it was dark enough that she could make it to the mausoleum without being easily seen from the house.

She picked up the box and tried to close the door again without attracting attention. There was a soft click as the door latched again. Nothing that they would have heard.

She hurried along the edge of the patio to the corner of the house. All she had to do is make it that far without being seen, and she could make it to the mausoleum.

She paused at the corner and looked back at the rooms along the back of the house. There was no sign that anyone had seen her. She smiled. Home free, she thought.

She hurried around the corner and immediately stopped dead in her tracks.

The mausoleum stood a couple hundred yards from the back of the house in the middle of the small cemetery. And she would have easily been able to make it there.

Except there was a crowd encircling the mausoleum. Thomas and Franklin had told her the Dead wouldn't let the box fall into the hands of the Wielders. And here they were.

The way to the mausoleum was blocked by a wall of Dead.

Chapter 51

Thomas waited in the conservatory. It was dark, and there were no lights on in the room. He simply stood there, listening.

They had been chasing Sara all over the house for hours without luck. He decided that, rather than chasing Sara, he would find a place that she was likely to go and wait for her to come to him.

So, there he was in the dark.

Then, he heard someone walking along the rooms at the back of the house, coming toward him. He moved quietly to the side door of the conservatory and waited for the person to enter.

The light came on in the room beyond the door, and a shadow appeared at the doorway. A hand reached in and flipped on the lights in the conservatory. Thomas stepped into the light.

"Thomas," Daniel said, taking a step back. "You scared me."

"I thought you might be Sara."

"I've been looking for you," Daniel told him.

"Why?"

"I'm going to help Sara. And I want you with us," Daniel said.

"She isn't going to win," Thomas told him.

"Maybe not on her own. She can if we help her."

"It's impossible."

"Listen to your heart," Daniel said.

"I'm dead, remember?"

"Well, listen to your head, then. We're family. Who knows what we can do together?" Daniel told him.

Thomas stood silently, staring at Daniel. Daniel looked over

Thomas' shoulder and then back at him.

"I think you have a visitor," he said. "Trust me. And trust Sara." He turned away and went back toward the front of the house.

Thomas watched him leave before turning to find Lucinda standing at the conservatory door.

"You should be outside with the rest of the Dead," Thomas told her. He went to the window and looked out. He couldn't see the Dead from there.

Lucinda went to him and put her hand on his arm. "Daniel is right," She said softly.

"They don't know what they're doing."

"They're following their hearts," Lucinda said. "They're trying to protect their family."

"They can't win."

"Maybe. They have a better chance if you help them."

He closed his eyes. "We can't let the box fall into the hands of the Sisters," he reminded her.

She squeezed his arm. "Then help them so that it doesn't."

Thomas turned his head and stared at her for a moment. Then he nodded.

Lucinda smiled. "I told Sara that she can put her trust in you. Let them trust you. And put your trust in them."

Sara sat on the floor of the balcony outside of Daniel's room looking out at the Dead milling around on the lawn behind the house. It was just after ten o'clock. She had less than two hours to find a way to get to the mausoleum.

The majority of the Dead were between the house and the cemetery. During the time she had been watching from the balcony, she could tell that there were plenty of guardians on the forest side of the cemetery as well as along the cliffs.

"There's got to be a way through," she whispered out loud to herself.

"It doesn't look like it," a voice whispered back from the balcony door startling her. She jumped to her feet.

She had kept the lights off in Daniel's room so that she could stay hidden up there in the dark. They were still off, but a dark figure stood in the doorway.

"Don't come near me," she hissed.

"I don't intend to," the person whispered and sat down on the floor of the balcony.

He was well away from her. He still blocked her from escaping back into the room though.

"Daniel?" Sara asked. The responding chuckle, though quiet, was familiar enough to confirm that she was correct.

Sara was not amused. "Why don't you just leave me alone and let me try to get Mom back?"

"Do you think you're the only one who wants to get her back?" Daniel whispered to her angrily.

Sara was taken aback by his response. "No," she said. "It would help if I didn't have to hide from you and Thomas too."

"We were trying to find you."

"And now you have. Are you going to go tell Thomas so that the two of you can stop me and let Mom die?"

There was a pause before Daniel spoke. "Nobody is going to let Mom die," He said. "I'm not going to tell Thomas. We don't see things the same way."

"Why are you here then?" Sara asked.

"We're family."

"So?"

"I think we need to get her back. Together," Daniel told her.

"Then help me get out to the mausoleum," Sara said.

"Believe it or not, that's why I'm here," he said.

"Well, we only have until midnight."

"They're a problem," Daniel said looking out at the circle of Dead.

"Any ideas?" Sara asked.

"How about a diversion?" Daniel suggested.

"What do you mean?"

"If we could distract enough by the cliffs or at the forest in the back, maybe you could get through and into the mausoleum before they can stop you?"

"What kind of distraction?" Sara asked.

Daniel thought for a few minutes. Sara stared at the yard below with a growing sense of dread. Daniel snapped his fingers.

"Shh," Sara shushed him.

"Sorry," He said. "I could try to get to the mausoleum with something that looked like the box. At the last second, I would run off into a different direction away from the cemetery."

"What would that do?" Sara asked.

"Maybe some will try to chase me and try to get the box I'm carrying. If we can get enough to follow me and leave part of the circle open, you can get through."

"Maybe," Sara said studying the swirling mass below them.

"We don't have many options right now," Daniel reminded her.

"OK," Sara said, finally. "Let's see what we can do." They both stood up, took one last look over the railing at what waited for them in the yard and then went back into Daniel's room.

Chapter 52

Sara set the box on the floor and closed the door to the balcony. She pulled the drapes closed.

"What are we going to use as the fake box?" Sara asked.

Daniel reached over and clicked the switch on the lamp next to the balcony door. The light didn't turn on.

"I don't know. It probably just has to be a similar shape and size. It will be too dark for them to tell it's a fake," he said.

He clicked the light again. It still didn't turn on.

"What's with the light?" Sara asked.

"Maybe the bulb's out," Daniel told her. "Let's just go."

There was a click and a lamp on a table across the room lit up. Even though it wasn't very bright, they blinked at the sudden light.

The Sheriff was sitting in the chair next to the lamp. He grinned at them, his one, white eye mercifully hidden in the shadows of his craggy face.

"What's all this?" he asked. "Sneaking around in the dark. Someone might think you're up to no good."

They didn't say anything. Sara stepped in front of the box, and Daniel eyed the door. They might be able to make it, he thought. They were standing, and the Sheriff was sitting. He glanced at the box behind Sara. Could she pick it up fast enough?

The Sheriff saw Daniel glance toward the door and the box. The smile left his face.

"I don't think you want to be doing that," he told them. "I'll tell you what. I don't have a grudge with either of you."

"Really?" Sara asked.

"Nah. If you just go on your way peaceably, I won't stop you," he said, smiling again.

"And the box?" Daniel asked.

"That would have to stay here with me," the Sheriff told him.

"So you can give it to the Sisters?" Sara asked.

"The Sisters?" he asked, surprised. "Now, why would I want to give something like that to them?"

"You want it for yourself," Daniel said. It was a simple statement of fact.

"I think it's time for me to retire," the Sheriff said. "And I bet that box would make that possible."

"You'll have to go through us," Sara told him. Daniel looked over at her. She had a determined look on her face.

"Well," the Sheriff said as he stood up. "I was kind of hoping you'd say that." He unsnapped his holster and drew his pistol. He aimed it at Sara.

Daniel looked at Sara. He could see that she was as scared as he was. He could also see that she was thinking.

"I wouldn't advise you to try anything," the Sheriff said. "It would only take a fraction of a second for me to shoot you."

"You're going to anyway," Sara said through clenched teeth.

"Not at all. I despise unnecessary bloodshed," he said. "I just wanted to point out the seriousness of the situation you're in."

"You're just going to let us go then? If we give you the box?" Sara asked. The longer she kept him talking, the better chance they had.

"Sure I will," the Sheriff said. "You don't have much time. The offer expires soon, and when it does, well—"

Daniel looked at Sara. She was still trying to think her way out. He reached out a hand to her.

"Sara, let's just go," he said.

Then, they all heard something. It was something unusual to the Sheriff and Daniel. It was something all too familiar to Sara. A low rumbling started to build up.

"What the hell is that?" the Sheriff asked to no one in particular. He glanced around and quickly brought his attention back to Sara.

Daniel wasn't sure what it was either, and he glanced around also. Sara kept her focus on the Sheriff and smiled at him.

"You know what it is," the Sheriff said to her.

Sara's smile just widened a bit. She could see that he was starting to get nervous. Behind her smile, she was nervous too. She just hoped that he wouldn't start shooting.

The rumbling stopped, and before anyone could relax it started again. The room shook causing all to brace themselves against a piece of furniture so they wouldn't lose their balance.

And then it stopped.

Matthew was standing by the door just behind the Sheriff.

Sara could see that Matthew had been surprised by the scene in front of him. The Sheriff was not yet aware that Matthew was standing there, and she was afraid that Matthew might say something.

"Shh," she said.

"What do you mean, shh?" the Sheriff demanded.

"I just thought you might be a little on edge after the earthquake," she told him. "I think we all should calm down."

She looked over at Daniel who was staring at Matthew in wonder.

"Daniel!" she hissed at him.

He instantly turned his attention to her. She shook her head at him.

"Focus on me," she told him.

She turned back to the Sheriff. Matthew was motionless behind him. What could he do against the Sheriff's pistol?

Then she saw Matthew's right hand. He was still holding the silver letter opener that she had given him the last time he had appeared. She looked over at Daniel. He was trying hard not to look at Matthew.

"What we need," Sara started to say, turning back to the Sheriff. "What we need is some calm."

As she looked at the Sheriff, she held her right arm in front of her and scratched at her wrist with her left hand. She shifted her eyes to Matthew. He was watching her. She tapped at her right forearm just above the wrist. He nodded once.

She shifted her eyes back to the Sheriff, but it was too late. He had seen it.

He quickly turned toward Matthew. Matthew was already in motion. As the pistol pivoted toward him, he slammed the letter opener sideways through the Sheriff's arm.

The Sheriff yelled in pain and his hand involuntarily flinched firing a bullet into some books on a shelf beside the fireplace. Then his hand fell open, and the gun clattered across the floor and slid under a nearby chair. He clutched at his bloody arm and the letter opener that was still stuck in it.

Matthew quickly recovered the gun and pointed it at the Sheriff.

The Sheriff glared at Matthew and groaned in pain.

"Let's get out of here," Sara told Daniel.

"No," Daniel said. "Take the box and go downstairs. I'll be down in a minute."

"What are you going to do?" she asked. With the grim look on Daniel's face, she wasn't sure what he had in mind.

"I don't want him to come after us," he said.

The Sheriff looked at Daniel and narrowed his eyes.

"You aren't going to," Sara picked her words carefully, "hurt him more, are you?"

"No," Daniel said. "I'm just going to tie him up. Get going!"

Sara grabbed the box and headed to the door. She had forgotten about Matthew. He was standing near the door looking at the blood on his hand. She set the box down again and went to him.

"I didn't know if I could do it," he said. "When he turned on me," his voice trailed off.

"You did just fine," she said and gave him a hug. She picked up the box again. "Thank you, Uncle Matthew," she said and left the room.

"Help me to find something to tie him up with," Daniel told Matthew. Daniel moved around the room keeping an eye on the Sheriff as he knelt on the floor bleeding. Matthew looked around also. However, he never moved from his spot.

A low rumble began. Daniel grabbed onto a nearby table just in case. It died off quickly.

"I'll be leaving now," Matthew said.

"You can't leave," Daniel told him. "I need your help."

"I don't have much choice." The rumbling started again.

Then there was another noise. A cry of pain brought Daniel's attention back to the Sheriff. He had pulled the letter opener out of his arm and with a swift backhand, threw it at Daniel.

He barely had any time to twist out of the way. The point of the blade glanced off his shoulder, and it flipped end over end until it clattered against the wall. He grimaced in pain. The tip had ripped through his shirt and sliced his shoulder.

The room started to shake, and since Daniel was already off balance, he stumbled and fell on the floor beside the bed.

Above the rumbling, he heard Matthew yell. "Watch out, Daniel." And then, the shaking stopped and the room was suddenly quiet.

"Matthew?" Daniel called. There was no answer.

Carefully, Daniel got up into a crouch and peered over the bed. There was no sign of either Matthew or the Sheriff. He stood up and moved around the bed toward where the Sheriff had been a minute earlier.

With an unearthly cry, a large mountain lion leapt up onto the bed from the far side. Daniel stumbled backward away from it. It leapt at him.

Daniel tried to duck to the side, but one of the big cat's paws caught him in the chest and the weight of the beast sent him backward onto the table behind him. It collapsed under him, and he fell amid the splintered wood and glass from the lamp that slid from the table with him.

The animal's leap carried him past Daniel. It lightly landed on the floor and turned back on him.

Daniel had the wind knocked out of him and was trying to catch his breath. He tried to push himself up and felt the metallic base of the broken lamp under one of his hands.

He rolled away from the cat just as it swiped at him with one of its claws. The nails scraped at his back. Even through the pain, Daniel managed to push up onto his knees at the end of the roll.

He sat back on his heels and held the lamp like a bat in front of him. The cord hung down on the floor.

He looked at the cat, and the animal looked back at him. He noticed the one white eye.

"So, you're a Shifter too," Daniel said to the beast.

In answer, the cat cried out, and then leapt at Daniel. He swung the lamp with all he had. The base of the lamp connected with the cat's head mid-leap and there was a sickening crunch as the impact sent the large animal sprawling to the side. It was slammed against the side of the bed. The bed shifted position.

Even with a large wound above its normal eye and blood dripping down onto the carpet, the cat was back on its feet at the same time as Daniel got to his.

Daniel held the lamp in front of him trying to keep the cat at bay while he tried to get around it to the hallway door. The cat would not let him get by.

Then, he had another idea. With one hand, he felt behind him and opened the door to the balcony. He kept the lamp in his right hand ready to strike if the cat made an attack.

He slipped through the door and after slamming it hard on the animal's paw as it tried to slash at him through the opening, he managed to close it with the cat inside.

He hurried to the end of the balcony and stopped when the lamp almost pulled out of his hands. He looked back to see that the door had closed on the cord. He dropped the lamp and quickly went to the railing at the end of the balcony.

It was about a five foot gap to the next balcony over. He was about to climb on the railing when he heard a crash behind him. He spun around.

The cat had leapt through the glass in the door and was facing him amid the shattered glass scattered over the balcony floor. In the light from the room, Daniel could see that the animal had numerous cuts across its head and front legs. There were even glints of glass still in some of the wounds.

He turned and vaulted up onto the railing. He was about to jump when the cat's front paws slammed into him from behind. He lost his balance and fell forward between the balconies. Both he and the cat crashed down and disappeared into the large bushes that lined the back of the house.

Several of the Dead, attracted by the noise, approached the bushes. When there was no further disturbance, they went back to the main group.

Hidden beneath the bushes, the bodies of Daniel and the cat lay motionless.

Chapter 53

It was almost 11:30. Rather than being a dark, peaceful place where all were resting up in their beds, the house was filled with activity.

Like Jason and Thomas, Kask had discovered the box missing but not until about 11 o'clock. He and Bramwell had spent the last half hour combing through the rooms on the main floor, especially those near the hallway that led to the storeroom.

Finally, Bramwell suggested that perhaps Sara had hidden away in the basement. Kask, desperate to find her, agreed with him, and they quickly headed off in that direction.

Although they were fairly thorough in their search of the rooms, they had overlooked the short, narrow door that stood partially hidden in an alcove. The rarely used broom closet was, in fact, being used as a hiding place.

When Sara heard them head off down the hallway, she emerged from her hiding place to take a quick look for Daniel. He told her that he would be only a few minutes. That had been quite a while ago.

She quietly moved down the hallway to the back door to look for him. She was almost there when a suit of armor along the hallway spoke to her.

"You are a hard one to find," a familiar voice told her. She was looking curiously at the armor display when a tall, thin figure stepped out from behind it.

"Thomas," she said, relieved. "I thought you were," her voice trailed off. She didn't even want to mention him out loud.

"Who?" Thomas asked.

"Nobody," Sara said. "So now it's your turn to try to stop me."

"Would it matter?"

"Trying to stop me?" Sara asked. "No, it wouldn't."

"You're going to try no matter what I say."

"Yes," she said through clenched teeth. She was watching him for any sign that he was going to try something.

"Then I guess," Thomas began. Sara tensed. "I better try to help you then."

Sara blinked. "Was it a trick?" she wondered.

"You'll help me," she said, unconvinced.

"I was told that individually, we will fail. Together," he began.

"We will defeat them." Sara finished the thought.

Thomas just nodded.

"Your friends out there are trying to stop me," she paused. "They're trying to stop us from getting out to the mausoleum."

"I know," Thomas said. "There is another way."

"How?"

"Come with me," he told her. "I'll show you."

They headed back up the hallway away from the back door of the house. When he pulled the tapestry away from the secret hallway, Sara stopped.

"Trust me," Thomas said. Sara looked at him for a long moment and then ducked through the opening into the dark hallway.

There was no movement under the bushes for a long time. Then, with a groan, the Sheriff was able to get to his feet. He was unsteady and leaned against the stone of the mansion for support.

He checked his injuries. There were mostly cuts and bruises. He put his hand to his head. Although, like all Shifters, he was a fast healer, Daniel had done some damage, and it would be a while before he fully recovered from it.

He looked around for Daniel. However, in the bushes and in the dark, he couldn't tell where he had landed. Daniel wasn't his only problem. He was standing naked in the bushes, and his clothes were up in the room where he had changed into the mountain lion.

Then he heard a low groan coming from a short way away in the bushes. He smiled to himself. He'll take care of the kid, he thought. And then sneak back to his car. He'll be the one to investigate the killings later. He'll deal with the clothes he left behind then.

The bushes moved in front of him, and he heard a deep grunt emanate from the spot. He stopped in his tracks.

There was something wrong, he thought. He was just thinking that he should turn around and get out of there right away when a large dark shape broke out through the top of the bushes.

A bear stood up on its hind legs and towered over the Sheriff. It looked at him and roared.

The Sheriff dove down into the bushes and started to crawl away from the bear. The bear shuffled forward batting at the bushes with its front paws trying to find the Sheriff.

It came down on all four legs and barreled through the bushes leaving a trail of destruction behind it. Then it heard movement ahead of it. Rather than charging ahead, it stopped. It knew that it was the Sheriff. The smell was wrong though.

It narrowed its eyes and took a step backward just as the mountain lion leapt from the bushes in front of it. The cat landed on the bear's back digging in its claws and sank its teeth into the back of the bear's neck.

The bear reared up again trying to shake the cat free. The cat held on, and whenever it got the chance, it would rip at the bear's back with its rear claws. The bear roared in pain and fell back onto its front paws.

The bear tried to pull the cat off. But, its paws weren't able to reach its back. Finally, the bear reared up again and staggered back into the wall of the mansion. The cat, seeing that it might be crushed between the bear's massive body and the stone wall, leapt off the bear at the last second.

They faced each other for another attack. The cat leapt at the bear's face. Its front paws latched onto both sides of the bear's head, and it was about to bite down on the bear's throat when the bear swiped one of its front paws into the cat's chest ripping it from the bears head and throwing it against the stone wall.

The cat landed on its feet and immediately launched itself at the bear again. The bear caught the cat in the chest with its claw and slammed the cat back against the stone wall.

The bear's claw broke the cat's ribcage and punctured a hole in its chest, disappearing into the cat until the nails scraped against the stone behind it.

The cat hung on the wall for several seconds as it shook from pain and looked down at the bear's claw sunk deep into its body. The cat looked up at the bear one last time and then the head slumped to the side and moved no more.

The one white eye continued to stare unseeing at the bear until it pulled its bloody paw away from the wall and allowed the cat's body to fall to the ground. It watched curiously as the cat, even in death, changed back into the Sheriff.

He checked the Sheriff just to be sure he was dead and then headed away to help Sara and Thomas, leaving the lifeless body alone in the bushes.

When Sara and Thomas reached the bottom of the steps, rather than going into the storeroom, Thomas stopped in the middle of the hallway. Sara felt cold air.

He pulled out a broken piece of stone and pressed his fingers into the recess behind it. There was a loud click. He pushed against the wall, and a section of it swung in. There was a slight shift in air pressure sending a thin cloud of dust out from the opening.

Thomas turned on a flashlight and shined it into the passage beyond. It was filled with cobwebs and, despite the light from the flashlight, it was still too dark to see clearly.

"This was used by the original inhabitants of this house to get out to the cemetery," Thomas told her.

"The original inhabitants?" Sara asked.

"When the mausoleum was built, the passage was incorporated into the plans," he continued, ignoring Sara's question.

"So we can get to it by going in there?" Sara said. She wasn't sure that was better than trying to get through the mob outside.

"Yes," Thomas said and started down the passage.

Sara watched him clear the cobwebs as he went. When he quickly started to disappear into the darkness, she followed him in and rushed to catch up.

Sara shivered in the cold air of the passage. She could smell the dampness and could hear water dripping slowly in the darkness.

"How did you know about this?" Sara asked.

"The Dead know about it. They told me to guard it," Thomas told her.

"Why don't they use it to get in the mausoleum?" Sara asked.

"They're not trying to get in," Thomas said. "They are trying to keep you out."

Sara thought about that. The Dead didn't want the box. They just didn't want the Wielders to get it.

"You're helping me get into the mausoleum," Sara said.

"We're family," Thomas said.

Thomas stopped. Sara could see that the passage ended ahead of them. There was a steep set of steps. They appeared to end at a blank wall.

"Wait here," Thomas said and climbed to the top of the steps. The wall at the top was short, and Thomas had to stoop to stand by it. He dug at the wall, scraping off layers of mud and mold that caked the walls of the passage.

"There," he said to himself and pulled on a handle that had been covered up. A small square section of the wall pulled open and light streamed in from the other side.

"Come on," he said and climbed through the narrow hole.

Sara climbed the stairs and pushed the box through onto a stone floor. She crawled through and stood up next to Thomas.

They were standing in the mausoleum. The passage led up under one of the marble tables and the hole exited through the side.

She looked around as her eyes adjusted to the light. The outside door was open. The inside metal bars were closed and locked. Then, as she continued to scan around the room, she saw them.

Her mother was on her knees at the far side of the mausoleum. Her hands and feet were bound. She looked at Thomas and Sara with scared, moist eyes.

Standing over her was a young woman who Sara had once thought was her friend.

"Francesca?" Sara asked.

"That's one of her names," Thomas said. "This is Dior. She is one of the Moira sisters."

Chapter 54

Sara's mind was swimming. With Thomas' help, she was able to get the box to the mausoleum so she could exchange it for her mother. When she finally came face to face with the person who was tormenting her family, she turned out to be someone she thought was her friend.

"Francesca," was the only thing she could say. She just stared at the woman.

"It's not Francesca," Thomas reminded her.

"That's not strictly true. Physically, I am what used to be Francesca," Dior said. "Yet I am not her."

"Who are you then?" Sara asked.

"As your brother said, I am Dior," she said.

"Well, whoever you are, I brought the box. Let my mother go," Sara demanded.

"How do I know you brought the right box?" Dior asked.

Sara picked up the box and set it on the table next to her. Sara stood behind it, and Thomas moved off to the side.

"It's the box you showed me when I was in the fountain, when you killed my brother," she said. "This is the box you wanted me to bring to you."

Dior nodded. The box that she had wanted for so long was there on the table.

"Do you have the key?" She asked.

Before Sara could answer, Thomas picked up the metal plate that at one time had sealed him up in the wall. He flung it at Dior.

Although she had her attention on Sara, Dior immediately waved one arm toward Thomas and the plate spun back toward him.

He ducked as it flew past him and it hit the wall behind them driving the edge of the plate between two marble blocks until only about half of it could be seen.

Dior's attention was diverted away from Sara, so Sara immediately took advantage of it and tried to send Dior backward into the wall behind her.

Except, Dior hadn't taken her attention away from Sara completely. Dior blocked Sara's attack and with a whirl of her finger, the dust in the room began to swirl into a dust storm. Sara and Thomas were blasted with wind and bits of dirt.

Sara could barely hear Dior's voice above the storm. "So you think your table moving parlor tricks are enough to beat me?" She laughed.

Sara had her arms up shielding her face. The pellets of dirt stung her arms, and the wind made it hard to breathe.

The force of the wind knocked Sara backward. She fell to the floor and rolled until she hit the wall behind her.

As suddenly as the dust storm formed, it dissipated.

Dior laughed. She waved a hand as if she were dismissing a servant and the sides of the marble table where the box sat exploded outward. Thomas and Sara flattened themselves on the ground and covered their head as they were sprayed with marble debris.

The end of the room filled with dust briefly, and as it settled, Thomas and Sara got to their knees and brushed themselves off.

The top slab of the table had fallen down on top of what was left of the bottom portion, sealing off any escape through the passage below.

Dior kept an eye on them as she stepped through the rubble of the table. Sara coughed several times to clear her throat of the dust. She glowered as the woman bent down and took hold of the box. She tried to get to her feet, but felt herself being forced back down on her knees.

"Stay where you are," Dior commanded. She picked up the chest and set it on the marble table at the other end of the room.

"Did you really think you could use the little bit of power you learned against me?" Dior asked her.

Sara didn't say anything.

"Why didn't you just take the box yourself?" Thomas asked.

"What would be the fun in that?" Dior replied.

"It's because you couldn't," Thomas said. "The box was protected as long as it stayed inside the mansion."

Dior ignored him and ran her hands over the box.

"Who's Francesca?" Thomas asked.

"Nobody," Dior told him. "Just a shell that I inhabit."

"She was somebody. Somebody you needed because you couldn't exist on your own."

"She was a nobody. I didn't need her. I'm just using her."

"You're just a parasite," Thomas said.

"Enough!" Dior shouted. She made a quick gesture and Thomas was thrown backward into the debris. He lay still.

"What are you going to do with the box?" Sara asked.

"I'm not going to do anything with it," Dior told her. "It isn't the box that important. It's what's inside the box."

"What's in it?" Sara asked.

"Haven't you looked?" Dior asked. "It's what I've been seeking for many, many years."

"So you can take over the world?"

"Take over the world? Why would I want to take over this pitiful piece of rock?"

"What do you want then?"

"To go home," Dior said.

"Where's that?"

"'Where' is such a primitive concept. There are so many things beyond this tiny world. The Norse Mythology talks about nine worlds or planes where the gods and men live. There are many more than nine. I come from one of these other planes of existence." She paused to look at the three of them. "A much higher one." She laughed. "Does that make me a god?"

"Why do you need the box to get back to your world?" Sara asked.

"Travel between these worlds is tricky. I can open a door. That would be like getting on an elevator and having it stop at a random floor. It probably won't be the floor you want, and it might be a floor that you truly don't want."

"So you need the box to," Sara prompted her.

"The box contains something like a beacon. It will help me home in on the right plane and open a door to it."

Sara was about to ask another question. However, Dior was done with her explanation. Dior held out her hand.

"Now all I need is the key," She said.

Chapter 55

L et our mother go," Sara said.

Dior glanced down at Mary still kneeling beside her. She almost seemed surprised that she was still there. Mary wasn't looking at Dior. She kept her eyes on Sara and Thomas.

"Do you have the key?" Dior asked Sara.

"Yes."

"Show me," Dior said.

Sara pulled it from her jacket pocket and enclosed the cross shaped portion of the key in her fist, letting the short wooden handle protrude through between her fingers. She hoped to prevent Dior from easily summoning the key with her powers. She held the key up so that Dior could see it.

"Bring it to me," Dior commanded.

Sara picked her way through the debris around the first table, and when she reached the second table, she stopped.

"I'll give you the key," she said. "First, you have to let my mom go."

"Give me the key and you can have her," Dior said.

Mary started to pull at her restraints and tried to speak. All that came through the gag was muffled grunts. She shook her head violently. However, Sara couldn't see her from where she was standing.

Sara moved to the last table and stood across from Dior. The box was set on the table between them.

"As soon as Thomas takes my mother out of here, I will give you the key," Sara promised.

"You can take her to the other side of the room if you like. You can't leave until I get the key."

Sara thought about it for a moment and then she nodded her

agreement. She motioned to Thomas to go get their mother.

Thomas quickly went to Mary and removed her gag. He then started to untie her legs and feet.

"No!" Mary shouted. "Don't give her the key."

Sara just stood facing Dior. Thomas finished removing her restraints and then helped Mary to her feet. He quickly helped her back to the other end of the room.

"You have your mother," Dior said. "Now give me the key."

Before Sara could answer, there was a metallic clang. Both Dior and Sara turned to look at the barred gate. Thomas had tried to open the gate so that he and Mary could escape outside. There was more than just the latch holding the gate closed.

"Uh, uh, uh," Dior said. "I said the other end of the room."

A moment later, with a metallic scream, one side of the double gate ripped off its hinges and flew toward Thomas and Mary. Thomas flung Mary down into the corner of the room and knelt down to shield her with his body.

The gate slammed sideways into the walls on either side of the corner burying the bars in the walls. It made a short, triangular space where they were huddled. Mary screamed.

Thomas found that he could move, and he stood up. While the bars formed a short wall across the corner, he could easily just step over it to get out. However, one of Mary's legs had been sticking out of the corner, and the gate had trapped it between its metal bars and the floor. Mary could not move.

Before Sara could react to her mother's situation, Dior grabbed Sara's wrist from across the table and slammed it down on the marble surface. Her hand automatically opened, and Dior plucked the key from it. Sara pulled her hand back when Dior released it. She didn't think it was broken. The pain was excruciating though.

"You said you would let us go," Sara said, rubbing her wrist.

"Sorry," Dior told her. "I can't do that."

Sara turned and rushed over to Thomas and her mother. Thomas was trying to move the gate. It was solidly wedged into the corner. Sara checked her mother's leg. Where it pressed her thigh into the floor, the gate had ripped the fabric of her pants as well as part of the top layers of her skin.

"Do you think it's broken?" Sara asked.

"I don't think so," Mary told her.

Sara was worried about the pressure that the gate was putting on her mother's leg. Although there was only a little blood, the skin under the gate was starting to turn a faint bluish color.

Sara tried to help Thomas lift the gate enough for Mary to pull her leg out, but it wouldn't move.

"Sara, go tell that rabble outside to clear out," Dior told her. "I can't hear myself think."

Neither Sara nor Thomas had paid attention to the noise outside that was growing. The crowd was starting to raise their voices. They couldn't tell what they were saying as the voices just blended together into a dull roar.

"Tell them yourself," Sara yelled back to her and continued to try to work Mary's leg out.

She thought she was making headway when the gate creaked and seemed to press down on Mary's leg harder. Mary screamed in pain. Sara jumped to her feet.

"Stop it!" she yelled at Dior.

"Go tell them to leave," Dior repeated.

Sara looked at Mary as she ground her teeth in pain holding both sides of her leg.

"Fine. I'll do it. Just stop," Sara said.

The gate stopped pressing down on Mary's leg. It still held it tight against the floor.

Sara went to the entrance of the mausoleum and slipped through the opening by the remaining gate and walked out onto the landing in front of the building.

As she stood there facing the crowd of Dead encircling the mausoleum, the prediction of Madame Zella, the psychic, came back to her.

"You were standing at the door of the mausoleum," the psychic had told her. "You said something to the crowd, and then you shut the door to it. The angry crowd started to close in on you and then I saw the most terrifying thing I've ever seen."

Sara would never forget what Madame Zella told her that day. The psychic had seen the building disintegrate in a fiery explosion

Sara raised her arms to get the attention of the crowd. The noise died away.

"Please," she pleaded with them, "You have to leave. If you don't, we will all be killed." She paused for a moment. The Dead have a different view of death, she thought. "We will all be destroyed." She corrected herself.

She turned and went back into the mausoleum. The roar of the crowd returned.

"Shut the outside door," Dior commanded.

Sara could see the crowd closing in on the small building. She quickly shut the door and latched it.

"How long will it be before the mausoleum explodes?" she wondered.

After she had slipped back through what was left of the inner gate, Sara glanced at her mother. She could tell that she wasn't doing well.

She looked over at Dior. The woman had her hand flat on the top of the box. Her eyes were closed, and she was smiling. She lifted the key up to put it in the keyhole.

I can't let her open the box, Sara told herself. Sara concentrated on the key.

Just as Dior was about to slide the key down into the slot, it suddenly ripped from her fingers and went clattering against the wall behind her. Dior's eyes flashed open, and she quickly searched the room. Her gaze fell on Sara, and her face darkened.

"How dare you?" Dior screamed at her.

Before Dior could do anything more, Sara concentrated on the box itself. As she moved toward Dior, she tried to send the box smashing against the wall too.

Dior recovered from the first attack and countered. The box slid quickly to the edge of the table. It hung there teetering for a moment before slowly moving back onto the table in jerking movements.

"Do you still think you can take me on?" Dior asked.

Without answering, Sara released the box from her power. It rushed back across the table, and almost went off the other end before Dior regained control over it and brought it to rest back at the center of the table in front of her.

Sara quickly grabbed a torch sconce from the wall and turned on Dior herself. She swung it at Dior's head. The metal club clanged as it hit. But it didn't come in contact with her head. It stopped just inches from it.

Sara swung again and again the sconce clanged against an unseen force.

Dior laughed. Then the humor faded quickly. Sara felt the sconce rip from her hands, and a moment later it slammed into her midsection sending her backward over the table behind her and dropping her amid the marble debris on the floor.

"Do I have to teach you another lesson?" Dior asked.

The screech of the gate was deafening as it pressed down on her mother's leg. Above the groaning of the metal, a definite snap could be heard. Mary's screams filled the small room.

Chapter 56

Sara groaned from the pain of landing on her back and coughed in the dust that was kicked up.

"Stop it," she tried to yell. It came out punctuated with her coughs. "Leave her alone."

"You brought it on yourself," Dior told her in a low voice. "Stop fighting me and I'll stop hurting her."

"OK. OK," Sara pleaded. She crawled on her hands and knees over to Mary and her brother. She blinked through the tears that were streaming down her dusty face.

"I'm sorry, Mom," she told her mother.

"Sara," her mother started to say. Her voice was choked off by the pain in her leg.

Sara reached through the bars and took her mother's hand in hers.

Dior ignored the three people in the corner. She had her palms on the lid of the box feeling the power around her. The part of her that was Francesca, the part that struggled against her many years ago, had died away long ago. The part of her that was Dior drank in the intoxicating energy.

She began a low chant. Nothing that was audible at first. To Sara, it was just a hum. As her voice rose and the strange words became more distinct, the lights in the mausoleum started to brighten slowly, becoming too bright to look at.

Wispy tendrils of mist began to form in the air, swirling around the room and gathering against the wall behind Dior. As her chanting became louder, more and more of the swirling mist appeared until a thick cloud covered the wall.

Suddenly, another noise could be heard over the chanting. A slow, rhythmic banging, like that of a gong, echoed around the room. Someone was banging on the outer metal doors.

Dior ignored the banging and her chant continued to accelerate. The cloud at the end of the room darkened and then a light appeared at the center and began to spread out, getting slowly larger until it was almost like a window with the dark mists as a frame around it.

The lights in the room crackled and blew out. Sara and Thomas found that they could still see though. The light coming from the mists had become brighter than the artificial lights had been.

In the light, they could see images materializing and then vanishing again only to be replaced by other images. Some things they recognized like oceans and mountains. Other things were strange and beyond their understanding. Once in a while, they glimpsed odd looking creatures. Most of the time, it was just empty landscapes.

Sara looked at Thomas and her mother. Thomas fearfully looked back at her. Her mother had her eyes closed and her hands on her leg. The pain had become her whole world, and she was not aware of what was going on around her anymore. She looked back at Thomas.

The chanting died away, and Dior stood back to gaze on the portal that she created. The room was silent except for the banging that continued on the outside doors.

"Almost home," she said aloud. Smiling, she retrieved the key from the floor and returned to the box on the table.

"All I need is the beacon," she said to herself. She looked at the cross on the key and held it over the slot in the lid.

A short metallic screech was heard as the outside door began to rip from its hinges. The pounding paused a moment and then continued on unabated.

Sara and Thomas returned their attention to releasing their Mom's leg from the gate. Thomas tried to kick one end of the gate to try to dislodge it from the wall. Sara looked around for something that could be used to pry the gate up off her leg.

Dior inserted the key into the slot and tried to turn it one direction and then the other. There was a click, and the lid came loose. She removed the key and set it aside. Smiling, she lifted the lid off the box and gazed at the contents.

The smile quickly faded from her face, and she threw the lid onto the ground. She reached into the box and felt around with both her hands.

"What is this?" Dior screamed. "Where is the beacon?"

Thomas looked at Sara. Sara shrugged.

"You took it, didn't you," Dior said, her gaze searching the room for Sara. "Didn't you." She yelled when she finally saw her.

Sara shook her head. "It was empty when I found it," she told her.

Nobody noticed that the pounding had stopped.

Dior strode over to where Sara had been digging through the debris. "Where is it?" Dior demanded. "Where did you put it?"

Sara quickly got to her feet and faced her. "It was empty. Whatever was in there was gone a long time ago."

"It can't be," Dior said. "That beacon is why there is so much power flowing through this town. It has to be here someplace."

Dior was suddenly lifted into the air. Thomas threw her body against the wall. Dior screamed as she hit and fell face down on the floor. Thomas rushed over to her. Before he reached her, she rolled over and with a gesture of her hand, sent him flying into Sara. Sara tried to duck. His body hit her, and they both sprawled out on the floor.

Dior stood up. She looked down at their mother lying on the floor next to her with the gate still pressing down on her now broken leg.

"You've taken the beacon away from me," she called to Sara and Thomas. "Now, I have to take something away from you." She reached down toward Mary.

The outside doors ripped open with a horrendous screech of ripping metal followed by a resounding clang as the two doors flattened against the side walls of the passage into the mausoleum.

Everyone turned to look at the entrance just as a large brown bear charged through the single remaining barred gate flinging it open with a crash. It glanced around the room, and when it saw Dior standing over Mary, it rushed at her.

Dior tried to block the bear, but the sheer force of a half-ton bear was too much for her and with one backhand swipe of its paw, she was flung halfway down the room and landed on top of the center table.

Thomas was back on his feet and reached Dior just after she landed on the table. The wind was knocked out of her, and Thomas tried to press the advantage. As he brought his fists down on what would have been her ribs, she had rolled away from him off the opposite end of the table. The impact of his fists on the table caused a crack that quickly snaked across the table top.

The bear turned its attention to Mary, and after sniffing at the gate that held her in place for a moment, it wrapped its front legs through the gate. With a loud cry, it pulled with all its weight and ripped the gate from the wall. It flung the gate down against the broken table. Sara rushed over to her mother.

The bear turned its attention back to Dior who had gotten back on her feet and stood up to face Thomas.

Thomas moved faster than Dior had seen anyone move before. And the way he cracked that marble table showed how physically powerful he was. Still, Dior knew that he was just a human and with a thought, sent him flying backward across the room and into the wall on the far side. He fell to the floor by Sara.

The bear was another thing. It collided with her just as Thomas came to rest on the other side of the room. She was knocked backward onto the floor. The bear took two quick steps. It leapt on her with its two massive front claws.

Dior held up her hands, and the bears claws came to a stop just inches above them. The bear looked as if it were standing on an invisible shelf above Dior's body.

The bear leaned down toward Dior and snapped at her arms, catching one of them. His sharp teeth cut through the skin and splattered blood across both of them.

She was able to dislodge her arm and rolled away from the bear. She stood up to face it. It raised itself on its hind legs. It couldn't stand to its full height because of the low ceiling. It roared at Dior, a frightening sound amplified by the small size of the room to an almost ear-splitting volume.

Sara knew that her mother couldn't walk with the broken leg. She wanted to pick her up and carry her from the room. However, she didn't have the strength. She looked around for Thomas. Rather than finding Thomas, her gaze fell on something else.

Thomas appeared next to her. She grabbed his arm and pointed to something behind her. He turned and saw that the gate had come to rest with one end resting on the floor and the other resting on the raised top of the broken marble table.

Thomas looked at her questioningly.

"A missile," she hissed.

He looked at the gate again and then at the other end of the room.

The sharp poles of the gate were lying like a rocket ready to launch. And it was aimed right at Dior. The only problem was that the bear was standing in the way.

"Can you do it?" Thomas whispered.

"Take Mom out of here. I'll wait for a shot," she whispered back to him.

Sara moved over to the gate while Thomas stood up and hoisted their mother on his back. He hurried toward the door of the mausoleum.

The bear lumbered toward Dior, and as he dropped on top of her, she raised her arms to ward him off. She went down under him as he dropped to the ground. Thomas paused at the door to see if the bear had killed her. Sara started to stand up to try to see too.

The bear was pushed back and then flew up and away from the woman on the floor. Sara backed up and Thomas flattened himself against the wall as much as he could while carrying another person on his back.

The bear landed heavily between the two remaining marble tables which caused the entire mausoleum to vibrate from the impact.

Dior was then up on her feet. She vaulted up onto the marble table so that she could look down on the injured bear. She held her fists out in front of her and rotated them in opposite directions as if she were ripping something apart with her bare hands. The bear began to howl in pain.

"Daniel!" Sara yelled.

"Sara!" Thomas yelled. "Now."

Dior suddenly stopped torturing the bear and looked up at Sara in alarm. It was too late. Sara sent the gate flying straight at Dior, and it caught her with two of the bars, one on either side of her chest. It continued straight through her and out her back until the first crossbar hit her and then took her body backward off the marble table. She landed on the floor and slid up against the gate, the upper part of her body raised up by the metal bars.

Sara rushed over to where she lay, and Thomas just stood and watched in horrific fascination. Dior moved her mouth as Sara came into her view. She spluttered out blood which dripped down and joined the growing puddle that pooled beneath her back.

There was a flash of light and rumble from the end wall. A shadowy figure appeared in the gate and bent down toward Dior whose shoulder was touching it. A misty claw grabbed onto her, and she began to twitch. Then they saw it start to drag Dior into the gate.

It took a moment for Sara and Thomas to realize that it wasn't actually Dior's body being pulled in, but a ghostly image of Dior being ripped out of it. As it stretched out from the body, a ghastly shriek emanated from the image rising to a horrifying wail. The image broke free from the body and disappeared through the gate, the wail dying off into the distance.

Dior's eyes rolled up. Her head fell back and she lay still.

They looked at the swirling mists and realized that what had earlier been a smoothly rotating portal was now breaking down and expanding to fill the room.

"Let's get out of here," Sara said.

"What about Daniel?" Thomas asked her. He stood over the bear. It was still breathing.

A lightning bolt shot across the room, and both of them ducked. It was accompanied by a tremendous boom that rocked the small building. The mists were now covering the ceiling and were streaming down the walls, blocking their exit out the door. It started to swallow up the table next to the bear.

The gate had become violently unstable. Sara suddenly realized that the gate was going to cause the explosion that destroys the mausoleum.

Sara tried to pull on the bear's paw. There was no response from Daniel. She looked up at Thomas with tears in her eyes.

"What are we going to do?" she asked.

Thomas just looked at her helplessly.

Chapter 57

Outside the mausoleum, the Dead had watched the bear bash its way into the building after which they could hear the sounds of a struggle.

After the boom of thunder in the mausoleum, many of the Dead started to rush toward the small building.

Kask and Jason were also running across the lawn toward the cemetery. They had watched the bear from a second story window as it enter the mausoleum, and they had hurried down to help.

They were halfway across the lawn, and the Dead were just entering the cemetery when everything suddenly and violently changed.

An explosion ripped through the mausoleum throwing everyone to the ground. They put their arms over their heads to shield themselves from the falling debris. When the debris settled, Kask looked up at the cemetery.

The mausoleum that had stood there for close to a century was a pile of rubble.

Chapter 58

Kask couldn't believe his eyes. It was just the darkness, he thought. And the dust hanging in the air. Still, the mausoleum had to be there.

He looked at Jason who was standing next to him. The boy looked as if he were in shock. He just stared out into the darkness. Kask saw his mouth move as he said something. He couldn't hear it though. His ears were still ringing from the explosion. Jason would have almost had to shout for him to have heard anything he said.

He looked back at the cemetery. They would need flashlights. That was the only way they would be able to find them out there, in the rubble, in the dark.

When he turned to go back to the house, he saw several people hurrying across the lawn toward them. Franklin, Bramwell, and Cook rushed over to them carrying the flashlights that they would need.

"Are you alright, sir?" Bramwell asked. He moved the flashlight over both Kask and Jason looking to see if they were injured.

"Yes. We're fine," Kask told them. "We need the flashlights. I think Mary and the kids were in the mausoleum when it exploded."

Cook gasped and looked wide-eyed at the cemetery. Bramwell took the flashlight from her and told her to call 911. She ran back to the house while Bramwell handed the flashlight to Kask.

The four remaining people started working their way out to the mausoleum. At first, the debris was extremely small. Although, there were a few pieces of marble here and there, there were not a lot.

As they got closer to the cemetery, the number and size of the chunks of marble increased.

When they reached the edge of the cemetery, they discovered that the short fence around it was bent and leaned out away from the center of the blast. The frame around the gate was twisted, and the gate itself lay on the ground, bent in half.

That was where they discovered their first casualty of the night. Three of the Dead were tending one of their own who was hit by debris. They each picked up a piece of the body and soon disappeared in the darkness.

They found more casualties from the ranks of the Dead here and there as they made their way through the cemetery. Each was being tended by other Dead. By one headstone, they found a pair of worn boots set as if an invisible person were standing there. None of them had the stomach to see if they were empty.

When they reached the mausoleum, they found that the walls had been blown out with much of the debris covering the ground around the mausoleum's foundation. It looked like the roof of the building had remained in place, and once the walls were gone, it simply dropped down and shattered over whatever and whoever was inside.

"Sara," Jason called out. "Sara, can you hear me?"

The three of them circled the rubble shining the flashlights everywhere, looking for any sign that someone could still be alive.

"Sara," Jason called out again.

"Thomas," Kask joined in. "Mary. Can you hear us?"

Once they had searched around the outside once, they started to step through the remains of the walls and work their way toward where the building once stood.

"If they're still alive," Kask said. "They're probably buried under the roof."

"They are still alive," Jason told him. There was an edge to his voice.

"Of course," Kask said softly. He put his hand on Jason's shoulder. "We'll find them."

They made their way to the heap that once was the mausoleum and began pulling pieces of marble away from the pile and tossing them behind them.

Jason kept calling for Sara. Kask started using a small piece of marble to tap on the larger pieces. He would tap three times and then pause to see if there would be any answer from beneath the pile.

One piece at a time, they cleared the steps and front platform. The only thing left of the columns that used to hold up the roof over the front doors were jagged circles of marble only four or five inches high.

To help them sift through the rubble faster, Bramwell stood and held two flashlights lighting up the area where the mausoleum door used to be while Kask, Jason and Franklin began pulling large chunks of marble off the pile and throwing them to the side.

They had cleared several feet toward the center of the building when Kask suddenly grabbed Jason's arm.

"Quiet!" he hissed at him.

They stood absolutely still, each trying to keep their breathing as quiet as possible. Neither heard anything.

"What was it?" Jason whispered.

"I don't know. Something like," he said. He stopped when they both clearly heard three slow taps. Kask picked up a small piece of marble and rapidly tapped three times.

They stood still again, waiting. A few seconds later, the three taps were repeated.

"It's coming from right in front of us," Kask said, and they doubled their efforts to pull the large chunks of marble off the pile.

At one point, Jason pulled a chunk away and caused a cascade of debris to slide down toward them. They both jumped back to avoid getting caught in it, and once it settled down, they began pulling pieces out again. Both of them wondered if the slide had further injured whoever was still alive. Neither said anything aloud.

Kask pulled a piece from the top of a large pile in front of him and saw a dark space rather than more debris behind it.

"Bramwell," he called, "Bring me one of the flashlights."

Bramwell handed him one and helped him climb to get a better look. He aimed the flashlight into the hole and put his face right up to it so that he could see inside.

"What the," he started to say. Then he jumped back down and shoved the flashlight back into Bramwell's hand. "Hurry," he said to Jason and Franklin. "We've got to get them out of there."

They started dismantling the pile feverishly. Even Bramwell set the flashlights down, so they were aimed at the pile and joined in moving the larger and larger pieces of marble.

It took several minutes. Soon they had cleared an opening that they could see into. Bramwell picked up the flashlights again and shined them into the opening.

It was a circular cave under the remains of the roof. Mary and

Daniel were lying on the floor. Mary's leg looked as if it were in bad shape. Daniel didn't have any visible injuries. He was unconscious and only wearing a jacket wrapped around his mid-section. Thomas was kneeling between the two.

Strangest of all, Sara was kneeling perfectly still in the middle of the cave. She had her eyes closed, and her arms were extended out slightly with one hand flat out, one palm down over Mary and the other over Daniel.

Thomas immediately picked up his mother and started handing her out over the rubble.

"Quickly," he said. "I'll get Daniel. Don't disturb Sara."

Kask and Franklin took Mary and lowered her down to the ground away from the pile. When they returned, Thomas handed them Daniel's body. They laid him down next to Mary on the cleared platform.

Thomas quickly returned to Sara. He told them to stand at the entrance and be ready to grab Sara from him. He looked up at the top of the cave and then back at Sara.

"Ready?" he asked, not looking at them.

"Ready," Jason replied.

Thomas scooped Sara up in his arms, and as he dashed toward the opening, tossed her out. Jason was able to catch her, although the impact caused him to stumble backward a few steps.

Kask was watching Thomas. As soon as he had moved Sara, it was like a bubble had burst and the roof of the cave started to collapse. At first, Kask thought he wouldn't make it out. Thomas was fast though. He moved faster than Kask had ever seen anyone move before.

Thomas dove out through the opening just as the cave collapsed in a shower of debris. Kask helped him to his feet.

"Are you alright?" Kask asked.

"All things considered," Thomas told him.

"Is there anyone else out here?"

Thomas looked toward where Dior's body had been.

"No," he said, "Nobody else."

Chapter 59

Several hours later, as the sky over the lake began to lighten, Kask and Sara were standing on the balcony of Daniel's old bedroom. Because of the damage to his room, Daniel had been moved across the hallway to a bedroom next to Mary's room. While the doctor was attending to his and Mary's injuries, they had come out on the balcony to view the damage.

The extent of the devastation became apparent in the light of the morning. Not only had the walls of the mausoleum been blown out. The remains that had been interred in those walls were strewn about the cemetery. Many of the headstones were also broken or knocked over.

For a moment, Sara thought she glimpsed a young boy with black hair with a brown and white dog just at the edge of the forest. When she looked back again, there wasn't anyone there.

Thomas and Franklin were talking with a number of the Dead who stayed behind. Kask wasn't sure what they were discussing. Thomas was gesturing toward the cemetery and talking to them seriously. The Dead seemed to be listening intently. They showed no emotion, which was normal for them.

A couple of highway patrol officers were standing below the balcony taking pictures and making notes. The Sheriff's body, enclosed in a black body bag, was being loaded into an ambulance.

Mason appeared from around the corner of the mansion and ran across the yard to the ambulance. He talked with one of the paramedics briefly and then they helped him into the back of the vehicle.

Mason stepped up into the vehicle beside the body as the paramedic unzipped the bag and pulled it back displaying the Sheriff's face.

Mason turned white and nodded his head. He turned away and began sobbing into his hands.

After the body had been secured in the ambulance, he turned back to speak to the paramedic who listened to him and nodded when he was done. He stayed in the back of the ambulance with his father as the paramedics closed all the doors and drove away with no lights and no siren.

Sara saw Mason's face at the little window in the back of the ambulance looking out. Although it was hard for her to tell, she felt that he was looking up at her standing on the balcony. She didn't speak until the ambulance disappeared around the corner of the house.

"I feel sorry for Mason," Sara said. "I know how it feels to lose a dad."

"Sheriff Marco was an evil man," Kask reminded her.

"I know. It doesn't matter. He still is your father. It still hurts.

"Be careful about feeling too sorry for him," Kask told her. "He knew what his father was."

Sara just nodded.

"I guess Shadow Bluffs is going to need a new sheriff," Kask said with a sigh.

"I hope it will be someone better than him," Sara said.

"I hope so too."

"They'll appoint one of his deputies, won't they?"

"His last deputy left about four years ago. He never appointed anymore."

"Why?"

"Don't know. The Sheriff said he was tired of replacing them all the time, so he just stopped."

They stood gazing out at what was left of the mausoleum. A thin tendril of smoke arose out of one corner of the wreckage.

"What about Jason?" Sara asked.

"What about Jason?" Jason asked. They turned to find him standing in the doorway of the room.

"He can be the new sheriff," Sara suggested. Kask looked at him thoughtfully.

"Whoa," Jason said. "I can't be a sheriff."

"Why not?" Sara asked.

"Because I've only been a police officer for less than two months," he told her.

"That's two months more than anyone else around here," she said.

"I don't know anything about being a sheriff."

"No. However, you have something that's more valuable to have in a sheriff than experience. It was something that Sheriff Marco didn't have," Kask told him.

"What's that?"

"Honesty," Kask said. "You are someone the people of Shadow Bluffs can trust."

The doctor called to them from Mary's room. He confirmed that her leg was broken, and she would need a cast. He was able to immobilize her leg until she can be transported to the hospital.

"I've given her some pain medication," the doctor told them. "And I've called for an ambulance."

"Will she have to stay in the hospital?" Sara asked.

"I don't think so. She should be back home in her own bed by this evening," the doctor assured her.

Sara went to her mother's room and found her sitting up in bed.

"I'm sorry, Mom," Sara told her.

"You have nothing to be sorry about," Mary said.

Mary looked up to see Thomas enter the room. She waved him over. He went to her and stood by her bed. She took his cold hand in hers.

"I appreciate what both of you did for me," she told them. "I'm proud of you, all of you."

Kask put his hand on Thomas' shoulder, interrupting the conversation.

"What did you find out?" Kask asked him.

"They were here to prevent the box from falling into the wrong hands." Thomas said.

"None of us wanted the Wielders to get the box," Kask said.

"It wasn't just the Wielders."

"Who then?"

"Shifters. Us. You," Thomas said.

"Me?" Kask asked. "I swore an oath to them to protect it."

"They don't trust anyone," Thomas told him.

"Well, they can rest easy," Sara said. "The box was destroyed."

"Are you sure?" Thomas asked her.

"What do you mean?"

"After the explosion, the box disappeared," Thomas said. "I looked and couldn't find even a piece of it."

"Believe me, it can't fall into anyone's hands," Sara assured him. "It was destroyed."

Thomas narrowed his eyes at her. He had never known his sister to lie. Still, he didn't quite trust her on this.

"It was," Sara repeated.

"OK," Thomas said.

"What do they think?" Kask asked Thomas.

"I told them that it was destroyed in the explosion," Thomas said.

"Did they believe that?"

"Not at first. I told them that I was there when it happened."

"They believed you, then?" Sara asked.

"I gave them my word," Thomas said. "They know that I brought you out to the mausoleum through the tunnel, so I'm not sure how good my word is. They seemed to accept it."

"As long as they're satisfied, maybe things can go back to normal," Sara said.

"They are satisfied," Thomas told her. "I'm not so sure about what normal is anymore."

Kask turned to the doctor. "What about Daniel?" he asked.

"Daniel is a curious case," The doctor said.

"What do you mean?"

"Well, I think it would be better if I showed you," the doctor told him and led them to Daniel's room.

Daniel was resting in his bed. He looked like he was asleep when they entered. He opened his eyes and gave them a half smile as they drew near his bed.

"How are you feeling?" Sara asked.

"I've been better," he joked.

The doctor pulled back the sheet. A good portion of his chest had been wrapped with bandages. There were some spots where blood had soaked through.

The doctor could see their worried looks. He shook his head.

"It's not as bad as it looks," he told them. "That's the strange thing."

He pulled some of the bandages down to look at the wounds. They all leaned closer to see some small red cuts underneath. He covered them again.

"What was strange about that?" Kask asked.

"They didn't look like that when I first treated him," the doctor said. "They were larger and deeper. They are healing at an amazing rate. I don't understand it."

"The gentlemen with the ambulance are here, doctor," Bramwell announced from the doorway.

"Oh. Thank you," the doctor said, still staring at Daniel's bandages.

"You go ahead with Mary," Kask told him. "We'll head out to the hospital shortly."

"Of course, of course," the doctor said, rejoining the conversation. He went into the next room to oversee the paramedics.

"We're glad you're OK," Sara told Daniel.

"What happened to the Sheriff?" Daniel asked.

"Don't you remember?" Thomas asked him.

"Flashes. I remember fighting with him in my room and falling from the balcony. Not much else."

"The Sheriff is dead," Sara told him. "He was found in the bushes behind the house. It looks as if he were attacked by a wild animal."

"Me?" Daniel asked.

Sara nodded her head. "They don't know that. They think it was a bear that was frightened by the explosion."

"They believe that?" Daniel asked.

She nodded again. "They are confused about why he was naked, though."

"Do you remember going into the mausoleum?" Thomas asked.

"A little. I remember trying to open the door. Bears have a hard time with doors," he joked. Sara laughed.

"Then I remember Mom was trapped under a something," Daniel said. "Not much more."

"She was trapped under a gate. You saved her. You saved all of us. If you hadn't broken in, I don't know what would have happened to us."

"I'm glad I helped, even if I don't remember it."

"How do you do it?" Thomas asked him.

"Do what?" Daniel asked.

"Change."

"I don't know. It just happens," Daniel told him.

"You'll have to work on that," Thomas told him.

"Excuse me," the doctor interrupted from the doorway. "We're heading to the hospital with your mother. You should let Daniel rest for a while, I think."

They thanked the doctor and told Daniel that they would check on him when they got back. He closed his eyes and settled back into his bed.

After they had left, he found that he couldn't sleep. He felt restless. He got up and stood for a moment to make sure he wasn't going to be dizzy. He felt like getting some fresh air, so he went out on the balcony.

He stepped out in the bright sunshine of the day and took some deep breaths. He listened to the sounds of the birds and the buzzing of insects. Then, he became aware of sounds that he never paid attention to before.

There were the calls of owls, squirrels and raccoons. The distant sounds of frogs, deer and even wolves were audible to him. He closed his eyes and let the sounds envelope him. Without thinking, he opened his mouth and let out a deep roar that reverberated through the valley below.

Chapter 60

They returned home in the early afternoon after Mary's leg was set in a cast. They helped her to a room on the main floor where she could recuperate until her cast was removed. Once they had her settled in her new room, they told her to rest for a few hours until dinner.

Thomas went upstairs to check on Daniel. Sara had some questions for her great grandfather. She pulled him aside and asked to speak with him. They went into the back parlor, and she closed the door.

"I had opened the box before I gave it to Dior," Sara told him.

"I see," Kask replied.

"It was the box that Dior wanted me to get for her. However, it was empty."

"Yes, it was."

"It wasn't always empty, was it?" she asked.

"No," he said.

"Dior said that there was something inside the box. Where is it now?"

"I removed it and put it in a vault. It is well hidden and protected," Kask told her.

"It was the real Pandora's Box, wasn't it?"

"Yes," Kask said. "When you described the outer box perfectly, I knew that it wasn't safe anymore."

"So you removed it and hid it again," Sara said.

"Yes."

"Where?" Sara asked.

Kask just smiled at her. "Where it will be safe," he told her.

By evening, the investigation was finished for the day. Those that lived at the mansion had retired inside for the night, and everyone else had gone home. Despite the destruction in the night, nature began to return to the yard of the mansion.

Bird calls could be heard over the sounds of the lake. Rabbits and squirrels darted about the yard, chasing or being chased. The wind rustled through the trees at the edge of the yard and blew leaves here and there amid the grass.

And the sun dipped down below the tree tops, sending shadows stretching across the yard and the broken pieces of marble that were still strewn about.

Even though everyone else had gone, two people stepped through the debris and entered the little cemetery. They had not been part of the investigation into what had happened during the night. They had not joined in the gathering up of bodies that had been displaced when the mausoleum exploded. They had not been seen by anyone else who had been there during the day.

Still, they had been there, hidden and watching. And now that it was empty, now that it was quiet, they made their way through the cemetery and up the steps to where the small building had stood just the day before.

Together, they began to look through the rubble that remained on top of the mausoleum's foundation. The small one moved what she was able to.

At one spot where a twisted metal gate stuck out from a pile of marble, they noticed a burnt piece of cloth visible beneath the pile. They looked at each other. Each recognized the fabric that matched the dresses that they wore. They began to clear as much marble as they were able to.

Finally, they had cleared enough to free what remained of the dress, as well as the gate from the pile of marble.

There wasn't a body in the dress. When they freed it from the gate, the charred material revealed nothing except a fine dust that began to blow around in the breeze.

The girl bent down and sifted through the dust until she found a ring with a dark ruby stone that flashed with light for a moment until she placed it in a pocket of her dress.

The old woman folded up the damaged dress and stood silently with the young girl over the charred shadow on the marble floor which was all that remained of their sister, Dior.

"I told you. You weren't ready," Piri said. Asami simply nodded.

Then they turned and made their way out of the cemetery and into the forest to make their way back to their apartment above the pawn shop.

The lab in the basement of the mansion wasn't as quiet as the rest of the house. A generator hummed in a corner, and every 15 seconds there was a crackling as electricity flowed through a maze of wires and then through small holes cut into the black body bag that was strapped to one of the center tables in the room.

Amid the crackling of the electricity, Peter was monitoring the readings that were being displayed on a computer monitor and double checked the wire connections. He also had the body bag partially unzipped so that he could keep a close eye on the face of the creature inside.

At first, Peter didn't hear the tapping at the door. The sounds in the room drowned it out. Soon the tapping became a knocking. Finally, it got his attention when it became a pounding.

Peter glanced at the door. He wasn't happy. He was right in the middle of an experiment and really didn't want to be disturbed. He thought about ignoring it and pretending that he wasn't there. He realized that the noise told whoever it was that he was there.

Swearing under his breath, he turned off the generator. The crackling ceased immediately, and the hum of the generator wound down until all that could be heard in the room was a beeping coming from the computer. He pressed a key and even that ended. He went to the door.

"What do you want?" he asked through the door.

"Mr. Kask has requested that you join the family in the front parlor," Bramwell said.

"Why?" Peter asked. He still didn't open the door.

"They are celebrating the end of the recent events and would like you to be present," Bramwell told him.

"It's really not a good time for me," Peter protested.

Bramwell didn't say anything. Peter wasn't sure whether he was even still standing outside the door.

"Bramwell?" Peter called quietly.

"I understand. I will tell him that you declined his request for you to attend."

Again, it was quiet. Peter looked at the equipment that he had set up for the experiment. He swore again.

"Fine. I'll be up in a few minutes," he growled.

"Very well," Bramwell said. "I will tell him to expect you."

Peter listened for a minute longer and still couldn't tell whether Bramwell was there or not.

He checked the equipment to make sure that everything was still connected and then made sure that everything had been powered off. He looked at the strange face in the body bag and shook his head in disappointment.

"I'll be back soon," He said to the creature.

He turned the main light off in the lab leaving the dim light from the computer screen as the only illumination in the room. With one last glance back at the equipment, he left the room and relocked the door before he made his way upstairs to the gathering.

Everything was quiet in the room as he ascended the steps. Then, suddenly, the body bag shuddered. The computer beeped once, and a spike of white line appeared in a black grid on the screen. The body shuddered again, and a beeping began, each accompanied by a white spike on the screen.

Inside the black bag, the face of the creature that had been motionless a moment before moved slightly and then two black eyes opened and stared at the ceiling.

THANK YOU

Thank you for reading Grimm End. If you enjoyed this book, please rate and review Grimm End on Amazon and Goodreads.

To get behind the scenes content, announcements of upcoming events, announcements of book releases and access to beta chapters of upcoming books, please sign up for my free Members-Only Newsletter on my website at STCameron.com. How do you become a member? Just sign up at my website, it's free.

OTHER BOOKS BY THIS AUTHOR

Inca Wraith

Eleven-year-old CJ Kask and his Young Explorer friends accompany their parents on an adventure to Peru in 1917 when they are sent to discover why an archaeological expedition has stopped sending reports on their dig at an Inca temple.

The Young Explorers discover that they must find the key to a mystery involving an Inca pyramid and the shadowy Wraith that is guarding it. Only then will they be able to not only save their parents but also prevent the Wraith from escaping its pyramid prison.

Phantom Express

When eleven-year-old CJ Kask and his Young Explorer friends help their archaeologist parents find artifacts from a steam train that crashed off a bridge in the early 1880's, they discover that the ghostly train continues to haunt the small town and crashes off the bridge again and again.

The key to unlocking the mystery of the Phantom Express involves a gold pocket watch and an unused ticket for the doomed train.

Will they be able to solve the mystery and put the more than one hundred souls on the Phantom Express to rest?

ABOUT THE AUTHOR

I tell stories and have adventures.

I have two Young Explorers adventures, Inca Wraith and Phantom Express, as well as the first Grimm End novel in a series of five books.

Outside of writing, I have adventures with Kay, my wife and future author of her own books, my two wonderful daughters and their families including four grand-children and ten grand-kittens. I also let people know what is going on with my writing at stcameron.com.